Her fingers traced the stern line of his jaw

McCai's cologne had a fresh, clean smell to it. Plain and simple...completely the opposite of the man wearing it. "Has anyone ever told you that you talk too much?" Jennie whispered, hoping to distract him from his incessant questions.

A ghost of a smile whispered its way across his sensuous lips. "Oddly enough, no." His mouth touched hers, then. Lightly...teasingly.

Jenny, her eyes closed, murmured a halfhearted protest. He responded by taking her lips in a hard, forceful kiss that was a mixture of painful longing and incredible excitement.

The kiss turned gentle, a wooing caress, then savage, then tender...back and forth, forging a need throughout her body Jenny made no effort to control.

Longing and excitement. Passion and desire. The perfect blending of the two.

McCai felt a hunger bone-deep. In his mind, he was afraid of the future. In his heart, he had a greater fear of what was happening right now.

ABOUT THE AUTHOR

Eleanor Woods is well-known to romance fiction fans as the author of thirty-five contemporary novels about love. The proud mother of two, Eleanor is an inspired homemaker who is not only a gourmet cook but an expert gardener, as well. She and her husband, Don, travel extensively on the dog show circuit and *Above Suspicion* reflects her insider's knowledge of the sport. Eleanor lives with her family in Mississippi.

Books by Eleanor Woods

HARLEQUIN SUPERROMANCE
307–SECOND TIME LUCKY

Don't miss any of our special offers. Write to us at the following address for information on our newest releases.

Harlequin Reader Service
901 Fuhrmann Blvd., P.O. Box 1397, Buffalo, NY 14240
Canadian address: P.O. Box 603,
Fort Erie, Ont. L2A 5X3

Above Suspicion

ELEANOR WOODS

Harlequin Books

TORONTO • NEW YORK • LONDON
AMSTERDAM • PARIS • SYDNEY • HAMBURG
STOCKHOLM • ATHENS • TOKYO • MILAN

Published March 1990

First printing January 1990

ISBN 0-373-70395-3

CHAPTER ONE

New Orleans
August 23

"KNOCK IT OFF!" Joey Tate yelled as he entered the kennel. It was early in the morning and the dogs were anxious to go outside. The moment they heard his key in the lock the noise level inside the building had increased significantly. Even to the most devoted dog lover, the excited barking of thirty-five dogs was, at best, nerve-racking.

Some of the dogs belonged to Joey, and some were boarders. Running a boarding kennel was hard work, but over the years he'd found that he preferred the company of animals to that of most people.

At the moment, most of the dogs were reared up on the chain-link runs, their tails swishing back and forth frantically as they waited for Joey to pet them. "All in good time, all in good time," he called out as he adjusted the thermostat, then slowly made his way across the room.

Joey's right leg was shorter than the left one, causing him to walk with a decided limp. A deep, ugly scar spread from the outer edge of his right eye into his cheek. The skin on either side of the scar was puckered and ugly, pulling at his mouth and creating a permanent grimace. Both the scar and the limp were the result of an auto accident.

Joey stopped at the first indoor run and petted an aging basset hound, then moved to the next run, which held two pugs. On and on he went, down the line of expectant faces and wiggling bodies, looking and watching, making sure each dog was in good shape.

Finally satisfied that all was well, Joey walked over to a circuit breaker in one corner of the kennel and pressed a button. Immediately, the door in the back of each run opened. The dogs, familiar with the routine, waited eagerly for their freedom. The moment there was enough space for them to get through, they scampered outside into the sunshine and left their master to the task of cleaning the kennel.

Once he'd taken care of the chores in the main area, Joey went into a smaller adjoining room also equipped with runs. "Oh my," he said as he closed and locked the door behind him, then paused, his gaze surveying the silent occupants. "Why is everyone looking so glum this morning? You really shouldn't do that, you know."

Joey slowly made his way down the aisle and examined each dog carefully. "Today you'll be going for a ride in the van. Won't that be nice? Even though it will only be a visit to the vet, I know you'll enjoy it. I'll be with you, so nothing will bother you." He stopped in front of the last run where a white standard poodle bitch was standing. Her head, with its long, lean muzzle, was tipped to one side, her intelligent dark eyes watching every move Joey made.

"You're the beauty of the lot, aren't you?" he said in a far less detached tone, his mood changing as quickly as the winds heralding a storm. "Do you think Joey walks funny? Do you think he looks odd with his mouth pulled all out of shape? No? Well, that's good." He reached inside the run with one slim hand and gently petted the dog. "That's very good. Perhaps I'll change my mind and keep you with me when I get rid of all this," he said, glancing around the kennel room. "Joey has plans and all of you are going to make them happen. Just a few more weeks," he added quietly, thoughtfully, "and I'll be starting a new life." He withdrew his hand, then glanced at the other five dogs.

"Now don't get your feelings hurt. You're all good dogs. I pick only the best. That's one thing people have never understood. I'm sure they wonder how stupid Joey always manages to get hold of such nice dogs. They should know by now that I have an eye for dogs. Perhaps your new owners will think more highly of Joey when they see you beauties." He was silent for a moment, his expression grim, his gaze becoming fixed. "I'll scrounge around out there for my monthly quota of mutts," he finally said, nodding toward the main room. "Some that are ugly...like me."

The sudden ringing of the telephone brought Joey out of his disturbing reverie with a start. It was just after seven o'clock in the morning. Who could be calling so early? he wondered as he limped hurriedly to answer.

"Hello?"

"I've been hearing rumors about you that make me very unhappy, Joey."

"Mr. Tremont. What a pleasant surprise. How are you?"

"I didn't call to exchange pleasantries, Joey."

"Don't you know you can't believe everything you hear, Mr. Tremont?" Joey said, the weak, sick feeling of fear pulling at him. He knew exactly what André Tremont was talking about, but nothing on earth was going to make Joey admit his guilt.

"You work for me, Joey. Have you forgotten?"

"Of course not, Mr. Tremont."

"Perhaps I should remind you that you are behind in your duties, and refresh your memory as to exactly what it is that you are paid to do."

"That's not nec—"

"That's what I was hoping you would say, Joey. Your carrying out your duties will ensure a smooth operation for everyone. Failure to do so will cause me to become very angry. Understand, Joey?"

"I understand, Mr. Tremont."

"When I hear rumors that any of my employees are dealing on the side, I get upset. If my people are making their own deals, Joey, then that means I'm losing money. Do you get my drift?"

"Perfectly, Mr. Tremont," Joey replied in a calm voice, trying to ignore the fear uncurling in the pit of his stomach. He'd seen how André meted out punishment to anyone caught double-crossing him.

"Good. I do hope you'll remember this little conversation." A sharp click sounded in Joey's ear, then the buzzing of the dial tone began. He replaced the receiver with a shaky hand, his palms wet with perspiration.

Joey continued to stand beside the telephone, wondering how André had found out. Perhaps he should just continue with his boarding kennel and photographic studio, and accept his life as it was. But the more he thought about it, the more determined Joey became to get enough money together to leave the country, enough money for the extensive surgery he'd been told would make his face normal again. He wanted a new beginning...a new life. Someplace where he wasn't known, where people would think of him as Mr. Tate that nice young man rather than Joey Tate the cripple with the scarred face. Not only did he want to go away, he thought, he would go away—in spite of André Tremont and his threats.

The thing he regretted most about leaving was having to give up his kennel. However, there was little he could do now. He'd already accepted deposits on certain merchandise. Those deposits meant his freedom, a freedom Joey had been craving for years.

Dallas
October 11

"GENTLEMEN," portly, balding Martin Scanlon began, "it is the opinion of the committee appointed by the companies represented here today that we hire an elite investigative firm to try and get to the bottom of our problem, before honoring the claims regarding the lost or stolen dogs that have been reported. Some of these claims date back over a sixteen-month period. That being the case, we need the best of the best to look into these mysterious losses. Don't you agree?''

Nodding heads accompanied murmurs of approval.

"Good, good," Scanlon continued. "At least we agree on that suggestion." He looked down at the sheet of paper bearing his notes. "Several names were considered. However, we thought our interests would be best served by hiring someone here in Dallas. After careful consideration, we decided on Jonah McCai, who's already been on the case a week. His firm, McCai Limited, has offices in Dallas, New Orleans and Chicago," Scanlon said, nodding toward the back of the room where a tall, broad-shouldered man leaned against the wall. His hair was dark and his eyes were smoky green. He was casually dressed in light gray slacks, open-necked white shirt and dark blazer.

McCai returned the openly curious stares leveled at him from the board members with his own cool gaze. He looked almost indifferent, as if he didn't give a damn whether or not they approved of him or found him acceptable, and as if he didn't wear a tie for anybody. That very same bearing also conveyed a message of authority not unlike that of a predatory beast's territorial imperative. A message that was immediately recognizable, even grudgingly accepted, by other males.

"I'm sure everyone here would be interested in hearing exactly how you're progressing with our little problem, Mr. McCai," Scanlon remarked. "Why don't you come on up here and field a few questions?"

A look of annoyance briefly registered on the rugged, tanned features of McCai's face before fading into the enigmatic mask that shielded his thoughts from the prying eyes of others. With an economy of movement, he pushed off the wall and made his way to where Scanlon was standing at the head of the table. He leaned slightly forward, his palms resting against the shiny surface and looked at the expectant faces of the businessmen.

"I'm really not prepared to go into detail at this moment," McCai said bluntly. "Our methods of investigation are a little different from those of our competitors. We employ a number of techniques not unlike the ones used by various law enforcement agencies. Obviously we've incorporated certain covert operations into our organization. Working undercover has proved to be a very valuable tool for our firm and we use it frequently." *What the hell do they want?* McCai wondered. Did they seriously expect him to stand there and give them a play-by-play of what he'd already done and what he planned on doing?

"Do you personally handle any of the cases for your firm, or do you merely act as a figurehead?" he was asked.

"Figureheads are a waste of time and money," McCai said shortly. "And now, other than telling you that this case is going to be a difficult one to solve, there's really little I can add at this particular time."

Martin Scanlon looked as if he wanted to press the issue, but after a quick glance at McCai's forbidding features, he held his tongue. However, after the meeting had been adjourned Scanlon did remind McCai that he, as chairman of the committee, was supposed to receive a weekly progress report.

"When there's something to report, Scanlon, you'll hear from me. You knew how I operated when you hired me. If you don't like doing business that way I suggest you get someone else to help you find your dogs."

"No, no," Scanlon said hastily. "We're aware of your unorthodox methods, McCai, but we want you anyway. Keep us informed as you see fit."

Later, as he drove back to his office through the murderous rush hour traffic, McCai considered calling Scanlon and resigning from the job. The group he'd just left struck him as a meddlesome lot that would do nothing but complain. He'd sensed it from the moment he walked into the boardroom. They were the sort of clients who wanted to tell him how to do his job. There was nothing that irritated McCai more.

He turned into the parking area back of his office, drove into the space bearing his name, then turned off the key in the ignition. For a moment he sat staring into space, still feeling strangely apprehensive about this latest job. For the life of him, he couldn't figure out why he felt differently about it than about any of the other cases his firm was involved with, especially in view of the enormous fee he'd quoted Scanlon.

But McCai knew money wasn't at the root of his apprehension. He was well established in his field and his personal wealth was secure. He didn't even bother to advertise his services to the public. Satisfied clients did that for him. But this case bothered him. There seemed to be something sinister about people stealing dogs—something that made the hair on the back of his neck stand up. The subject conjured up all sorts of unpleasant pictures in his mind.

McCai was an animal lover. His own German shepherd, Max, afforded McCai many moments of pleasure. He'd read some of the horror stories that circulated from time to time about dognappers and such, and he'd been repulsed. But like most people when faced with a really unappealing and controversial issue that didn't affect them directly, McCai tried either to put such grim happenings out of his mind or to rationalize the situation by acknowledging that without animals, certain aspects of important scientific research would be brought to a virtual standstill and mankind would be the loser.

McCai exhaled roughly as he opened the door of the dark Mercedes and got out. From every lead he and his staff had pursued, he needed to go to New Orleans.

Jefferson City, Louisiana
October 28

JENNY CASTLE, a frown on her pretty face, cradled the receiver between her chin and shoulder while she wrote with her right hand, and tried to arrange a bouquet of flowers with her left. She squinted her dark blue eyes as she reared back her head in order to get a better view of the arrangement.

"Yes, Mrs. Petty.... No, Mrs. Petty," she said, absently brushing back a curly strand of dark hair that had escaped the neat French braid. "Of course you can bring your dog to our guest house. But you will be asked to crate it when you bring it inside, or we can keep it in the kennel for you. I do hope you understand." *Shades of a super nightmare,* Jenny thought. How could people be so thoughtless? She'd been the pet route before and had almost suffered a heart attack at how careless some owners could be. Experience had brought with it determination she hadn't known she possessed.

"Quite the contrary, Mrs. Petty," Jenny replied. "I adore dogs. In fact, I have eighteen of my own. That's correct, eighteen." Rather it used to be eighteen, Jenny thought, before she lost Dulcie. "As I was saying, I only allow one of them the run of my private quarters. The others are kept in the kennel. The Arbor was built in the 1840s, Mrs. Petty. We're lucky enough to have some of the original furnishings here, plus some very fine antiques dating back to that time. I won't allow my animals to harm them, much less a customer's. I do hope you understand."

The conversation continued for another few minutes. By the time Jenny hung up the receiver, she wished devoutly she'd been in a position to tell Mr. and Mrs. Augustus Petty and their dog to take a fat hike!

"Problems, Jenny?" That question came from Dolly Yates, who'd been cook and jack-of-all-trades at the Arbor for close to fifteen years.

"The Pettys are again favoring us with a visit. Possibly two weeks this time," Jenny remarked dryly. "Can you believe our good fortune?"

"How nice," Dolly said flatly. "They are two of the most aggravating people we've been unlucky enough to have as guests. But," she said, shrugging, "they stay long and pay well. So . . ."

"This is true," Jenny agreed, "and I most definitely need the money."

"In spite of everything that's done," Dolly said, sighing, "this place seems to have an insatiable appetite for dollar bills. I can't figure out why Kathleen left such a crazy will."

"Neither can I," Jenny agreed. "Leaving me this huge ancient turkey without the money to operate it seems almost a joke. What it really needs is a major overhaul to get it even close to tip-top condition."

"Just out of curiosity, after the three years are up will you keep it or sell it?" Dolly asked.

"Unless I lose complete control of my faculties, I fully intend selling this money-hungry monster," Jenny said firmly. "There are taxes, utilities, insurance and always a monthly bill to either the plumber, the electrician or the carpenter. I feel as if I'm about to sink any minute."

"Can't say that I blame you," Dolly remarked. "It wasn't any better when your aunt was alive."

"And yet she stuck me with her burden," Jenny said thoughtfully as she rearranged the flowers. "Frankly, I like the place, Dolly. I could really get used to living here. And I even applaud Aunt Kathleen's wanting to preserve our family's heritage. It was an admirable gesture. But for me to continue running the Arbor at the expense of everything else in my life has another name...it's called dumb." She finally stood back and stared at her floral creation, then slowly shook her dark head. "You know, some people can wear a blindfold and make a bunch of bitterweeds look good. But my talent is unique, Dolly. I can take roses, and in less time than I care to think about they look worse than the bitterweeds."

"Don't be so hard on yourself," Dolly replied, chuckling. She reached for the vase of flowers, her deft fingers pushing and pulling here and there, then announced, "They look fine." She walked over and placed the vase on one end of the mantel. "See? That's just—" The sound of a car door slamming interrupted Dolly's flow of words. She leaned her head to one side and stared out the window facing the parking area beneath the large live oaks. "Oh, good grief!" she exclaimed. "Company, when we need it least. Matilda Atwood is coming up the walk. I'll give her five minutes, then rescue you."

"Thanks," Jenny remarked just as the front door could be heard opening and closing.

"Good morning, Matilda," Jenny said the minute her visitor appeared in the double doorway. "How are you?" Matilda was short and plump with a face that reminded Jenny of a Rockwell painting depicting the archetypal grandmother. Jenny had always been a little puzzled at how a couple as genuinely nice as the Atwoods could have produced a son as nerdy as Joseph. He was a policeman in Jefferson City, and had tried to date Jenny for years.

"Good morning, Jenny," Matilda returned in her usual sunny manner. "I'm fine, thank you." Without waiting to be asked, she settled herself on a Queen Anne love seat and crossed her trim ankles. "As you know, for some time now we've been making plans for the Fall Fete. This year we've decided on a masked ball. Don't you think that will be exciting?"

"Oh, yes," Jenny said, nodding. "It'll be nice... very nice."

"Since you were so gracious last year in allowing the Arbor to be on our list of homes open for viewing, and allowing us to have our grand tea here, we thought we would allow you the chance to exercise your generosity again."

Bull! Exercise my generosity indeed, Jenny thought. "I'm afraid I can't help you this year, Matilda."

Matilda, not in the least fazed by the negative response, remained undaunted. "Of course you will, honey. I realize that the fete is only two weeks after Thanksgiving and that it puts a lot of extra work on you, but we need your support. Your aunt was a founding member of the Sweethearts of the Nathan Bedford Forrest Society. Have you forgotten?"

"No," Jenny said, remembering precisely how devoted her aunt had been to the group. "I haven't forgotten that Aunt Kathleen was a member, Matilda. But neither have I forgotten that I've only just this month made the last payment to the bank on a loan I was forced to make in order to pay for damages to the Arbor during last year's tour and the tea. Damages that I duly reported to your group as per our agreement, and the same damages that were just as duly ignored by your group. To put it bluntly, Matilda, I simply can't afford to participate this year. I'm sorry."

"I'm sorry about the society not paying that bill, Jenny. The committee handling it treated you badly. But I'm sure you'll want to reconsider and help out. After all, being Kathleen's blood relative entitles you to membership in the society. With that membership come certain responsibilities. I'll have the caterers meet with you later in the month so that you'll be able to join in the discussion of the menu."

As Matilda went on and on with her plans, Jenny propped one elbow on the counter and rested her chin in her palm. Matilda was on a roll and Jenny knew what that meant—a long, boring lecture that could last forever. As she listened, Jenny wondered how it was possible for supposedly sane and intelligent women to feel such fervor and loyalty toward a man who had died in 1877? Had they been his descendants she could have understood. But they'd simply chosen a hero from the Confederacy, sworn devotion to that person, then gone about the yearly backbreaking task of presenting the fete—a week of parties and pageantry between Thanksgiving and Christmas that included several teas, a ball and a number of tours of local historic homes. Though small, the group was indefatigable in its efforts to honor its chosen one. Jenny, on the other hand, wasn't particularly taken either way with the deceased general. If he could have helped her pay for the upkeep on the huge white elephant she'd inherited, then she would have been glad to sing his praises. However, since that wasn't the case, she felt she had about all she could take with the problems of day-to-day living.

"I'm sorry, Matilda," Jenny said the moment she was able to get a word in. "I simply can't participate again this year."

"But, my dear, are you aware of exactly how much the fete benefits the city financially? How can you be so insensitive to the efforts of the society?"

For one crazy moment Jenny was tempted to tell Matilda that she considered the society to be a royal pain in the behind, but she didn't. Matilda was a darling. She was honest and sincere in her efforts, and was simply doing what she believed in.

"I'm positive Jefferson City appreciates the society's efforts in attracting tourists, Matilda. So do I. But even that fact doesn't change my mind. I can't participate this year. I've recently taken on a project at the nursing home and this happens to be our busiest season here at the Arbor."

"Would it be possible for the nursing home project to be looked after for a few weeks by your kennel help, Jenny?"

"I suppose it would, but I don't want to handle it that way. The patients I see are all quite elderly, a couple of them in very poor health. They've gotten to know me and my dogs and they look forward to us visiting them. I wouldn't disappoint them for anything in the world.''

"Well, I'm sure your Aunt Kathleen would really appreciate your doing your civic duty. But when it conflicts with the fete, I do think she would want you to let the fete take priority.''

"I'm sorry, Matilda. I simply can't take on anything else.''

Matilda tut-tutted for a moment or two, then rose to her feet. "Naturally I'm disappointed in you, my dear. I'm sure—at this very minute—Kathleen is spinning in her grave at your callous treatment of her dear society. Why I—''

"Excuse me,'' came a deep voice from the doorway. "While the unfortunate Kathleen is spinning, perhaps one of you ladies would be so good as to tell me where I might find a Ms Jenny Castle?''

Jenny looked across the room and found herself staring at a tall, broad-shouldered man standing in the doorway, quite obviously listening to Jenny and Matilda's conversation. For someone so large, he'd certainly moved quietly.

"I'm Jenny Castle," she told him. "How can I help you?''

McCai's long easy stride carried him into the room, his cool gaze going from the obviously annoyed Matilda to Jenny, who also appeared to be short on patience at the moment. "My name is Jonah McCai, Ms Castle. If you can spare me a few minutes, there's a matter I'd like to discuss with you. In private," he added pointedly.

"I'll be in touch with you, Jenny," Matilda said quickly, then turned on her heel and marched from the room, as stiff and erect as a general reviewing troops on the parade grounds.

While Matilda was leaving, Jenny sneaked a quick glance at Jonah McCai. Under similar circumstances the absence of a tie on any other adult male wearing a suit might have stood out like a sore thumb. But the large man taking up considerable space in the middle of her front parlor looked as if he'd been dressed by Bond Street tailors. He was what Jenny called sexy casual, and on him the look was terrific.

Other features about him that caught her eye were the faintly visible wings of silver in his dark hair that followed the curve of his sideburns and faded over his ears. She liked the stubborn set of his chin, and the determined thrust of his head. His rugged features reminded her of a man who had lived life hard and taken the good and the bad without complaining.

Suddenly she found herself vastly amused by her thoughts. Just when had she become such an expert on how men of Jonah McCai's ilk went about life or anything else for that matter?

"Ms Castle," McCai said as he walked over to where Jenny was standing behind the mahogany piece that served as a front desk. "I understand you lost a dog a few weeks ago. Am I correct?"

"Yes," Jenny said quickly, hope instantly flaring to life inside her. "How do you know about Dulcie? Are you from the police? Has she been found?"

"No, no," McCai said, shaking his head and at the same time reading disappointment in her eyes. Eyes the same color as dark swirling clouds on a stormy day. Their grayish-blue hue struck McCai as unique. Her disappointment also left him feeling uncomfortable. "I'm sorry, Ms Castle. I'm not from the police, and I have no news about your dog."

"Then exactly what is your connection, Mr. McCai?" Jenny demanded. For a brief second she had allowed herself to think she just might possibly get Dulcie back.

"I represent several insurance companies, Ms Castle. I'm looking into the disappearance of top show dogs."

"I'm familiar with the problem. The dog world has been thrown into chaos. In fact, the stealing of dogs during the past eighteen months has left most people in the fancy more than a little nervous. But I'm afraid you're mistaken on one point. My Dulcie wasn't insured."

"I know," McCai said, nodding. "But she had done quite a bit of winning, hadn't she?"

"Yes. Dulcie was doing quite well. Though I must confess she was far from being in contention for top dog. However, being an owner-handler, I was very pleased with her wins. But tell me, Mr. McCai, why are the insurance companies launching the investigation?'' Jenny asked. "Surely they don't suspect the owners of turning in bogus claims, do they?"

"At this point, Ms Castle, everyone is a suspect," McCai answered. "Even you."

CHAPTER TWO

"I BEG YOUR PARDON?" Jenny asked, disbelieving. Was the man serious? Did he honestly suspect her of stealing dogs?

"Until we get the case solved, Ms Castle, no one is excluded," McCai said bluntly, gesturing with one wide hand, the tanned back of which Jenny couldn't help but notice was covered with dark hair. For a split second she wondered if the hair would be silky to the touch or if it would be coarse. "I wasn't accusing you personally of stealing the animals."

"How considerate of you, Mr. McCai. However, I am one of a group of suspects, correct?"

"That's about the size of it."

"Well, even if I'm not considered the top thief of the dog world, would you please explain what you could possibly want from me?"

"Hopefully, your help, Ms Castle," McCai said thoughtfully as he clasped his hands behind his back and began walking about the room, punctuating his flow of words with short nods. "With a little cooperation from you and others, and the help of a friend of mine who lives in New Orleans, I might be able to get to the bottom of this damn mess. Personally, I happen to think that whoever took the dogs is incompetent and crazy as hell.''

"Well, I'm not so sure I'd go that far, Mr. McCai. We thieves prefer to be thought of as crafty rather than crazy,'' Jenny countered. In spite of his being about the rudest character she'd ever run into, there was an aura of sensuality about the man that held Jenny's attention. "But I would like to know why you consider this particular thief—or thieves—to be incompetent. They stole the dogs, didn't they? And they haven't been caught, have they?''

McCai favored her with a dark look that expressed more clearly than words exactly what he thought of her remarks. "They're incompetent, Ms Castle, because of the number of dogs they stole, and all within a few days,'' he told her. "And yes, I do think one person or group is responsible for taking all the dogs.'' He paused in front of the desk, then turned and faced Jenny. "How can the thief not be aware that the theft of one top dog, or any show dog for that matter, would send shock waves throughout the sport. That being the case—for someone to steal three at one time...'' He shook his head. "That's incredibly stupid. They have to know that eventually they'll be caught.''

"I agree with you to a point,'' Jenny admitted. "However, I'm not so sure the culprits think they'll be caught. Aren't most crimes committed by people who believe they have *the* perfect plan? Perhaps this person feels the same way. At any rate, how do you figure I can help, Mr. McCai?'' she asked. ''Especially in light of you considering me a suspect?''

''Suspect or not, Ms Castle, I'll accept help from anyone. I figure that since you also lost a dog, perhaps you're a bit more anxious to find the thief than the average person would be. That is, of course, if you really did lose a dog. Secondly, in order to check out certain leads that I feel are vital to the case, I need someone who knows their way around the dog game, someone who knows the reputable kennels and the not so reputable ones. Import-export records have to be checked and veterinarians interviewed. Considering your own . . . er . . . loss, it stands to reason that you'd be more cooperative than most.''

''And I get the distinct impression that you never lose the chance to capitalize on another's misfortune. In this particular case, my misfortune—genuine or suspect—is heaven sent. Right, Mr. McCai?''

''I couldn't have put it better myself. If I think that misfortune can be of use in solving my cases, then no, Ms Castle, I don't hesitate a moment in using it. After all it's results that count, not playing Mr. Nice Guy. And remember, the people who hire me usually are victims of misfortune as well. From where I stand it all equals out in the end.''

''Is being rude and suspicious a prerequisite for someone in your profession, Mr. McCai, or are you simply obnoxious by nature?''

McCai felt the corners of his mouth twitch. His report hadn't indicated that Jenny Castle had a temper. He liked a woman who wasn't afraid to speak her mind. He also liked the way her eyes took on that stormy blue-gray hue when she was angry. And she was definitely angry with him at the moment.

"A little of both," McCai said with a straight face.

"So after weighing my certain desperation against my possible involvement, you've decided you can trust me," Jenny remarked coolly.

"More like your input would be beneficial, and I hope I can trust you," McCai corrected her.

They stared at each other then, each assessing, each measuring the other for flaws or weaknesses upon which to pounce.

Jenny saw a tough, hardened male in his late thirties . . . maybe early forties. But male in every possible sense of the word. She wondered what he would be like without the fifty-pound chip on his shoulder and the fist-size cocklebur under his ornery hide?

McCai saw dark shiny hair pulled back in a French braid, with soft wispy tendrils framing a heart-shaped face. He saw beautiful blue eyes, a small straight nose and a full, generous mouth. Jenny Castle was a very pretty woman, McCai quietly mused. He wondered why she wasn't married. From the investigation he'd had run on her, he knew she had no family in the vicinity and that she had been dating a man named Edward Bayliss off and on for three years. McCai wondered if she and Bayliss were lovers?

"Oh . . . all right," Jenny remarked, breaking the tense silence. She had a feeling she was getting nowhere fast by trying to figure out the darned man's motives. And really, she reasoned, why should she even try to figure him out? She wanted results in his investigation just as much as he did. If she helped him, there was a distinct possibility she could learn something about Dulcie, perhaps even get her back. If he chose to think of her as one of the suspects, so what? "I'll help you," she said finally.

"Good," McCai said. He pushed back a white cuff and glanced at the gold watch on his wrist. "Would you have lunch with me so that I can fill you in on a couple of ideas I have? You can also give me two or three names so I can begin checking kennels in the area."

"I'm afraid lunch is out of the question, Mr. McCai. I have an appointment in thirty minutes."

"Can't you break it?" McCai asked impatiently. He knew he was being pushy, but nothing about the damned case had gone as it should and he was frustrated. Every lead he'd gotten so far had pointed to New Orleans. Yet for the life of him, McCai couldn't put the first piece of the puzzle together.

"No," Jenny said, shaking her head. "Short of my being ill, this appointment doesn't get broken. I take puppies and dogs to a local nursing home three times a week for the patients to play with. This is one of the days I do that."

"You actually take dogs into a hospital environment?" McCai looked at her as if he considered her more than a little bit nuts for doing such a thing.

"Yes," Jenny replied, nodding her dark head. "As I just told you, three days a week. And a nursing home is not a hospital, Mr. McCai." Jenny knew that she'd never met a more hostile person than the man facing her. She wondered what circumstances had shaped Jonah McCai into such a hard, cynical individual?

"Nursing home...hospital...call it what you will. Don't you think it's generally accepted that the residents are nothing more than statistics waiting to die?"

"I suppose that's one way of looking at it," Jenny said softly, wincing at the cold edge to his voice. "But I choose to think of it as a place where older people are cared for, Mr. McCai." She didn't bother to tell him that the grandmother she'd been so fond of had been one of his "statistics." Simply because Jenny's parents had neither the time nor the patience to bother with the older woman, she'd died a sad, lonely death. Jenny, twelve years old at the time, hadn't been able to do much about the situation. Now, however, each time she saw one of the patients at the nursing home smile or heard them chuckle at the antics of one of her puppies, Jenny knew in her heart that she was taking the time to care because of her grandmother.

"Ms Castle, if looking at the world through rose-colored glasses makes you happy, then who am I to disagree?"

"Who indeed, Mr. McCai, who indeed?" No, she told herself, her association with Jonah McCai wasn't going to be an easy one. But if he could help her find Dulcie, then she would gladly tolerate his bad temper.

Later, as she and Phil, one of the two college students who alternated days helping her with the kennel, were overseeing some of the patients at the nursing home play with the dogs she'd brought, Jenny couldn't help but remember Jonah McCai's caustic remark. Perhaps she did look at the world through rose-colored glasses, but in her opinion it was far better to do so than to be as cold and uncaring as an iceberg.

"Is she too rough for you, Mr. Harper?" Jenny asked an elderly man in a wheelchair, who was holding a boisterous ten-month-old golden retriever puppy. She'd been watching the twosome rather closely because the puppy was an extremely playful one, and Jenny didn't want Mr. Harper to be scratched nor the puppy dropped.

"No," the man answered quickly—too quickly, or so it seemed to Jenny. He glared at her for several moments, then dropped his gaze and clutched the puppy to his chest with his left hand.

Jenny squatted beside the old man, her heart going out to him in spite of his grouchy personality. He looked so lonely. Lonely and afraid. She wished there was some way she could bring him out of his shell. About the only thing she did know abut him was that he didn't talk much. He usually spent most of the day in his room, sitting in his wheelchair, staring out the window.

"I bet you used to have dogs, didn't you, Mr. Harper?" Jenny asked quietly, rubbing the head of the puppy as she spoke.

The old man nodded, but not before Jenny saw his lips quiver. To her acute embarrassment, she saw tears slowly stealing down his lined cheek. The tears became blended with the day-old stubble of gray beard on his face, giving him an unkempt look. *Oh no!* Jenny thought. She hadn't meant to make him cry.

She placed her hand over his. "Mr. Harper, I'm so sorry. I didn't mean to pry. Please forgive me."

Suddenly the man thrust the dog at Jenny, causing her to fall backward in a sprawling heap onto the tile floor. Like an absolute fury, he spun around in his electric wheelchair and fled from the room.

"Don't pay any attention to him, honey," spry, seventy-two-year-old Edna Davis remarked as Jenny— with Phil's help—struggled to hold on to the wriggling puppy while getting to her feet. "If you ask me, he's just plain spoiled. He won't talk with any of us. Especially the girls. We won't bite him, you know. We're just curious, that's all. My goodness, if we don't pry into each other's lives and business, what else are we going to talk about?" She turned back to stroking the six-year-old beagle she was holding. "He's just a silly old fool, isn't he, Mildred? Just a silly old fool like the rest of us. We all know we're just idling away the time here till we die. Yes," she said softly, gazing thoughtfully into space, "that's what it's all about in this place...dying. Can Mildred stay with me today, Jenny?"

"Er...thanks, Phil," Jenny murmured to the young man, completely thrown off stride by Mrs. Davis's ramblings. "I'm afraid not, Mrs. Davis," she said gently. "But I'll be sure to bring her back to visit you on Wednesday. Will that be all right?"

"Sure, honey. Wednesday will be fine. I'm not going anywhere, you know. I'm not going anywhere at all," she said softly, her green eyes staring off into the distance. "I'll be here . . . for a little longer."

"Of course you will," Jenny said brightly. "Why, you're the resident clown, Mrs. Davis. This place couldn't operate without you. You make everyone laugh."

"But nobody makes me laugh, Jenny, nobody makes the clown laugh. I want to laugh, too."

"Mrs. Davis, could you . . . I mean . . . do you think you could try to talk with Mr. Harper?" Jenny asked, thinking it best to change the subject. She didn't want Mrs. Davis to become upset as well. "He seemed really depressed. Maybe he'd like to talk with you but doesn't know how. Perhaps he had a dog once and still misses it. Could be he just needs to tell someone about his problems."

"Well, I'll try, honey. But I've never been one to chase the guys, you know. Always let them do that. Do you suppose he'll think me forward if I approach him? Maybe I should wait till I get my hair fixed," she murmured thoughtfully, her hands caressing the sleeping Mildred. "The hairdresser comes on Tuesdays."

"Your hair looks lovely, Mrs. Davis. And I'm sure Mr. Harper wouldn't think you at all forward if you spoke with him. He's a very handsome gentleman, you know," Jenny told her, smiling.

"Shame on you," the older woman answered, favoring Jenny with one of her brightest smiles. "You wouldn't be trying to play Cupid, would you?"

"You never know, Mrs. Davis, you never know," Jenny replied, breathing a quiet sigh of relief as she returned Mr. Harper's puppy to its crate, then took Mildred from Mrs. Davis and crated the beagle, as well. "You'd better start picking up the others, Phil," she prompted her helper, who was talking and laughing with a group of elderly men absorbed in a hot game of checkers. "I'll be ready to go as soon as I have a word with Marge."

"Sure thing, Jenny."

Jenny finally found the director, Marge Williams, in the dining room. "I'm sorry, Marge, but I think I upset Mr. Harper," she said, then explained what happened.

"He's one of the most difficult patients we have to work with," Marge said thoughtfully as she pushed her reading glasses on top of her head. She was an attractive woman with prematurely gray hair, and was truly devoted to her profession. "He's had very few visitors since he came here two years ago."

"Does he have any family?" Jenny asked.

"A nephew. He lives in New Orleans. I think he's a photographer, but I'm not sure. He sends the obligatory box at Christmas and a present on birthdays, but he's certainly lax about visiting his uncle. At first I wondered why Mr. Harper didn't choose to live with the nephew. But now, seeing how infrequently the nephew visits, I understand. We have quite a few like that. A tendency to forget seems to be the norm in this business."

"I know, and it's sad," Jenny murmured, remembering her grandmother and how difficult her last days must have been.

Marge looked at her sharply. "You aren't going to quit on me, are you? This program of yours is one of the most wonderful things I've seen come through the front door of this nursing home."

"I'll have to admit that there are days when it gets to me, Marge. Like today...Mr. Harper so withdrawn and crying, and Mrs. Davis...we all know she has a bad heart and can't live much longer. She knows it. Yet most of the time she's joking...finding something to laugh about. There's tiny Mrs. DuPree, speeding up and down the halls in her wheelchair like a small motorized gnome, always fussing that I never give her a *good* dog, yet crying like a baby when I take it away."

Jonah McCai's remark that the patients at the nursing home were waiting to die was true, but Jenny hated to admit it. She also hated to admit that, while some of them had family who visited daily or weekly, there were many others who had been forgotten by their loved ones. Some would die alone, or with a stranger holding their hand—possibly pretending to be a beloved son or daughter or simply just standing by, quietly waiting.

"Of course it's difficult, Jenny. Why, there are days when I think I'll scream if I don't get away."

"I find that hard to believe," Jenny told her. "You always seem so in control, so calm. I've only been coming here a few months and already I'm emotionally involved with so many of them. Sometimes their faces haunt me."

"I see those same faces, honey. They look at me and it's as if they're begging for another chance at life, pleading with me to do something to make the nightmare they're living go away. Conversely, I see flashes of anger and resentment in those same eyes. But I know it's nothing more than frustration. These are their last days, Jenny, and some of them are fighting so hard to live and, at the same time, maintain their dignity. When there are no letters or visits they look to me or some other member of the staff to take away the hurt. Sometimes we can, sometimes we can't. Why, there are moments when I even feel guilty because of my health, guilty because of my youth." She grinned crookedly. "Admittedly a thirty-five-year-old isn't a teenager to most people, but behind these walls it's like being the baby on the block."

"That's certainly true," Jenny agreed. She glanced at her watch and groaned. "Dolly's going to kill me. It's almost two o'clock, and we have three new guests arriving this afternoon. I really must go, Marge."

"Have you heard any news about Dulcie?"

"No, but there's an insurance investigator in town, so I'm still optimistic. He stopped by the Arbor this morning. Hopefully he'll be able to shed some light on the mystery, even if he does think I'm guilty."

"What on earth are you talking about?"

"Jonah McCai, my dear, doesn't trust anyone. If you own a dog, then Sherlock McCai automatically suspects you."

"I see. Sounds like a very serious-minded individual."

"That's an understatement."

"The serious-minded part reminds me of you. What do you do for fun?" Marge asked her.

Jenny was thoughtful for a moment. "I've honestly never thought about it before," she answered truthfully. "It always seems I'm going off in four or five directions at once. I suppose it comes from being forced at an early age to look after myself. My parents were very wrapped up in their careers."

"You're too young to live by such a rigid schedule, Jenny," Marge persisted.

"Okay," Jenny said, laughing. "I promise that one evening real soon—rather, as soon as Ed gets back from his guard duty—I'll slip into something sexy and have him take me out on the town. Will that do?"

"Perfect."

For the rest of the afternoon Jenny was kept too busy to give even a fleeting thought to her promise to Marge. In addition to last-minute preparation of the guest rooms and the daily trip to the supermarket for the fresh meat and vegetables that Dolly insisted on, she still had to make a list of kennels and breeders in the area for Jonah McCai. From her brief meeting with the man, she wouldn't be at all surprised to find him—at any moment—in her front parlor, demanding to know why she hadn't done as he'd ordered her.

WHILE JENNY WAS INVOLVED in her role as innkeeper, McCai was busy setting up what he hoped would become a valuable information network in a less opulent section of New Orleans than he usually frequented when in the Crescent City on business.

He'd learned long ago that if a person was willing to pay, he could get just about anything he wanted. There had been numerous occasions during the course of his career that such a weakness in the human makeup had made his job much easier. So for more than an hour McCai sat at the bar in the dim, smoky confines of a seedy nightclub, nursing a Scotch and water while talking with the bartender.

A really reliable snitch could be an invaluable asset, McCai thought later as he walked outside the club after leaving his card with the bartender. He paused on the sidewalk, taking deep breaths of cool fresh air into his lungs to clear away the stench of the club. He caught the lapels of his sport jacket, hitching the collar more snugly into place while flexing his shoulders. Where he'd been for the past hour brought back memories of his childhood that McCai had tried hard to forget.

He couldn't begin to count the number of nights he'd curled up in a corner of just such a sleazy dump and gone to sleep while his alcoholic father gambled and drank himself into a blind stupor. When the elder McCai was almost incapable of standing, he would awaken his son and have the child lead him to wherever they happened to be staying at the time. The scene had been repeated many times, in many different cities across the country.

Those early years and the beatings he received from his father had had the effect of turning what could have been a normal, laughing little boy into a tight-lipped, watchful child. It was then that he started distrusting people. McCai's green gaze narrowed now against the wind suddenly gusting through the narrow streets of the French Quarter. So far he'd met only two or three people whom he trusted. That left a hell of a lot to be desired of the human race, McCai thought disgustedly as he shouldered his way into the late-afternoon crowd of sightseers and people getting off work.

Minutes later McCai rang a bell set to the right of a tall wrought-iron gate that blocked a long, narrow alley in the heart of the Quarter. Damned if he could figure out why anybody would want to live behind bars like this. Perhaps attempting to adapt to a supposedly civilized life after years of working for the government had turned his friend, Nate Jones, into more of an eccentric than he already had been. McCai had to admit that becoming established in the private sector had given him his own moments of unease. Maybe that was why he'd chosen a line of work that wasn't totally unlike the international witness protection program he and Nate had been associated with for a number of years. However, investigative work was free of the constant peril.

"Let's hear it," said a deep, impatient voice.

"Happen to know a good place where a man could put up his heels and relax for an hour or so with a cold beer?"

"Through the gate facing you and at the end of that alley is a little corner of paradise, my friend."

"Sounds interesting. I think I'll take a look."

"Well, it's sure as hell about time."

Suddenly a distinct clicking noise could be heard beneath McCai's hand, which was lightly grasping the handle of the gate. "Bring your ugly carcass in here and let's do some serious talking."

McCai grinned as he walked down the brick-lined alley. He knew exactly what he and Nate would talk about. It was five . . . close to six years since they'd retired, yet their conversations rarely varied.

When he reached a six-foot brick wall at the end of the alley, McCai turned right and found himself in a courtyard complete with fountain and tubs of greenery. Even to McCai's demanding taste, the setting was pleasant.

"Thought you'd like it," said someone from the second-story balcony overlooking the courtyard. "I even put in that tacky fountain you kept harping about. Damned thing cost me a fortune, too. Cursed you for a week after getting the bill." McCai stared up at the tanned, dark-haired man with the heavy mustache who was grinning down at him.

"Them's the breaks, my friend."

Nate Jones walked down the flight of stairs at one end of the balcony, his hand outstretched. "You're looking dour as usual, McCai," he remarked as they shook hands and clapped each other on the back. It would have been obvious to anyone that Nate Jones was one of those select few McCai trusted. "How's life treating you?"

"No complaints," McCai answered.

"You opened a branch of your company here nearly a year ago. Why haven't you gotten in touch with me before now?" Nate asked as they made their way across the courtyard and entered the house.

"I really don't know," McCai told him, without even bothering to offer an excuse. Nate understood the response. There was no room for pretense between him and McCai. Not after what they'd shared.

A short while later they were sitting on the back porch in comfortable rocking chairs. Their heels were propped on the sturdy railing while they sipped their drinks and enjoyed the gentle breeze of the ceiling fan whirling above them.

As usual, they reminisced about the years they'd spent risking their lives working for the government in practically every country in the world. They remembered the good times and the bad and agreed unhesitatingly that they must have been crazy as hell to stay in that particular line of work for as long as they had. McCai brought the conversation back to the present by telling Nate about the case he was working on.

"You're chasing dog thieves and I'm chasing illegal aliens. That's one hell of a comedown, McCai, for two old reprobates like us. Seems to me there has to be some kind of psychological mix-up in there somewhere," Nate said, chuckling. "Am I correct in assuming you want my help with this dognapping case?"

"How easy would it be for you to do some check-ing on import-export records in the area?"

"Shouldn't be too difficult," Nate told him, nod-ding. "As you well know, some government agencies cooperate readily, while others act like they're mem-bers of the Communist party. Exactly what am I sup-posed to check on?"

"Dogs," McCai said, then told him what he wanted. "Throw in anything else you think will help. It's numbers, dates and names within the past two years that I'm mainly interested in."

"Give me three or four days."

When McCai left Nate, he went back to the office to make some calls and do some planning and think-ing. It was well past two o'clock in the morning when he let himself into the apartment he'd taken during his stay, showered, then dropped, exhausted, into bed.

LATE AFTERNOON the next day, McCai found his way to Jefferson City and the Arbor once more. As he walked toward the wide cypress steps of the antebel-lum house, he noticed the soft glittery glow through the beveled-edged glass of the oval fanlight above and the panels on either side of the wide front door. There was the smell of smoke from the fireplace in the air, and through the floor-to-ceiling windows onto the verandah he could see into the front parlor.

The secure, homey scene pulled at a well-hidden core of wistfulness deep inside McCai. For a fleeting second—and in spite of his silent protestations to the contrary—he couldn't help but wonder what it could possibly have been like living and growing up in a house like this.

"Good evening," an elderly man said as he walked past McCai and entered the Arbor.

Another setting, not nearly so pleasant as the one he was now in, came to his mind as he nodded, then saw the man disappear into the house. A setting where he saw a skinny, little boy watching other children as they played, and envying them. A little boy who, instead of joining in those childish games, learned how to pick pockets with the lightest of touches. He also learned as he continued to grow that life was a game, a game of survival in a world that was harsh and cruel.

While McCai was remembering the bitter moments of his childhood, Jenny hurried from her bedroom, pulling over her head a bright yellow T-shirt with Life Is a Bitch scrawled across the front in bold red print. She had a spare forty-five minutes, and she desperately needed to work with the standard poodle puppy she was hoping to show. Lately, she didn't seem to have enough time to breathe let alone work with her dogs. And if that wasn't enough, she still had to get together that list of kennels for Jonah McCai.

Just as she stepped from her private apartment onto the wide veranda that wrapped around the sides and front of the house, she saw the object of her rather harried thoughts standing at the bottom of the front steps, a grim expression etched in the roughness of his features.

Jenny paused, unconsciously holding her breath as she watched the tall, wide-shouldered McCai. The moment was quite obviously a private one for him, and she didn't wish to intrude. But while she was waiting for him to come out of his reflective mood she saw no reason why she couldn't enjoy looking at him. She was still puzzling over what there was about the man that appealed to her.

He was curt, all business and blunt to the point of rudeness. Her mouth took on a rueful twist when she thought of what his reaction would be to her not having had a chance to get the information he'd requested. She had a feeling—no, she quickly corrected herself, it was more than a feeling. She *knew* that he was going to be properly put out.

"Mr. McCai," Jenny finally called out and walked forward to meet him. He'd made his way to the top step and was staring at the house as if he hated it. "I'm afraid I haven't had time to make a list of the kennels for you," she said, favoring him with her nicest smile. "But I promise to get it done this evening."

"Apparently you aren't as interested in finding out what happened to your dog as I thought you would be, Ms Castle," McCai replied, frowning as his annoyed gaze swept over the snug fit of her T-shirt and the length of shapely thigh beneath faded jeans. Any other time he would have been more appreciative of a good-looking woman with a nice figure standing not more than three feet in front of him. At the moment, however, McCai felt like throttling the female, who was looking so innocently at him.

"Whether you believe me or not, Mr. McCai, I want Dulcie back with all my heart. Losing her was like losing a member of my family."

"You certainly have a strange way of showing your grief."

"And I suppose always doing exactly what you want and when you want to do it—is another McCai law. Right?"

McCai propped one solid shoulder against a white column and studied the blue-gray eyes that had gone from friendly to cold in a split second. Though he was annoyed as hell with her, he couldn't help but admire her. He liked her spirit.

"Of course, Ms Castle."

"Then please let me be the first to inform you, Mr. McCai, that there are those of us who aren't as fortunate. This," she said sternly, waving one slim hand toward the house, "in case you haven't noticed, is a bed and breakfast. It requires considerable work on my part and on the part of my small staff to keep it operating and at the same time show even a small profit. That leaves very little time for other things. And you and your demands definitely fall into the category of 'other things,' Mr. McCai."

"I'm sorry, Ms Castle," McCai surprised himself and Jenny by saying. What was wrong with him? he wondered. Apologies certainly didn't come easily. So why now? And why, of all people, to Jenny Castle, a woman he barely knew? "This case is very frustrating. I'm afraid my patience is worn a little thin."

"Apology accepted, Mr. McCai," Jenny said on a less hostile note.

Out of habit, McCai quickly and thoroughly considered the tone of her voice. He wasn't accustomed to such generosity in people. Especially women. "You're mighty forgiving."

"Not really. Don't you find it difficult to stay angry with a person or carry a grudge?"

McCai found the question amusing. He crossed his arms on his chest and inclined his head to one side. "I really can't say that I do."

"No," Jenny said softly, after thoughtfully regarding him for a moment. "I don't suppose you do at that. I'm sure you're the off-with-his-head type of person and would never give the incident another thought. By the way, would it be all right for me to call you Jonah rather than Mr. McCai? And do you think it would be asking too much of you to call me Jenny? I'm afraid we're not very formal here in Jefferson City."

"Then by all means let's omit the formality," McCai told her. "My friends call me McCai."

"It suits you." Jenny glanced over her shoulder, then back to McCai. "I was about to go out to the kennel and work with a puppy I plan to show. Would you care to join me? Perhaps there are some questions I could answer that would help you with the investigation."

"Perhaps," McCai agreed and fell into step beside her. They left the veranda and walked to a square brick building, shaded by three large oaks, at the back of the property.

"Looks like a nice setup you've got here," McCai remarked after entering the kennel and looking around for a moment or two. From his firm's previous investigation he knew Jenny had lost a black standard poodle bitch. But from what he could see of the dogs in the indoor runs, there were only four poodles—three adults and one active puppy. He looked at a number of other dogs, then back to Jenny. "I wasn't aware that you were interested in so many breeds. Is this the norm for people involved in your particular sport?"

"Yes and no," Jenny said, smiling. "Which really isn't an answer, is it? Actually this is a hodgepodge collection. One beagle and one of the goldens need only a point or two to finish their championship. They belong to clients, and showing them helps me with my own show expenses. The poodles are mine, and all have a number of points except the puppy. As you can see, some of the others are purebred and some are mixed breeds. Aside from the dogs being shown, I pick my nursing home dogs from all the others."

"Did you buy the dogs for that project?"

"No, but I pay the feed and vet bills. Actually, I get the dogs here and there. Sometimes a friend will have one they feel is well suited for the project and will call me. I've even taken in a couple of animals who were hungry and roaming the neighborhood."

Now that he could believe, McCai thought. "I'm sure that helped."

"At any rate," Jenny said, shrugging, "the program leaves me with a zillion dogs to take care of, but I honestly think it's worth it."

McCai walked over to the runs where the poodles were watching him with quiet dignity. "They're beautiful animals. I'm sorry that you lost your dog."

"So am I," Jenny answered. She walked over to stand beside him, reaching through the chain-link barrier to scratch furry ears.

Jenny had found that just before she went to sleep was when she missed Dulcie the most. She bowed her head to hide the sudden rush of tears in her eyes, but not before McCai noticed. "Dulcie was very special to me, McCai. When she was a puppy, she was constantly getting into mischief. Rescuing her became a daily occurrence. From the time she was three months old she slept at the foot of my bed every night. Not only was she my dog, we were best of friends." Jenny looked up at him then. "Believe me, I want to find Dulcie just as much as you want to succeed for your clients. And yet I'm so terribly afraid I'll find out she's dead."

Though only moments ago he'd been thinking her a thief, something about the sadness in Jenny's eyes pricked at McCai's heart, he, the man who considered himself immune to any and all feminine wiles, not to mention the varied and sundry forms of entrapment used by the females of the world to lure men into doing their bidding. Without thinking, he reached out and brushed the backs of his fingers along the underside of her small, determined chin. "I understand. I have a dog of my own, and if I lost him, it would really bother me. I'll do my best to find her. Okay?''

One minute he was feeling like a gold-plated fool for letting her get to him. The next found him comparing the texture of her skin beneath his fingers to warm satin. For the second time in two days he wondered about her relationship with Edward Bayliss.

"Okay," Jenny said softly. There was something about the stern, hard-featured Jonah McCai offering comfort that—combined with her missing Dulcie—left Jenny wanting to bawl her eyes out. She wondered why.

Since forming his own company McCai had found missing art treasures, diamonds worth a king's ransom and even people who wanted to disassociate themselves from the world and everything in it. Yet not a single case he'd taken so far had been as irritating as this one. And not a single client so far had been half as intriguing to him as Jenny Castle. Was she for real or was she nothing more than an enchanting crook?

CHAPTER THREE

McCai knew the man was scared. He knew it with every fiber of his being. He knew it because the back of his neck was tingling and because of that old familiar gut feeling.

Those sensations were reminiscent of other times and places in McCai's life. Times when—at certain moments—his very survival depended as much on his reacting instinctively as on his following through with any display of physical strength.

"Should a new client happen to bring in any dog of these three breeds that you consider to be above average, I'd appreciate it if you would take the time to check for tattoos on the Lab and the terrier. And don't forget the microchip implant on the poodle," McCai reminded the veterinarian, then handed the man his business card. McCai extended his hand to the tall, lanky Dr. Moreau. "Thanks for taking the time to see us."

"My pleasure," the vet said, his dark eyes shifting back and forth between McCai and Jenny. "And good luck with your search."

The moment they were on the sidewalk outside the clinic, Jenny looked up at McCai. "I'm sure you're

much better at reading people than I could ever be—
your profession demands that you be. But did you get
the impression that Dr. Moreau was extremely agi-
tated?''

McCai had been in New Orleans almost a week
now. On several occasions during that time Jenny had
gone with him as he visited the long list she'd supplied of local kennels and veterinarians. During their
time together she'd gained a new respect for people in
the investigative field. Gleaning even the tiniest bit of
information was a painstaking, not to mention frustrating, ordeal.

"You're a fast learner, Jenny," McCai told her. He
cupped her elbow, then escorted her the few feet to
where his car was parked at the curb. "The man
was . . . is, frightened. But of what?" he asked as he
opened the door on the driver's side, then slipped behind the steering wheel. They sat in thoughtful silence for a moment.

McCai couldn't help but wonder if Moreau's nervousness was because he and Jenny were partners?
Had seeing Jenny with McCai been the reason for the
vet's tension?

"We merely asked him to look at the photos of three
different dogs," McCai murmured. "We didn't ac-
cuse him of anything, yet he acted as if we'd caught
him red-handed." McCai glanced at his wristwatch.
"Let's grab a bite of lunch. I don't think too well on
an empty stomach."

"Neither do I. I'm also curious about something,
McCai," Jenny began slowly. "Is it a trade secret, or

would you mind telling me exactly why you decided to begin your investigation in New Orleans?''

"Is your Good Samaritan's conscience bothering you, Jenny? Are you asking if I have a legitimate lead? Or am I simply running up an enormous bill for my clients?''

"Something like that," Jenny replied, grinning. So much for subtlety. She'd already learned that bluntness was as much a part of McCai's makeup as breathing or blinking his eyes. Yet his critical remarks were just as often directed toward himself as they were toward others. It was simply the way he was. But now that she'd been around him for several days, Jenny found that his sharp tongue didn't bother her nearly as much as when she first met him.

"We learned through one of our operatives in Mexico City that a surprising number of dogs—and quality dogs at that—were being shipped into that country from New Orleans. It's also rumored that someone in this area is supplying dogs for several research labs in the Southwest. And considering that two of the three show dogs recently stolen were taken from here, I couldn't think of a better place to start snooping around."

"McCai," Jenny began as she slipped her foot from her shoe and rubbed her aching toes against a navy slacks-clad leg, "I truly hate to shatter your sizable ego, but you do not snoop. You interrogate like Attila the Hun. By the way, I think I'm going to bill your firm for several trips to the podiatrist. What on earth possessed me to wear new shoes today?"

"I'm surprised," McCai remarked, teasing. He watched her brace her heel on the edge of the seat, then continue to massage her foot. "I can't imagine the efficient Ms Castle not being in total control."

"Since he'd met Jenny Castle, she'd shown him more sides to her personality than a multifaceted diamond. Usually the women of his acquaintance found his marital status and wealth to be a challenge they couldn't ignore. So far that didn't appear to be the case with the down-to-earth Jenny. Being with her was different from being with any of the other women he knew—a difference McCai found to his liking. But only for a short period of time. From experience, he'd learned that no matter how appealing a woman seemed in the beginning, she usually slipped up somewhere along the way and let the true side of her personality show. Unfortunate, he thought matter-of-factly, but true nevertheless.

"Mustn't be cute with your main gofer, McCai, I just might resign," Jenny replied, favoring him with a narrowed glare.

"Well, so far, gofer, you haven't been very productive," McCai returned in an amused tone. "That tall, nervous fellow we just left is the first weak link we've seen in this operation."

Jenny's hand on her foot became still, and she stared into the distance. For a brief moment she closed her eyes and saw Dulcie with her favorite squeaky toy hanging from her mouth, her head tipped to one side as she stared back at her mistress. An involuntary sigh slipped past Jenny's slightly parted lips. She hadn't missed McCai's remark about the dogs that were sent to the research labs. But that hadn't happened to Dulcie. She had to be alive—she *was* alive, Jenny told herself. She refused to believe anything else. When she turned her head and looked at the silent McCai, she found him studying her with that deep intensity to which she was slowly becoming accustomed.

"You're thinking of Dulcie, aren't you?" he asked roughly, almost accusingly. Then he started the engine and pulled away from the curb. The traffic was murderous, but during the past week Jenny had seen that McCai—though not a patient driver—was a careful one.

"Yes," she said softly when she'd managed to swallow the lump in her throat. "How did you know?"

"You have a very expressive face, Jenny. It's like an open book. If you want to protect yourself in this world, then you've got to learn to shield your emotions."

"Is that what you do, McCai, shield your emotions so that no one ever knows the real you?" Jenny asked in a stinging voice, then turned and stared out the window. She didn't understand his sudden anger and it hurt her. It was her dog that was lost, so why was *he* acting like the injured party?

"I haven't thought about it in years. But yes, I suppose that is what I do."

Jenny wanted to ask what on earth there was that could possibly hurt Jonah McCai, but she didn't. He was uptight because of the seemingly blank wall that existed between him and the answers he was seeking. She was on edge because she was terribly afraid she might never see Dulcie again. And surprisingly enough, Jenny found that she simply didn't want to hurt McCai.

"I'm sure that in your line of work it's a necessary precaution," she remarked.

McCai didn't comment and for a moment or two an awkward silence hung over them. Jenny found herself searching for and discarding topics of conversation like a rather frantic but dedicated shopper at a rummage sale. Then in the midst of her mental shenanigans her gaze met McCai's calm one. A ghost of a smile hovered around the edges of his lips. Without any other sign from him, Jenny felt the awkwardness leave as quickly as it came. Suddenly she felt a quivery rush of contentment stealing over her. Light and airy, but as warming as a soft blanket in a cold night. And all because Jonah McCai had almost smiled? she asked herself.

THE MINUTE MCCAI AND JENNY left his office, David Moreau pulled the telephone toward him, then dialed a number.

"Jo-lane-Lane Kennels."

"An insurance investigator just left my office, Joey," the vet practically screamed, his voice tight with anxiety. "When we started this business you assured me there would be no problems."

"An insurance investigator?" Joey felt the same wave of fear swamping him that he'd experienced when he spoke with André Tremont. He ran a thin hand across his face while he tried to think. With André snooping around and David Moreau running scared, if he wasn't careful all his plans could go up in smoke.

"Yes. His name is Jonah McCai, Joey, and he acts like he knows something. I don't like it. I tried to play it cool, but I don't think I fooled him at all."

"For God's sake, Moreau, don't panic. Just stay calm and this McCai dude will leave you alone. There's no way in this world he can possibly know a thing—no way at all."

"But what if somebody saw you take one of those damn dogs? And why the hell did you take dogs that were insured? That's the dumbest thing I've ever heard of."

"Oh yeah?" Joey yelled. "How was I to know they were insured? Besides that, I'm already working on a deal to sell the dogs McCai's looking for. There's no way he can find them, so that means he won't be coming back to you. You'll be getting your money within the week."

"Forget the money, Joey. I want out."

"Oh no. We made a deal and you're sticking with it."

"But I didn't agree to go to jail. All you said you wanted from me were a few health certificates now and then. You didn't say anything about any investigators coming around."

"We'll have more problems than insurance investigators, Moreau, if you panic. Just keep quiet and everything will be fine."

Joey continued talking till he'd calmed the nervous veterinarian. However, once the conversation was over there was his own fear to be dealt with. He knew the smart thing to do would be to combine the show dogs with the ones he'd collected for André and distribute them to the research labs. Yet the more Joey thought about it, the more determined he became to stick with his original plan. There were overseas markets that would pay top dollar for the six dogs he had in the back room of his kennel. Hadn't he sold the others through the same channels? With the money he'd get out of the deal, he could live like a king in Mexico. He could have his surgery and enjoy the kind of life that should have been his all along.

WHILE JOEY PONDERED his future plans, McCai and Jenny were on their way to lunch at an out-of-the-way restaurant that enjoyed a brisk local trade. During the quiet drive, McCai resisted the urge to probe Jenny Castle's ability to turn his dark moods into sunny ones. He even refused to give her credit for making him smile when he was around her—in spite of his firmly telling himself *not* to smile.

"Am I to understand that the specialty of the house is gumbo, gumbo, and gumbo?" McCai asked in amusement after glancing around the interior. He studied the chalkboard listing the bill of fare that was hanging amid the numerous pictures of past and present New Orleans Saints football players. The owner of the restaurant was an avid fan of the local professional team and promoted them vigorously.

"Gumbo and oysters on the half shell, and if you happen to be a football fan it helps," Jenny said, nodding. "You know, I really should have asked what kind of food you liked. I'm sorry, I wasn't thinking. Would you rather go someplace else?"

"Don't worry about it," McCai told her. "They're two of my favorites." He then proved his point by ordering a large bowl of the thick, dark seafood gumbo and a dozen oysters on the half shell. Without hesitating Jenny followed suit, ignoring McCai's surprised look till the young waiter left their table.

"Something wrong, McCai?"

"Certainly not," McCai said with feigned innocence. "All the women I know eat like stevedores."

"I'm a hardworking country girl, McCai. My day begins at six o'clock each morning and doesn't end most days till after midnight. Cottage cheese and salads won't sustain me over such long hours."

"That's a tough schedule for anyone, Jenny. Why don't you hire additional help?"

"Because additional help costs money, McCai. Need I say more?"

"I figured a bed and breakfast in an antebellum home would have the tourists flocking to your door. Doesn't the Arbor operate in the black?"

Jenny inclined her head, her lips pursed in resignation. "That's really a difficult question to answer. If you were to trade off guests against actual expenses for said guests, then yes. There would be a nice profit. However," she said, grinning, "until you've lived in a house built in the 1840s, you can't possibly understand my dilemma. I'm convinced there's a huge, black hole somewhere in the house that continuously sucks in every penny of my money. The upkeep is enormous."

"Then get rid of it," McCai advised her.

"Oh, but therein lies the rub, McCai. I can't."

"Of course you can. It's yours, isn't it?"

Jenny nodded.

"You don't enjoy working yourself to death for nothing, do you?"

"No."

"Then find some sucker who's hooked on historical houses and make his dream come true."

"If I were to do that, then I'd lose the Arbor and the five acres surrounding it." She went on to tell him how her Aunt Kathleen had stipulated in her will that Jenny, her favorite relative, must keep the business going for three years. At the end of that time she would receive thirty thousand dollars and full ownership of the property. If she failed to do as her aunt wished, the Arbor would become a historical landmark belonging to Jefferson City, and Jenny would lose out all the way around. "So you see, there really is very little I can do."

McCai couldn't help but chuckle. "That's the craziest damn thing I've ever heard. Was your aunt an eccentric?"

"In a way. She was also a member of the Nathan Bedford Forrest Society."

"Ah yes," McCai nodded. "Now I remember. Your friend . . . Matilda something-or-other, wasn't it?"

"Yes."

"How much longer does your sentence last?"

"An eternity. I've only been an innkeeper for seven months. Just long enough to get my kennel situated and to almost work myself to the bone. Before I became a member of the landed gentry—and I use the term loosely—I was a legal secretary during the week and showed my dogs on weekends. I was happy, had very few problems and didn't know beans about running a bed and breakfast."

"Has it been a bad experience?" he asked curiously.

"Not really. Although I have loving parents, they're both professors, busy with their careers and just as eccentric as my aunt was. I grew accustomed to expecting the unexpected at an early age. So the way I figure it, if dear Aunt Kathleen thought she would bamboozle me out of that money, then she's in for a surprise. I'll run her darn bed and breakfast just as she wanted. And when my sentence—as you call it—is up, I'll collect the money, sell the joint, then go on my merry way."

McCai laughed. He couldn't believe that he was actually sitting across from a woman who wasn't afraid to work for what she wanted, nor was she bending his ear with complaining. "Are you involved with a particular man?" he suddenly asked.

Jenny merely shook her head as she stared at the sexiest, most complex man she'd ever met. "McCai, you give new meaning to the word *blunt*."

"Ma'am," he replied in what Jenny knew had to be the worst Southern accent she'd ever heard. "I truly resent that. Why, I distinctly remember saying 'involved.'"

"When what you really wanted to ask was, am I sleeping with anyone. Right?"

"I'm shocked."

"In a pig's eye! To answer your question. I'm not 'involved' with anyone at the moment. I go out with Edward Bayliss occasionally, but at the present time he's away for three months at some sort of National Guard camp. Edward is gung ho on anything to do with the military."

"And you aren't?"

"Not really. It's a necessary evil to protect our country and I support the concept, but that's as far as it goes."

McCai leaned back in his chair, his elbows resting on the arms, his fingertips pyramided beneath his square chin. His green eyes were openly appraising the pretty woman seated opposite him, and he wasn't even attempting to hide that fact. "You give the impression that life is one huge bowl of cherries and that you are as uncomplicated as whipped cream. Are you aware of that?"

Jenny stared thoughtfully at McCai as she considered the remark. "I've never really thought about it," she replied just as the waiter appeared with their food.

Why did she feel that McCai hadn't meant anything even remotely complimentary by what he'd just said.

That thought remained in the back of Jenny's mind while she listened to the waiter and McCai discussing the Saints football team. She found herself thinking that the word *uncomplicated* could never be considered an appropriate description for McCai. He was an entirely different kettle of fish from Ed. She knew what Ed was thinking even before he spoke. They'd gone all through school together, and their relationship was about as romantic as one between two posts, but they were comfortable together. And at the moment that kind of relationship suited Jenny just fine.

McCai's large presence in her life, on the other hand, was causing some very odd moments. Moments when she found him staring at her for no apparent reason. Moments when he cupped her elbow to assist her in and out of the car, or moments when she felt the steady warmth of his large hand at the small of her back as they walked along together.

No, Jenny reasoned, Ed Bayliss and Jonah McCai were poles apart in many different ways, and so was her reaction to each of them. "The very first time I met you, McCai, you accused me of looking at the world through rose-colored glasses. Is that what you mean by 'uncomplicated'?" Jenny asked, smiling, choosing to ignore her initial reaction to his remark.

"That day I spoke out of frustration," he said gruffly, eyes flowing over her as if he couldn't get his fill of looking at her. Dear heavens! Jenny thought, forking a plump oyster into her mouth. The man's moods were as changeable as a chameleon, and she was aware of every single one of them. One minute his voice had an edge when he paid her a rather dubious compliment. The next minute found him staring at her as if she were a piece of his favorite pie and he was starving. "The case was giving me a hard time—still is—and I'm afraid I took my anger out on you. I couldn't believe you considered going to a nursing home more important than helping me find your dog."

"It was really quite simple, McCai. The nursing home took priority."

"Do you honestly enjoy going over there three times a week?" he asked. McCai liked things neat and tidy. Nothing irritated him more than not being able to figure out how and why a person did certain things. Jenny Castle was beginning to irritate him with her Pollyanna personality and with her noble ways, he thought. Nobody was as good as she tried to be. She had flaws and McCai was determined to find them.

"It's one of the most difficult, yet rewarding, things I've ever done in my life," Jenny said honestly, warming to a subject that was very dear to her heart. "You have no idea how looking into the faces of those old people can get to you. They were babies at one time, McCai. Tiny babies held in their mothers' arms. Perhaps their parents didn't look at life as we do today, but they were that generation's future. Now they're old and broken. Once they were teenagers—falling in love and playing pranks on their friends. They became married couples and raised families.

They contributed something to this country. Now they're old, and in most cases, forgotten. That's sad, McCai, by anybody's yardstick.''

''You can't take the burden of the elderly on your shoulders, Jenny,'' McCai replied in a gruff voice.

''I'm not trying to, but I am trying to make a few of them a little bit happier. Frankly, I think they're getting a bum rap. Do you realize that most other countries care for their elderly much better than we do here in America?''

''I've never really thought about it.''

''Why not, McCai,'' Jenny demanded. ''Do you have something against old people? Have you had all your elderly relatives banished from your sight?''

''No.''

''How kind. Do you ever visit them?''

''No.''

''Why not?''

''To my knowledge I don't have a single living relative, elderly or otherwise,'' McCai said.

''Cute, McCai,'' Jenny said sternly. ''Real cute. Why didn't you tell me to begin with?''

''And miss seeing you get up on your soapbox and blast me?'' he asked, chuckling. ''No way.''

This time it was Jenny who leaned back in her chair in a thoughtful pose as she considered the teasing man seated across from her. ''Tell you what, McCai. You're such a tough, cynical individual, I think it's time you saw how another group of our society lives. A group of the virtually helpless. Why don't you come with me to the nursing home tomorrow afternoon?''

"You suspect one of the patients of being a dog-napper?" he asked silkily, and Jenny knew immediately that she had annoyed him.

"You're the detective, McCai. That'll be for you to find out. Well?" she persisted. "Do you have the courage to come with me?"

"Perhaps some other time," McCai answered. "I have several appointments tomorrow."

"Sure," Jenny replied, nodding. "That's the stock answer. I hear it all the time. But I'm surprised at you, McCai. Somehow I had you pegged as being different."

"That's called life, Jenny," he irritated her by saying. "Seldom do we hear or get what we think we deserve. I'm simply not as interested in visiting nursing homes as you happen to be."

For a moment Jenny was tempted to come back with the stock reply that he would be old someday, but somehow the argument had lost its zest. She'd learned, much to her dismay, that a surprising number of people wanted to forget that places like nursing homes existed.

"Sorry," Jenny murmured. "As you said, I suppose I do tend to get on my soapbox. But if you ever decide you'd like to go with me, the invitation is still open."

Conversation after that lagged somewhat, and neither of them seemed interested in correcting the situation. Jenny found herself feeling depressed. She was disappointed that McCai hadn't agreed to visit the nursing home. For some strange reason she'd been anxious to show him what she did for the old people. It was as if she wanted his approval, wanted to hear him say that he thought she was doing a terrific job.

McCai felt like a jerk. The invitation appeared to have been an honest gesture of friendship, but he—being so wrapped up with his suspicions of Jenny—had turned into his usual blunt, critical self. He'd known the woman barely two weeks, but he felt like a royal ass for having disappointed her.

When McCai took Jenny back to the Arbor, he caught her hand as she started to get out of the car. It was only the second time he'd purposefully touched her, and the quick rush of awareness she felt took Jenny by surprise.

"Wh-what is it?" she asked, looking over her shoulder at him. She'd already opened the door and had one foot out of the car. Dear heaven! He had the most gorgeous eyes she'd ever seen. What a pity that they were often so cold and indifferent.

"I've hurt you, haven't I?"

"Maybe. But it doesn't matter. I shouldn't have pushed you." She tried to ease her hand from his, but his grip tightened. He wasn't about to let her go.

"It does matter, honey," he corrected her, using the term of endearment without even being aware that he'd done so. "You were trying to share something with me, and I acted like an ass." McCai ran his other hand over his face, then clasped the back of his neck. He'd never been in a situation quite like this one. "There are certain things and events in my past that make me suspicious of people, Jenny. I don't mean to be that way, it's just one of those things. Plus, I've been alone most all my life and I'm not used to sharing. In some ways, I suppose you could call me a selfish person."

"Not everyone is out to get you, McCai," Jenny said gently. "There really are some decent people around. You just have to learn to recognize them."

"Tell me something, Jenny."

"If I can."

"Were you raised in a house like that one?" McCai asked, nodding toward the Arbor, which was nestled beneath the spreading branches of centuries-old live oaks.

"Not that old, but a house of the same type. Why?"

"You've already told me that your parents are eccentric, but loving. Right?"

"That's correct."

"And when you were hungry, you automatically went into the kitchen and fixed yourself something to eat. Right?"

"Of course, McCai. Doesn't everyone?"

"No, Jenny," he replied, "everyone doesn't. For some there are no kitchens, there are no houses and there sure as hell aren't any loving parents—eccentric or otherwise. As your T-shirt says, life really can be a bitch. But little girls like you have never seen anything but the good side."

"Am I suppose to cover myself with sackcloth and ashes just because I wasn't deprived as a child?" Jenny demanded, then jerked her hand away from his larger one. She got out of the car and turned to face him.

"Perhaps it's time someone showed enough interest in you to tell you a few home truths about yourself, Jonah McCai. You are the most cynical, hard-nosed, mean-tempered human being I've ever met. No matter what anyone tries to do for you, you automatically think they're out to get you. Now might be an excellent time for you to take some of your own advice and join the real world, my friend. We've all had problems we've had to learn to deal with, but some of us have managed to do so without letting those problems turn us into bitter, suspicious people. Drop me a line in about twenty years if and when you finally grow up." She slammed the car door, then turned and ran up the walk to the front door of the Arbor.

McCai sat in stunned silence for several moments, not believing he'd actually sat and let someone say such things to him. Had it been another man hurling such insulting remarks at him, then that individual would now have been on his way to the hospital. As for Miss Jenny Perfect, well, she could go to hell for all he cared. Let her bore Ed Bayliss to death with an account of all her charitable works. If they'd been dating for as long as his report indicated, then McCai was certain they must share a lot of ideas. He wished them well. They deserved each other.

McCai reached out and turned on the engine, then jammed the accelerator to the floor and spun out of the parking area. The smell of rubber lingered long after the car disappeared from view.

"I DON'T THINK this one likes me, Jenny," Mrs. Dupree remarked, her mouth settling in an unhappy pout as she held a bone for the adorable rust-colored puppy that seemed more intent on taking a nap than playing with the bone.

It was the day after Jenny's quarrel with McCai, and she found her spirits lower than they'd been in ages. She'd just gotten the patients settled down with their dogs, but today her heart wasn't in her work. "Of course she does, Mrs. Dupree," Jenny assured the tiny woman, "but I'm afraid she's sleepy." She reached down and petted the puppy on the head. "Wake up, Snuggles, and play with Mrs. Dupree. She thinks you're mad at her."

Snuggles responded by opening one eye, yawning and then immediately going back to sleep.

"Don't let it bother you, Mrs. Dupree. She'll probably wake up before we leave."

Jenny moved on to where another patient was laughing at the antics of a more active puppy. "Don't let her tire you, Mrs. Morrison," she cautioned. "And if you get a scratch, let me know."

"Don't worry, Jenny," the woman said happily. "As you suggested, Marge fixed all of us these long-sleeved smocks to wear when the pups visit us." She hugged a squirming puppy to her bosom. "This is the most enjoyment I've had since I came to this place a year ago."

When Jenny turned around, she found McCai blocking her path. He was dressed casually in navy-blue pants, pullover shirt and windbreaker.

She met his hard green gaze with her own steady one, not knowing what to say. She felt as if someone had just handed her a million dollars. "Hello, McCai."

Her voice was soft and gentle and made McCai want to look away so he wouldn't see the sudden light of happiness in her eyes. She really was glad to see him, he realized.

"Jenny," he said stiffly. "I wasn't sure what time you usually came over here, so I took a chance." He did look away then, seeing close to a dozen old people holding dogs of various sizes on their laps. "So this is what you do three afternoons a week."

"Yes," Jenny murmured. There was a huge lump in her throat and she was having a difficult time speaking. On impulse, she caught his hand in hers. "Come with me. I want you to meet Mr. Harper. He's my number-one problem."

"Oh? Why? Doesn't he like the food?" McCai teased as they made their way through the haphazard alignment of chairs. His sharp gaze caught the way the patients smiled at Jenny. Some grabbed her hand and pulled her down so that they could whisper in her ear. Others had her pet the dogs they were holding, and some simply brushed their hands against her arm as she passed. McCai found himself dealing with an emotion unfamiliar to him. He was moved by the patients' show of affection toward Jenny—just a smile or a touch or a word from her seemed to bring joy to their eyes. McCai was afraid that if he wasn't careful, he, too, could be caught up in the web of golden sunshine she spun.

"Mr. Harper," Jenny said when they reached a patient seated a little apart from the main group. "I'd like you to meet a friend of mine. This is Jonah McCai. He heard so much about you guys, he wanted to come and meet you for himself."

McCai extended his wide tanned hand to the older man. At first he, and Jenny, thought the gesture would be refused. But after a moment or two, Mr. Harper shook his hand.

"Why don't you talk with Mr. Harper, McCai, while I check on Mrs. Davis. She seems to be missing from the group today."

"She had a flare-up with her heart last night," Tom Harper said in his stern voice.

Surprise registered on Jenny's face. It was the first time the man had said more to her than just a yes or no. There was also concern for Mrs. Davis. She was Jenny's favorite. "Can she have visitors?"

Tom nodded, keeping his eyes trained on the puppy he was holding on his lap. Jenny waited, but he offered nothing further. She turned to McCai.

"Do you mind waiting here with Mr. Harper?" she asked, then nodded at the young man helping her. "Phil is right over there."

"Don't worry," McCai told her. "Mr. Harper and I will get along fine."

When Jenny entered the room that Edna Davis shared with another patient, she saw the thin, frail body lying still and quiet beneath the sheet. Jenny's walking shoes were noiseless as she moved to the side of the bed, then stood and watched the older woman's shallow breathing while she slept.

Jenny wondered if Edna's daughter had been called? From what she'd heard Marge say once before, the daughter only visited two or three times a month even though she lived in New Orleans. After a few more minutes of quietly watching, Jenny left the room.

As she stepped into the corridor, Jenny almost collided with a woman who looked to be in her late thirties. She, too, had stopped at Edna's door. "She's sleeping right now," Jenny told the woman. "If you're from one of the church groups that visit the patients, perhaps you could see her tomorrow. She loves company."

"I'm Marie Gordon, Edna's daughter. I'm afraid I haven't met you. Are you new to the staff?"

"I don't work here, Mrs. Gordon," Jenny told her, then explained who she was and how she came to know Edna. "I'm so glad you could get over today. She really misses you."

"And I see all manner of condemnation in your eyes, Ms Castle, because I don't visit her more often," Marie replied matter-of-factly.

"Please . . . I—"

"And I suppose some of it is justified," Marie Gordon continued. "Don't for a moment think that I don't love my mother—I do. But have you ever tried to juggle a full-time job as a schoolteacher, raising four teenagers and taking care of a husband who's a diabetic?''

"It sounds terrifying," Jenny admitted.

"It is terrifying, Ms Castle," Marie Gordon agreed. "It broke my heart to put my mother in this place...and this is one of the best ones. The very words *nursing home* always struck fear in my heart. I felt I had betrayed her. For months after I brought her here, she would barely speak to me. It's only been in the past year that we've gotten back to being friends.''

"Really, Mrs. Gordon, you don't have to explain any of this to me."

"But I want to explain to somebody, so please listen. Perhaps it will relieve some of the guilt I still feel. At any rate, I was trying to run mother's home and mine—meals, cleaning, the whole smear—all because she refused to move in with me or allow anyone to live with her. If I didn't cook for her, she didn't eat. If I didn't see to her bath, she didn't bathe. Once she learned how bad her heart condition was, she simply stopped cooperating. Finally my body rebelled and I collapsed. At least now I know she's being fed and looked after. Most likely not the way I would personally do it, but enough so that she's not suffering. Does that make me a mean person, Ms Castle?''

"No, Mrs. Gordon, it doesn't. It makes you a very concerned and loving daughter. But the picture you've just painted of your mother is so different from the Edna Davis we see. In here she's the one who cheers everyone up and makes the others fight to live. She's the leader. I've only seen her depressed once. And then it was for only a minute or two.''

''You don't know how glad I am to hear that.''

''I have to go, Mrs. Gordon,'' Jenny told the woman, ''but I've enjoyed our visit. You take care.''

The first thing Jenny saw when she returned to the activity room was McCai and Tom Harper laughing and talking as if they'd been friends for years.

''Looks like your young man knows what it takes to get that old sourpuss to smile,'' Emily Dupree remarked to Jenny. ''They've been going at it ever since you left. He could spread himself around a little, though. Tom Harper isn't the only person who needs cheering up.''

''You're right, Mrs. Dupree,'' Jenny agreed. ''You're absolutely right. It wouldn't hurt him at all to mingle.''

When it was time for Jenny and the dogs to leave, McCai followed the van back to the Arbor, then joined Jenny on the old-fashioned swing on the front porch.

There was no mention of the argument they'd had the day before, and neither seemed anxious to bring up the subject. Simply by his being there, Jenny felt McCai had said he was sorry. At least she preferred looking at it that way. It also showed her that though he tried hard to be a cold, uncaring person, Jonah McCai had a gentleness about him as well. She'd caught glimpses of it once or twice, and he'd shown it with the patients at the nursing home. When she as good as told him the same thing, McCai frowned.

"Actually, it wasn't as bad as I thought it would be. I feel sorry as hell for your Mr. Harper, though. He was a farmer, used to walking over his property, fishing in his pond and running his Walker hounds when the stroke happened. When he left the hospital he was supposed to go to his nephew's place. The nephew said he couldn't manage, so Mr. Harper went to the nursing home."

"He told you all this?" Jenny asked, amazed.

McCai nodded.

"How? What did you do to get him to open up? He's been there for almost two years, and Marge and the rest of the staff have to practically pull every word out of him."

"I honestly don't know," McCai confessed. "I don't have some special affinity with the elderly, believe me. Oddly enough the old fellow and I hit it off." He looked away from Jenny. "I promised I'd visit him again."

Jenny was surprised. Had she actually heard Jonah McCai—the world's most cynical individual—admit that he was going to visit Mr. Harper again? "I'm sure he'd like that, McCai," she murmured.

The silence stretched on and on, leaving Jenny tongue-tied. She hadn't the faintest idea what to say.

McCai could feel the tension hovering all around them like invisible tentacles holding them in their grip. He tried telling himself that he couldn't begin to understand why he'd felt compelled to visit at a nursing home, particularly one in a strange town. But he knew he was lying to himself. He'd gone because Jenny had asked him to.

He looked at her then. "Okay. You can have your laugh now."

"I beg your pardon?"

A large tanned hand moved easily to cup her nape, the pad of his thumb lightly caressing the gentle curve of her jaw. Her skin was so soft, so warm . . . he could almost feel it pulsing with energy. At that moment McCai had to use every ounce of self-control he possessed to keep from sweeping her into his arms and kissing her till she was speechless. "I did as you wanted. Aren't you going to gloat?"

"Oh, McCai," Jenny whispered, closing her eyes. For a moment she rested her cheek against his arm, absorbing the silky-rough texture of dark hair covering his skin as it brushed against her face. "You try so hard to be bad, when all the while you're a good, decent person."

McCai stared at the face resting innocently against his arm. The next minute he was kissing a mouth he'd watched and wondered about for days.

Jenny's eyes flew open in surprise and her mouth unwittingly followed suit. McCai took full advantage of the situation, thrusting his tongue deeply into the dark sweetness he knew he would find waiting. Her tongue met his, hesitantly at first—then boldly. She became a seductress. McCai's senses were filled with the taste and scent of Jenny Castle. Jenny was heady with the total sensual essence of Jonah McCai.

When he slowly raised his head, Jenny saw, for the first time, warmth and a hint of disbelief.

She reached out and cupped her palm to his cheek. "I'm curious about something, McCai. How does this move figure in with your case?"

"Danged if I know, Jenny Castle, but if it's a new investigative technique, then I'm definitely all for it."

CHAPTER FOUR

"JENNY? JENNY, you have a phone call," Dolly Yates called from the side veranda of the Arbor.

Jenny, on her knees planting tulip bulbs for the following spring in a newly prepared bed, looked up at the older woman through the slats of the railing. This was the fourth or fifth interruption since she'd started working outside, and she was beginning to think she would never finish. "Who is it, Dolly?"

"Wouldn't give her name. Just wanted to know if I was the lady that put the ad in the paper about a dog, and asked if there was still a reward."

"Just say you're the one responsible for the ad. If someone's really got information about Dulcie, they'll tell you."

"Probably just another crank call," Dolly remarked as she turned and went back into the house.

"Probably so," Jenny repeated, returning to her gardening.

Since Dulcie's disappearance the ad had generated from two to six phone calls daily. A few of the callers were sincere in their efforts to help. Unfortunately, a large majority of them were interested because of the five-hundred-dollar reward.

"Jenny!" Dolly yelled a short time later, the sound of her footsteps echoing across the cypress boards of the porch. "I think you'd better come inside and talk with this woman. From the way she sounds, she could have found Dulcie."

The next few minutes were a blur for Jenny. One minute she was setting out tulip bulbs. The next minute she was talking on the phone, listening to a woman describe a dog that sounded remarkably like Dulcie.

What condition is she in, Mrs. Delacroix?" Jenny asked.

"Other than being real thin, she looks fine to me. 'Course, all that long hair she's got on her makes her look fat. My daughter has a poodle, and she said this one would probably be really pretty if the hair on her face was trimmed off."

"Your daughter is absolutely right, Mrs. Delacroix. But listen, do me a favor, please. My dog's name is Dulcie," Jenny said excitedly. "Would you mind calling the dog by that name and see what kind of response you get?"

"Certainly, Ms Castle. Hang on a minute." In the background Jenny heard the woman doing as she'd been instructed, the sound of several voices speaking at once and a dog barking, then the sound of footsteps closer and closer to the phone. There was a rustling noise as the receiver was picked up. "She wagged her tail when I called her, Ms Castle, and came to me. Do you want us to bring her to you?"

"Oh no," Jenny quickly assured her. "Please, you stay put. I'll come to you. If it really is Dulcie, then I don't want to take the chance of her getting away from you. Where do you live, Mrs. Delacroix?''

A short time later Jenny and Dolly Yates were in the van headed north on the interstate toward Tuckerton, a small community approximately fifteen miles from Jefferson City.

"Poor Dulcie," Dolly said. "I wonder how she got so far from home?"

"Well, according to Mrs. Delacroix, she's very thin, which makes me wonder if she was actually stolen or simply managed to get out of the kennel," Jenny said thoughtfully.

"Mmm…" Dolly murmured. "The last time we saw Dulcie was the day the new kid started. Remember? Frankly, I always wondered if he left the gate open for her, and was too scared to tell anyone."

"It could have happened that way," Jenny agreed. "Maybe that's the reason he quit. Even Phil couldn't understand when he didn't show up two days later. He said the kid really needed the money for tuition."

"Knowing that Dulcie was a show dog, he might have gotten it into his head that you were going to make him pay for her. Let's just hope this trip won't be in vain."

"Amen," Jenny said fervently.

By the time they found their way to the attractive house a mile off the interstate, Jenny was as tense as a post. The tips of her fingers were white from gripping the steering wheel so tightly.

What if it wasn't Dulcie? What if it was yet another blind lead? But the woman had sounded sensible enough—so different from all the other callers. Hadn't she?

Dolly, too, was staring with interest at the house. Finally she turned to Jenny. "Well? If Dulcie is there, she isn't going to come out all by herself."

Jenny nodded. "I know."

"Do you want me to go?"

The offer touched Jenny deeply. "Thanks, Dolly, but I'll go."

Mrs. Delacroix opened the front door just as Jenny reached out her hand to press the doorbell.

"You must be Ms Castle? I've been watching for you."

"Yes, I am," Jenny said to the attractive older woman. "I came to look at the d—"

The sentence was cut short by a barking black flash that shot past Mrs. Delacroix, and hurled itself against Jenny.

"Dulcie!"

The next few minutes were a mixture of tears and laughter. Jenny was so happy, she was barely aware of writing out the check for the reward or of Dolly having followed her into the house and restraining the jubilant Dulcie.

The return trip to Jefferson City was made in record time. The first thing Jenny wanted to do when they arrived at the Arbor was to take Dulcie to the kennel and groom her.

"Unless you need me to help you with dinner?" she asked Dolly.

"I don't need your help," Dolly told her. "Go pamper your baby."

"I intend doing that," Jenny said happily.

Dolly chuckled at the young woman's joy. "I think it's wonderful. You go and get started. I'll call you when dinner is ready."

JONAH MCCAI SAT back in his chair, his alert gaze reading and rereading every single bit of information collected so far on the dognapping case. In his opinion the results were pitiful. He hadn't learned much more than when he'd first arrived in New Orleans. And he was accustomed to being much further along in his investigation of a case.

McCai reached for the phone. He punched in the numbers, then leaned back in his chair and propped his feet on a corner of the desk.

"All right?"

"It's nice to know that some things never change," McCai remarked.

"Meaning?"

"You still sound like a bear when you answer the phone."

Nate Jones laughed at the comparison. "My friend, that's an excellent example of the pot calling the kettle black. Why don't we get together for a drink?"

"What time?" McCai asked.

"Meet me in an hour at Ralph and Kacoo's on Decatur. We can have a drink, then pig out on crayfish?"

"Sounds great. By the way, I could enjoy my crayfish a whole lot better if I knew you had some information for me."

"I've got some, and more will be forthcoming."

"Good," McCai said, breathing a sigh of relief. "See you at six." He dropped the receiver back in its cradle, then crossed his hands behind his head.

McCai stared at the ceiling. He had one nervous veterinarian. Why the man was nervous, McCai couldn't say, but he would keep on digging into the vet's affairs till he came up with some answers.

Then there was Jenny Castle. Pretty, sexy Jenny Castle. McCai never knew from one minute to the next how he was likely to find her. Was she saint or sinner?

So far there were three facts about Jenny that worried McCai. One was her "friends" who kept her supplied with dogs, ostensibly, for the nursing home. Were they obtaining those dogs through less than honest means, and was Jenny aware of those circumstances—perhaps even a willing helper? Secondly, she traveled, showing her dogs. Was that all she did—just show her dogs? And last, but certainly not least, Jenny Castle was—if indeed she turned out to be the dognapper—certainly knowledgeable enough about canines to procure only the best. It was the first and last facts that bothered McCai most.

The abrupt sound of the telephone ringing interrupted McCai's train of thought. He reached for the receiver and raised it to his ear. "McCai."

"You're obviously of Scottish descent, McCai," Jenny informed him. "You possess a certain economy with words that gives new meaning to the phrase, *not having much to say*."

"Bad day at the Arbor, Ms Castle?" he countered.

"Quite the contrary. It's been a fantastic day, Mr. McCai."

"Did you discover that your eccentric aunt really did leave a sensible will, and you can now sell your white elephant?"

"It wasn't quite that good a day, McCai. But from a personal viewpoint, I think it's grand. I found Dulcie."

McCai was silent for a moment. His mind, which had been trained for years to think the unthinkable, to suspect the most unsuspecting, went into overdrive. "Er...how? When?"

"In the most unlikely place, naturally. You know I've been running the ad in the paper ever since Dulcie disappeared."

"And?"

"Well, today I got a call from a Mrs. Delacroix in a small town a few miles north of here. Dolly and I rushed up there and...I've just spent the past couple of hours bathing and brushing one very tired, but very happy poodle."

"What kind of condition was the dog in?" McCai asked. Was she telling the truth?

"Other than being pitifully thin, she seems fine. I'm afraid her coat isn't too great at the moment. But with care that will grow back."

"And I assume the woman who called you was a complete stranger?"

"Completely. Isn't that wild?"

"I'm happy for you," McCai said.

"Well, I was beginning to wonder," Jenny confessed, puzzled by his lack of enthusiasm. Of course, she reasoned, since he considered her high on his list of suspects, he probably didn't believe a single word she'd told him. "By the way, how's the case coming? Any likely suspects—besides me?"

"There've been no changes" was McCai's curt reply.

"Oh my! I think I hit a nerve. By the way, if you don't have other plans, would you like to eat Thanksgiving dinner at the Arbor? I realize it's a way off, but it doesn't hurt to make definite plans."

For a moment McCai closed his green eyes in angry frustration. Jenny knew she was a suspect, yet she was inviting him to share Thanksgiving dinner with her.

How was it possible for him to be so attracted to her, and at the same time be more than casually suspicious of her involvement in the case he was working on? Situations like that simply didn't happen—at least not to him. But this one had happened, he quickly told himself, this one sure as hell had happened.

"I wouldn't want to intrude," he said stiffly.

"Is that a polite way of telling me to go to the devil?"

"Is that the way it sounds to you?"

"Of course it is. Plus cautious overtones regarding my supposed guilt thrown in. The least you could do is share a meal with a condemned woman, McCai."

McCai had to grin at that remark. Even knowing he considered her capable of stealing dogs, she refused to be intimidated. He liked that. He also wondered, if she did turn out to be the culprit, would he be tempted to look the other way?

"Then by all means include my considerable appetite when you buy the turkey. Will your parents be there?"

"Oh yes. In fact, they're flying in two days before the big day."

"You make them sound ominous."

"They are, but in a friendly sort of way. You haven't lived till you've met my parents."

"Are you busy tomorrow evening for dinner?" McCai suddenly asked.

"No . . . why?"

"Will you have dinner with me?"

"Should I?"

"What the hell is that supposed to mean?"

"Are you asking me out for a pleasant dinner, or is it just an excuse to ask me more questions? Think about it, McCai. I've got to scoot. See you."

McCai held the receiver in his hand, a frown creasing his wide brow. The question she'd asked was an uncomfortable one, and one he really wasn't ready to answer. He turned his thoughts instead to Jenny's news, which seemed to point an incriminating finger at her. Wasn't it odd that of all the dogs that had been stolen, Jenny Castle's was the only one recovered? He thought for a moment longer about the other names on his present list of suspects, then reached out and pressed two numbers on the phone panel.

"James Baldwin."

"I need some surveillance work done, James."

"When?"

"As soon as possible. Why don't I walk down to your office and give you the details," McCai suggested.

"Come on," James agreed. "I just had coffee and sandwiches sent in. We might as well snack while we talk."

"See you in about five minutes," McCai told him, then sat back in his chair. It was possible that the break he'd been waiting for was about to happen. So why wasn't he happier, or at least reasonably pleased? Why wasn't he making plans to go out and celebrate? He wondered why none of the aforementioned ideas appealed to him?

Why?

One word. One lousy three-letter word. But in his line of work it held a wealth of meaning. And in this particular instance, the importance it carried was beginning to gnaw at his peace of mind.

As McCai and James Baldwin were discussing business, Joey Tate was finishing with a customer in his studio.

"Here you go, Mrs. Brown," he said, smiling at the elderly lady as he handed her a small bag with the logo of his shop printed on one side. "The photo came out nicely. I hope you have a lovely trip."

When Mrs. Brown was safely out the door, Joey locked it, then walked over to where Phyllis Gliden was gathering up the receipts and bills she collected each week.

"How's Noah doing?" he asked while studying the appointments for the next day. Juggling his time between the studio and the kennel was hectic at best, but by having an answering service take his calls at the studio, Joey managed. He had to. He needed every penny he could get his hands on if he wanted to realize his dream.

Attractive blue eyes regarded Joey over the top of black-framed reading glasses. "Fine. He's a precious little guy. I'd like to keep him with me forever."

Immediately Joe's lips formed a thin line. "I've told you a hundred times not to become attached to him," he said sternly. "You'll get hurt when he goes. Noah already has a home, and a very nice one at that. At the moment his folks are away. Surely you haven't forgotten?"

Phyllis shrugged, just as disapproving of Joey's rules where Noah was concerned, as he was of her sentimentality. "How can I? You remind me almost every day."

"It's for your own good. I'll drop by your place later, and check on Noah," Joey told her as he started to leave. "Will you be in?"

"I'll be there," Phyllis murmured, then picked up her purse and left the studio.

She took a deep breath as she walked toward the bus stop, then exhaled slowly. At times Joey Tate had to be the most irritating person to work for in the entire world. Why she put up with him, she wasn't sure. If she had any sense at all, she'd tell him to get himself another bookkeeper.

But even as she was thinking such negative thoughts about her employer, Phyllis knew that one of the main reasons she continued with Joey was that, in spite of his erratic behavior at times, he was good to her.

When she came to work for him more than four years ago, she'd been on her fifth job within a six-month period. Total deafness was a handicap most people were uncomfortable with. Phyllis read lips, but even with that accomplishment under her belt and having gotten her degree in accounting, she had had difficulty finding steady employment.

But Joey had hired her, and recommended her to other small business owners. No, Phyllis thought, no matter how he annoyed her, she wouldn't leave him. Besides, she loved it when Joey let her go over to his kennel and play with his dogs. Sometimes he would even give in to her begging and let her keep one for a few days. Yet when she thought about it, it seemed odd to Phyllis that she'd been allowed to keep Noah for so long. After all, it had been several weeks. What kind of trip had his owners taken?

ON THE WAY HOME, Joey took the time to shop for a few groceries. His conversation with Phyllis had left him in a bad mood. She was almost like a child, and he hated to see her disappointed. That was why he continually cautioned her about becoming attached to the dogs.

Later, after he'd eaten and showered, he took down a manila folder from the bookcase in the living room. He carried it to the table in the kitchen, sat down and opened it.

In spite of the unfortunate distortion of his facial features, Joey looked happy as he touched his fingertips carefully, lovingly, to the colorful brochures of coastal Mexico he'd collected over the years. There were a number of photographs, as well, that he'd taken while vacationing in the country. His eyes darted from one to another.

Lord! The color. The natural beauty.

Joey felt his heart beat faster, felt perspiration dampen his palms. Deep, quivering excitement added an extra sparkle to his eyes and lent a flush to his cheeks. This was going to be his, he told himself, his. He traced the line of a sandy beach with the tip of his finger, pausing at the emerald-green water's edge. He closed his eyes and felt the coolness of the waves rushing over him, felt the heat of the sun warming his thin, crippled body. It felt so good . . . so good.

No, Joey vowed determinedly, there was no way on earth he was going to abandon his goal. Slowly, reluctantly, he replaced the brochures, closed the folder, then got up and returned it to the bookcase.

Joey looked at his watch. He was surprised to see that it was almost nine o'clock. As he started toward the door, he hoped Phyllis hadn't given up on him and gone out.

One good thing about Phyllis, Joey thought while driving to her apartment, was her loyalty. Not once during the time she'd been with him had she refused to help out, no matter what she was asked to do. That one trait alone made Joey a little sad. He wasn't accustomed to such dedication. Phyllis was like him; she was alone. Like him, she was one of the imperfects, placed on the earth to do the bidding of others. When his dream materialized and he left New Orleans, Joey couldn't help but wonder how she'd fare. Where would she go? What would she do?

Those thoughts and others were on his mind when he reached Phyllis's place. He knocked on the door, a brooding look adding to the harshness of his face.

When the door opened, Joey took one look at Phyllis and demanded to know what was wrong?

"Wh-what do you mean?" she managed to ask. Joey muttered something ugly under his breath and brushed past her into the room. Phyllis was steadily wringing her hands. Her face was puffy from crying and her eyes were still brimming with tears.

"It doesn't take a genius to figure it out, sweetie," Joey countered impatiently. "Come on, talk."

"You aren't going to like this, Joey," she said in a quivering voice. She raised her hand and pushed back the hair that had fallen over her forehead. "You really aren't going to like it."

"Give me a chance."

"I don't—"

"Talk!"

"Okay!" Several tense moments of silence followed her response. "Noah's gone."

There, Phyllis thought, her agonized gaze watching Joey, hoping to gauge his reaction in time to make a run for it if he became violent.

Joey hoped he'd heard wrong. He prayed that the words that issued from Phyllis's mouth had been some horrible joke. But the longer he stared at her, the more convinced he became that she'd spoken the truth.

A cold, limb-weakening sensation began to permeate Joey's very being. His heart beat as rapidly as it always did when he looked over his beloved brochures. But this time the increased acceleration was due to fear, not enjoyment.

IT WAS CLOSE TO MIDNIGHT when McCai opened the door to his apartment and sprinted across the living room to answer the telephone.

"McCai," he said briskly.

"Jonah McCai?" a man asked.

"Yes. What can I do for you?"

"It just might be that it's the other way around, Mr. McCai," the man said. "I'm Richard LeJeune, a veterinarian. My clinic is over on Veterans Boulevard. You and a young lady were in my office several days ago asking about specific breeds of dogs. I believe the dogs had been stolen. Correct?"

"Yes," McCai answered quickly. "Do you think you've found something?"

"I'm positive I have," the vet told him. "A wire fox terrier was brought in approximately three hours ago with a broken leg. I've just come out of surgery, and I think he's going to make it. He also has a number tattooed just inside the hairline on the right side of his stomach. I wouldn't have found it if I hadn't shaved the area before operating or if I hadn't specifically looked for it." He repeated the number he'd found, one McCai had committed to memory.

"That's the one, Dr. LeJeune. I'd like to ask you to cooperate with me in this matter. There are other dogs involved, and we think the base of operation is here in New Orleans."

"What do you want me to do?"

"For the moment, would you consider just keeping the dog at your clinic without letting the owner or anyone else know that you have it?"

"Be glad to."

"Good," McCai said, relieved. "I'll be by first thing in the morning to fill you in on the investigation. And thanks, Doctor. I appreciate your calling."

After talking with the vet, McCai showered, then tried watching TV. But instead of keeping his mind on the fast-moving mystery unfolding on the screen, he found his thoughts taken over by the real mystery he was struggling to unravel.

Jenny's dog had been returned and the wire fox terrier had been found. Two very unexpected occurrences, and two rather suspicious ones as far as McCai was concerned. Both dogs had been recovered in the vicinity of New Orleans. He asked himself the same

question he'd asked before. Had Jenny's dog been returned by an innocent person or was Jenny involved
in the dognappings? And now the terrier was in a veterinarian's clinic. Was she somehow involved in that,
as well?

CHAPTER FIVE

McCAI'S FIRST ORDER of business the next morning was to phone Scanlon in Dallas, and update him on the case.

"You really think it would interfere with the remaining investigation for us to let Mrs. Jones know we've found her dog?" Scanlon asked. He was on the hot seat from his board of directors for a progress report. He wanted to press for more definite action, but from the rumors he'd heard regarding McCai and how the man worked, Scanlon knew it would be pointless. McCai seemed to be a law unto himself.

"Among the people in the dog world, good or bad news travels faster than sound, Scanlon," McCai remarked dryly. "I wouldn't want to risk the woman keeping her mouth shut. Right now it's a wait-and-see game. The thieves know they've lost the dog...that's all. Let's leave it that way. As soon as we get through talking I'm on the way to see the vet. I'll try to convince him to cooperate with us. I'll get back to you as soon as anything new develops."

On that abrupt note McCai ended the conversation, then called in his secretary. After giving her a quick briefing on his plans for the day, he left. Dur-

ing the drive to the veterinarian's office McCai remembered how amused he'd been a few months ago
when he first talked with Scanlon about the dognapping case.

McCai had honestly been amazed at the amount of
money involved with the "dog claims," as he'd come
to think of them. Even the staff in the Dallas office
had joked about the firm going to the dogs. But the
longer McCai had studied the case—trying to decide
whether or not to take it—the more he saw that it involved more than just a few dogs being stolen. He decided he was dealing with a well-thought-out
operation, a very lucrative business, running into
hundreds of thousands of dollars a year, possibly
more.

"From what I was told by the woman who brought
him in, he was hit by a car," Richard LeJeune said to
McCai a few minutes later as they stood in front of an
aluminum crate containing a wire fox terrier. The dog
was sleeping on a bed of shredded paper, his breathing regular. The right rear leg was in a cast and resting parallel with the dog's body. "I even found the
small half-moon chip in the right incisor."

Suddenly McCai looked closely at LeJeune. "You
did get the woman's name and address, didn't you?"

The vet, a sandy-haired man in his mid-thirties,
grinned sheepishly and shook his head. "I was afraid
you'd ask me that. You have to understand, Mr.
McCai, all this happened between six-thirty and seven
o'clock last night. I was late closing and was about to
go home, when the young woman burst in, carrying

the dog.'' He nodded toward the sleeping terrier. ''She was hysterical, and kept muttering 'He's going to kill me.' Once I saw the condition of the dog, I didn't take the time to ask a lot of questions. Wouldn't have done me much good if I had,'' LeJeune remarked, then turned and walked back to his office.

''What do you mean?'' McCai asked.

''I immediately rushed the dog to an examining room. Naturally I assumed the young woman would follow me. But when I looked around to ask her a question, she was gone.''

''Would you know her if you were to see you again?''

''I think so,'' LeJeune said after pausing only a moment. ''She was on the petite side and rather plain except for her eyes. They were a deep blue. I don't recall any distinguishing marks. Do you think she stole the dog?''

McCai paced slowly while he thought, as was his habit. He made one or two laps around the office, one hand thrust finger-deep inside a back pant pocket while the other hand rubbed at his chin. ''That would be the logical assumption. But at this point I honestly can't say. You said she kept mentioning something about someone going to kill her. Are you sure she didn't mention a specific name?''

''I'm positive,'' LeJeune said firmly. ''A veterinarian learns to develop a keen ear to pick up information from incoherent owners. I distinctly heard her say *he* was going to kill her.''

"Apparently *he*, whoever he may be, didn't know she had taken the dog out."

"Of course. By the way, do you have the name and address of the owner of the dog?" LeJeune asked. "I'll need to get in touch."

"That's something I want to talk with you about, Doc," McCai said. "Your cooperation in this matter would be greatly appreciated."

WHILE MCCAI WAS USING his powers of persuasion on Richard LeJeune, Jenny found herself acting as referee between two stubborn factions at the nursing home.

Edna Davis, back to being her perky self as well as the spokesperson for her group, wanted to have a Christmas dance. John Rankin, reigning checkers champion and his cronies, wanted to have a quiet party without a lot of irritating noise giving them headaches.

"You're nothing but a stubborn fool, John Rankin!" Edna said, firing another volley of insults at the stern-faced gentleman glaring at her from across the room. "All you want to do is sit at that table and play checkers. Even the television bothers you."

"Now, Edna," Jenny began, "you know you don't mean—"

"Can a man be blamed if he likes his peace and quiet?" John countered. "If it's partying you want, Edna Davis, then why don't you open a nightclub?"

"Mr. Rankin," Jenny said and smiled her nicest smile, "I'm sure we can—"

"It's none of your business, young woman," John Rankin snapped. "That woman," he said, pointing a finger at the unflinching Edna, "is determined to keep some sort of ruckus going all the time. Why can't you people leave us alone?"

"Because we don't want to be left alone, John Rankin," Mrs. Dupree spoke up, much to Jenny's surprise. "Don't be such an old fool. If we wanted to be by ourselves, we wouldn't be so glad to see people like Jenny here, or her animals, or the children who come to sing to us during the holidays."

"I don't want a pack of kids yelling in my ear," John Rankin maintained. "As for the animals, I guess they're okay."

"May I make a suggestion?" Jenny spoke loudly, for most of the people surrounding her had some degree of hearing loss.

Edna nodded her snow-white head and glared at John Rankin. "Go right ahead, honey, speak."

"Mr. Rankin?" Jenny asked, looking questioningly at the elderly man. "Do you mind?"

A short nod was all the indication John gave, but Jenny figured it was at least better than another round of tempers flaring.

"Why don't we incorporate both Edna's and Mr. Rankin's suggestion into our plans for Christmas?"

"How can we do that?" Mrs. Dupree asked suspiciously. "I can tell you right now, I don't intend to spend Christmas playing checkers."

"No, no," Jenny said, quickly jumping into the conversation before a spluttering Mr. Rankin could throw in his own choice remarks. "This room has sliding doors that can easily make it into two rooms."

"So?"

"So, why don't we work with that in mind? Let's arrange it so that those of you who want to dance can do so, and the ones who would rather watch television or play cards or checkers can also do that. Think about it. Okay?"

"I'm tired of all this talk about Christmas. We haven't even had Thanksgiving yet," another gentleman spoke up. "Aren't we going to get our dogs today?"

"You certainly are," Jenny assured him, motioning for Phil to begin distributing the animals to their "owners." "But since you did ask me to help you with the party, I thought it was best to get our discussion out of the way first." Jenny couldn't help but be amused at the low-voiced muttering that followed that remark. In many ways the residents reminded her of small children bickering among themselves.

When the docile dog, Mildred, was placed in Edna Davis's lap, all the woman's anger toward John Rankin was momentarily forgotten. Hands that weren't as steady as they once had been—hands that were misshapen with arthritis—gently stroked and petted the sleek, contented Mildred. Edna crooned and talked as if she had a little child on her lap instead of a dog.

When the last pet had been distributed, Jenny paused for a moment and listened. Edna wasn't the only one making affectionate noises to the animals. Almost without exception the old people were talking to their pets, and producing various treats out of their pockets—a small doggie treat here, a rubber bone there, even a piece of meat that had been wrapped in a napkin. Though some of the old people's minds weren't as sharp as they'd once been, they had all remembered that they would be spending time with the dogs.

Jenny was thoughtful as she went about helping with the small problems that arose during the course of each visit. Suddenly, in the midst of her mental probing of the relationships between the elderly and animals, she found one face missing.

She walked over to where John Rankin was sitting, extolling the virtues of his Labrador puppy to another older man. "I don't see Mr. Harper, today, Mr. Rankin. Is he ill?"

"He's got a visitor," she was told.

"How nice," Jenny said. "I hope it's a relative."

"It is."

"Then I'm sure he's pleased."

"Can't say for sure. There are all kinds of relatives," John Rankin remarked, regarding her with eyes that—though some of their sparkle had dimmed—were still sharp.

"Well, I'm sure he's enjoying whoever it is."

"I think you should go tell him that his dog is here," Mr. Rankin told Jenny. "He sets great store by how quickly that puppy took to him."

"But I don't want to interrupt his time with his family," Jenny pointed out. "I don't think he gets very many visitors, Mr. Rankin."

"Suit yourself," the old man said, shrugging. "If it were me, though, I'd let him know about his dog. They're in room 14. It's just down the hall there," he said, nodding toward the corridor where the individual rooms were located.

"Maybe I will," Jenny told him, then walked over to where Marge Williams had just finished with one of the aides. "Got a minute?"

"Certainly."

"Busy day?"

"Aren't they all?" Marge laughed. "Trying to keep the patients and the staff happy is almost impossible. So... what can I do for you?"

Jenny told her the situation, adding that in view of Mr. Harper's not having that many visits from his family, she hesitated bothering him.

"Ordinarily I'd agree," Marge said, nodding. "But since he's been in your program, he's really come out of himself. Why don't you go tell him? That way he can make his own choice. There's no reason his visitor can't come with him. I'd like to talk longer, Jenny, but I'm supposed to be in three different places at once."

It really wasn't a big deal, Jenny thought as she made her way to room 14. However, it did seem to her unfair for poor Mr. Harper to have the only two things that brought him any pleasure at all happening on the same day.

She started to knock, then paused, her hand in midair.

"I don't care what you say, I'm not signing any damned fool papers," Jenny heard Mr. Harper saying in a loud, angry voice. His tone caught and held her full attention. "I'm not interested in selling off that piece of property, Joey. I have enough to take care of me. You'll just have to wait till I die to get your inheritance."

"It's for your own good, Uncle Tom," another man said soothingly. "Why, that land has tripled in value within the past two years. The shopping center has sent every bit of real estate in that area sky-high. Of course, they won't wait forever for an answer."

"There was no call for them to be waiting on me at all," Mr. Harper maintained. "I don't have the slightest intention of selling off my property. Wouldn't have sold that other piece a few months back if you hadn't kept on insisting. Who knows, I might recover enough to go back home. If that does happen, then I want to find everything just as I left it."

"You're being unreasonable, Uncle Tom. However, I didn't come to argue with you. Just sign the papers and I'll leave you alone."

"You know perfectly well I can't see without my glasses, and I told you that I broke them. It'll be tomorrow before I get them back. Till then I'm not signing anything I can't read. Now get out of here, Joey, and leave me in peace."

"Not on your life, old m—"

Suddenly Jenny's fist made several quick knocks against the door, her knuckles smarting from the force.

"Who's there?" the stranger demanded.

"Mr. Harper? It's Jenny Castle. Your puppy is waiting for you. Do you feel like joining us today?"

"Sure thing, Jenny," Tom Harper called back, the sound of his voice coming closer. Suddenly the door was flung open and the wheelchair whizzed past her so quickly that Jenny jumped back to keep her toes from being run over.

Jenny's gaze swung from the back of the retreating Mr. Harper to the scarred face of the individual staring at her from inside the room.

She'd seen the face before . . . but where?

A shiver of fear ran over her as she took a tentative step forward. "H-hello. I'm Jenny Castle."

The man ducked his head to one side, mumbled something unintelligible beneath his breath, then brushed by Jenny and hurried out of the room. Jenny turned and watched his uneven stride as he reached the door at the end of the corridor and left the building. Something wasn't quite right between Mr. Harper and his nephew, Joey, Jenny decided.

That day the time with the dogs ran over schedule. Jenny tried to speed things up, but for some reason everything seemed to go wrong. In addition to the residents' heated discussion at the beginning and Mr. Harper's mysterious visitor, Mrs. Dupree got a scratch on the arm from her puppy that had to be attended to. And as if that wasn't enough, Edna Davis and John Rankin got into another argument about the Christmas party.

"I thought we were going to let everyone decide on that," Jenny reminded them, while trying to keep the fight from getting any worse. "I really do think everyone interested should vote." She looked resignedly from Edna to John. Frankly, she thought, she was to the point where she wanted to send them both to their rooms. "Would the two of you be willing to abide by that decision?"

"I suppose so," Edna said stiffly.

"Mr. Rankin? Would you go along with the idea?" Jenny asked.

"Well . . ."

"Yes or no, Mr. Rankin."

"I'll go along with it," he grudgingly agreed.

"Good," Jenny said, relieved. "We'll be sending around slips of paper for each of you to vote."

Even though she'd stayed longer than usual, when Jenny started to leave she stopped to speak to Mr. Harper, who was sitting by a window. She went down on her knees beside his chair. "Mr. Harper," she said softly, "I'm glad your nephew came to see you today. It's too bad I had to interrupt the visit. I'm sorry."

The expression on the old man's face didn't change. Nothing moved in the network of lines marking the surface of his face but his eyes—sad eyes that were trained on the wooded area beyond the grounds of the nursing home.

"I appreciate your coming to get me, Jenny." Though the words were stilted, Jenny detected a trace of warmth in his voice. It was certainly a vast improvement over their first encounter.

"Mr. Harper," she said cautiously, praying she was doing the right thing, "it's none of my business, but I couldn't help overhearing you and your nephew arguing. If he's trying to make you do something against your will, please let us help."

The old man looked at her then, resentfully. "Don't you ever think that Tom Harper is too old to look after his affairs, missy," he said. After delivering these short, blunt words, he abruptly turned his chair around and left the room.

Jenny walked away slowly, self-consciousness mirrored in her eyes. But there were no recriminating stares, no embarrassed looks leveled at her. Her offer of help and Tom Harper's curt remarks hadn't made the slightest ripple in the ebb and flow of the lives of the elderly people seated around the room. If the incident had been noticed by anyone at all, then it had been only for a brief moment. The residents were old and tired, and what little time they did have, had to be reserved for the struggle of simply staying alive.

THAT EVENING when Jonah McCai arrived at the Arbor to take Jenny out to dinner, he followed the sound of loud voices to the kitchen.

"The front door was open, so I came on in," he remarked to no one in particular. He stopped in the doorway, summing up the emergency involving a burst pipe that had Dolly and his dinner date, clad in a very sexy beige slip, drenched to the skin. Jenny was crouching in front of the opened cupboard beneath the sink as if worshiping some invisible god.

He quickly removed his coat and tie, rolled up his sleeves, then, for the moment, took over placing buckets underneath the gushing pipe and emptying them into the sink. "Get me some tools," he said to Jenny. "Where's the cutoff?" he asked Dolly the same moment a spurt of cold water hit him squarely in the face.

Dolly grabbed a handful of paper towels to dry her face and arms. "Straight under there in the basement," she told him, pointing toward the floor of the cabinet beneath the sink. "It's not that hard to get to, but we couldn't let go up here long enough to take care of it."

Jenny ran back into the room, panting. "Here are the tools. I'll take that," she said as McCai snatched the tools from her and handed her the empty bucket. After removing the full pail beneath the sink, she put the empty one in its place. Dolly reached for the full bucket and poured the water down the drain.

"Seems like we've done this before," Dolly said with a shrug.

"This is probably Aunt Kathleen's punishment for my not allowing the Nathan Bedford Forrest Society to hold their tea here," Jenny remarked grimly. She grunted, then lifted another pail to Dolly.

"Could be," Dolly agreed, as she completed the bucket ritual. "There are times when it strikes me that your aunt really didn't die. I'm convinced this house simply absorbed her."

"My sentiments exactly," Jenny said, nodding. She was still breathing hard, her back felt as if it were breaking and the damned bucket was full again. "If that's the—"

Her flow of words were interrupted by a peculiar rattle, followed by the abrupt halting of the water flow from the faulty pipe joint beneath the sink.

Jenny and Dolly stared at each other, then back at the innocent-looking piece of metal. When it appeared that the water was truly stopped they dropped their buckets, then hobbled over to the table and sank wearily into chairs.

Only a few minutes passed before McCai joined them, the immaculate condition of his once white shirt marred by several dirty smears and a sizable rip across the back. There was a smudge on his face and a wispy cobweb clung to his dark hair.

Jenny stared at his less than spic-and-span appearance, then groaned. She wondered how much McCai had paid for his shirt?

McCai grasped the back of a straight chair and leaned on it, his wide shoulders thrown slightly forward, his green eyes taking in the delightful way the silky material of the damp slip clung to Jenny's body. Her nipples looked like hard, tight pebbles beneath the fragile cloth barrier. They looked as tempting as anything McCai had ever seen. At that precise moment he was swamped with an almost uncontrollable desire to catch that pebbled hardness between his lips.

"Ms Castle," he finally said with mock sternness, "have you any idea how expensive my time is? Especially the time I spend tending to plumbing problems. Not to mention the cost of replacing ruined clothing." The question was so far from what he was really thinking, McCai almost laughed.

"No," Jenny murmured. "But I have a feeling I'm about to learn." She recognized that look in his eyes, and knew it for what it was. Any woman would have. Pure feminine instinct enabled her to recognize a male's appreciation of a woman's body. His look was open, appraising. It was exciting, sensual. She could almost feel his eyes burning her skin as his gaze skipped back and forth across her dampened body, then returned glance after shuttered glance to her breasts.

Touching without physical contact . . . warming her with his eyes . . . bringing her to an awareness level that Jenny had never known.

She was tempted to cross her arms over her upper body, but she didn't. She was clothed as much as or more than when wearing a swimsuit. *Play it cool,* she kept telling herself. *Play it cool.*

"Mr. McCai," Dolly spoke up, blissfully unaware of the sexual tension between McCai and Jenny. "We can't possibly thank you enough. If you hadn't come along when you did we'd still be catching water. I told Jenny earlier that I honestly think her Aunt Kathleen's ghost haunts this place."

"Perhaps it does," McCai said, nodding. He straightened, then held up his hands. "If one of you ladies will show me to the bathroom, I'll wash up."

Jenny rose to her feet. "Dolly, you'd better get into something dry before you catch a cold. I'll call the plumber." She motioned for McCai to follow her. "If you hadn't come along when you did, McCai, I don't know what we'd have done," she said over her shoulder, painfully aware of his towering presence only inches behind her. "And of course I'll replace your shirt." When she was alongside the bathroom door, she lightly tapped on it with the tips of her fingers. "I believe you'll find everything you need in there. If not, sing out."

She was walking toward her own apartment when she suddenly realized that she wasn't alone.

With a supreme effort at casualness, Jenny stopped, then slowly turned. In the moments that passed while her eyes met those of the man behind her, her face took on a mask of politeness. "Guests usually use the bathroom I just showed you."

McCai took another step... another... and yet another.

When Jenny would have widened the narrowing space between them, McCai reached out and clasped her upper arms. "I don't think you really want me to do that." The words were plain and to the point, but Jenny didn't feel insulted.

"How would you know what I want?" One part of her wanted to indulge in the flirtatious fencing, while another part of her wanted him to take her in his arms and make love to her.

With infinite ease McCai drew her toward him till her breasts were pressed flat against his chest. He slipped a hand beneath her chin, then studied her for what seemed like an eternity.

"What are you, Jenny Castle? Who are you?" he finally asked in a gruff voice.

Jenny caught the ambiguous overtones in the question, but tonight she wasn't in the mood to try to allay his doubts where she was concerned. His body heat was warming her to a fever pitch, and she didn't care if he considered her the biggest crook in the world. All she wanted was for him to kiss her. She'd deal with his lack of faith in her later.

She raised her hand, the fingers splaying against McCai's nape; her other palm gently curved to follow the stern line of his jaw.

His cologne had a fresh, clean smell to it. Plain and simple, the complete opposite to the man wearing it. "Has anyone ever told you that you talk too much?" Jenny whispered.

McCai inhaled the special scent of her; he'd have recognized it anywhere in the world. It had been indelibly stamped on his brain since the first time he held her in his arms, and nothing he had done erased that memory.

A ghost of a smile touched his sensuous lips. "Oddly enough, no." His mouth claimed hers then. Lightly, teasingly.

Jenny, her eyes closed, murmured a low protest. She exerted her own pressure to his neck. McCai followed her gentle urging by taking her lips in a hard, forceful kiss.

Passion and desire. The perfect blending of the two.

The kiss turned into a gentle, wooing caress.

Passion and desire became savage then gentle...
back and forth, forging a need throughout her body
that Jenny made no effort to stop.

Mouth to mouth.

Heart to heart.

McCai felt a quiver, gut deep. He tightened his arms
around Jenny.

In his mind he was afraid of the future.

In his heart he was terribly afraid he was beginning
to care for Jenny.

CHAPTER SIX

JENNY'S RESPONSE took McCai by surprise. He felt it in the soft pliancy of her body as her slight curves blended into the muscled wall of his build. He heard it in the irregular sound of her breath as it rushed past her lips. He saw it in the flush on her cheeks, saw it in the expression of her eyes, which were dulled with passion.

Instinctively, McCai lifted a wide hand to her face. He smoothed the line of her jaw with his work-toughened fingertips. Touching Jenny was fast becoming a favorite pastime of his. How curious, he mused. Of all the women he'd known over the years, he'd never paid much attention to the texture of their skin. Skin was skin, or so he'd thought. But caressing Jenny was comparable to dipping his finger deep inside a velvet-throated blossom.

That sensual comparison took McCai's thoughts on another pleasure-ridden excursion. He imagined making love to Jenny, even to the point of how perfect it would feel to plunge himself into the hot, satiny sheath of her femininity.

"You make a man's work very difficult, Jenny Castle," McCai said in a rough whisper. Her head was resting in the crook of his arm, and his lips were slowly teasing the smooth skin of her forehead. And though holding Jenny in his arms and kissing her was something he was quite sure he could do for the rest of his life, the ugly implications of the present began encroaching upon the moment.

Once again McCai found himself wondering if Jenny was involved with the mystery of the wire fox terrier. Was she the respectable front McCai figured the dognapping business needed? Yesterday Nate had given him some rather startling figures regarding the number of dogs shipped out of New Orleans to foreign countries, especially Mexico. Was Jenny's personal involvement with dogs nothing more than a clever cover for a very lucrative, very dirty business?

"Only to men who think of me as a thief," Jenny replied lazily. "You're the one who's making your work difficult, McCai. I'm perfectly innocent." Jenny also knew that nothing would have pleased her more at that moment than for him to have affirmed his belief in her.

"That's what they all say," he murmured huskily, the sharp edges of his teeth nipping the tender lobe of her ear.

"Starting to get kinky, McCai?" Jenny asked teasingly, then stepped out of the circle of his arms. McCai really was beginning to feel the pinch of the situation. Tsk tsk! How sad, Jenny thought, tongue in cheek. She wondered if this was the first time he'd become involved with a suspect? Most likely it was, she decided. McCai didn't appear to be the kind of person to stray from the rules and regulations. She hadn't the slightest difficulty imagining the struggle he was having with his go-by-the-book conscience. Knowing him as she did, Jenny decided that he probably consulted his investigator's code of ethics each morning, then immediately inflicted appropriate punishment upon his person for each rule broken.

She was at the top of his list of suspects. Yet in spite of that fact, he was attracted to her. Considering the black-and-white code by which McCai lived, he had to be in a very difficult position.

He was a man who seemingly went to great lengths to distance himself from normal human conflicts and feelings. Jenny had seen a perfect example of that when he'd learned she took animals to the nursing home. But, as she'd observed once or twice since meeting him, McCai had shown a side of himself to Mr. Harper that was completely opposite to the tough-as-nails impression he tried hard to create.

Other softer aspects of his personality had been revealed when he kissed her, Jenny thought. And in her opinion, McCai, as a lover, was devastating!

McCai reached out and tapped the tip of her nose. "Just a little reminder that you aren't in control of the situation nearly as much as you'd like to think you are."

Jenny stared at him for a moment or two longer, finding it difficult not to laugh in that face she found so incredibly sexy. "I refuse to dignify that remark with a reply, McCai," she said briskly. "If your dinner invitation is still open, then let's get on with it.

Otherwise I can spend the time working with my dogs.''

McCai returned her hostile gaze without the slightest show of embarrassment. "Speaking of dogs," he said smoothly, "how are your dogs? I find it something of a miracle that you got your Dulcie back, don't you agree?"

In a pig's eye! Jenny wanted to yell at him. Again she'd gotten the unexpected from the infuriating giant standing before her. "An absolute miracle. Er...we were discussing dinner, McCai? How about it?"

"Of course dinner is still on, Jenny. Even a condemned man...er...excuse me, woman, deserves to be fed."

Ohh! Jenny turned on her heel and marched down the hall to her private quarters. Jonah McCai was the most arrogant, the most aggravating man she'd ever met in her life, she thought, and she kept reminding herself of that glaring fact while she showered and dressed.

The few pieces of the puzzle she'd been able to put in place, where he was concerned, were small and insignificant in relation to the overall picture of the man. The brief glimpses she'd seen of a warm, caring human being were at times so overshadowed by his obnoxious nature, it was difficult to believe that he possessed any genuine redeeming qualities.

But she also knew another McCai who kept himself hidden from the world, a tiny voice whispered. A McCai who—in spite of his size and obvious courage—seemed terrified of allowing anyone to get close to him. He spent so much time and effort keeping the world at bay, Jenny wondered how he managed to run his business.

Suddenly it dawned on her that getting to know the real Jonah McCai was becoming something of an obsession.

Why him?

What was so fascinating about a man who considered her a thief?

The questions were ones she really didn't have answers for at the moment . . . or so she told herself. She settled instead for the belief that even the hardest of rocks had a weak spot. With that questionable theory firmly in place, she was determined to find McCai's weak spot and prove to him that not all the people in the world were cold and uncaring.

"In the meantime," she muttered as she reached for her cologne and applied a light spritz to her neck and shoulders, "I'll try not to kill the overbearing ass."

However, her resolve was strongly tested a while later when she learned McCai's plans for dinner.

"Unless there's been a time warp and the world has changed drastically," she said crisply, "this is not the way to Galatoire's."

"Brilliant deduction, Ms Castle," McCai replied, raising his eyebrows and casting her a glance that was meant to irritate.

"May I be so bold as to inquire what your plans are for our dinner?"

"Certainly. I'm taking you to my apartment," McCai replied in the same tone as the question had been asked. "I had a hard day at the office. After wrestling with your plumbing," he told her, and the preponderance of evidence against you, he wanted to add but didn't, "I'm dog tired, no pun intended. And so, I think, are you. That being the case, I took it upon myself to change our plans." The car slowed and McCai looked at her again. "If you don't like the idea, I'll take you back home."

They stared at each other for what seemed to be aeons, but in reality was nothing more than the space of a few tension-filled heartbeats.

Jenny saw a man who intrigued her, a man who had begun to fill her thoughts and her dreams . . . dreams made up of wild and exciting fantasies in which she and Jonah McCai were the only players. She was aware of her reputation for being a gentle person, something of a do-gooder. It was a label she'd been forced to contend with for most of her life. Yet little did the people responsible for such judgments realize what a determined individual she really was. Perhaps it was time she let the world see that there was another side to her personality.

McCai saw a woman who—without his ever intending it to happen—had insinuated her way into his heart. He saw her fragility as an entrapment, her gentleness as a guise that enabled her to weave a spell to capture the hearts and souls of unsuspecting victims. He saw her as an enemy—a beguiling enemy, but one he was finding it more and more difficult to deal with.

"As you say, McCai, you asked me to dinner, and it's dinner I want."

There was no way in the world Jenny was going to be intimidated by his sharp tongue. She thought she saw one corner of his mouth quiver, as if he was trying not to laugh, but she couldn't be certain. In fact, there wasn't much about him she could be certain of.

It wasn't often that McCai met a woman who dared to argue with him. Truth was, he mused, it was years since he'd found one willing to do such a thing. And, he had to admit, most of the women he'd been associated with during his adult life had been the sort he wasn't overly attracted to.

Till Jenny, that was. Jenny Castle most definitely argued with him. She also shot to hell his modus operandi with the opposite sex. Underneath that gentle mask she presented to the world, McCai was well aware of a tough, stubborn female who never failed to give his ulcer an extra twist. She was also a suspect in his case. She knew she was one, and she tried to pretend she didn't give a tinker's damn. But McCai knew better.

During the remainder of the time it took to drive to McCai's apartment, conversation lagged, but more from weariness than from tension. They were two people tired from the ups and downs of a difficult day, their fatigue compounded by acute awareness of each other, and of the traps they considered each other more than capable of setting.

After they reached McCai's apartment, Jenny made herself at home in the living room while her host showered and changed. The room's decor was boring and more appropriate to an institution or an office than a home—all neutral colors and contemporary furnishings. Not the worst she'd seen, but certainly not something she'd want to live with for the rest of her life. Even before she inherited the Arbor, her apartment had been a blend of Early American style and a few antiques.

She walked out onto the terrace and leaned against the stout railing. Whatever the apartment's decor lacked was more than made up for by the view. It was perfect.

The crescent bend of the river hugging the outline of the city shone like Cupid's poised bow. To her right were the Pontalba apartments, the majestic beauty of St. Louis Cathedral and Jackson Square. The moonlight touching the water, and the mournful sounds of the small squat tugboats slowly moving their mammoth trails of barges northward through the treacherous waters of the Mississippi River, added a melancholy flavor to the atmosphere.

Jenny sighed wistfully as she stared several stories down at the large number of people getting an early start on an evening of the special magic the French Quarter offered. Though she had been born in New Orleans and knew its faults, she still loved the city. Its slightly tarnished image reminded her of that of a naughty lady who possessed endearing qualities as well.

Jenny thought about McCai's appearance in her life. He, along with certain other people and circumstances, was beginning to upset the natural ebb and flow of her daily existence. The Arbor was turning into much more of a burden than she'd bargained for from a financial viewpoint. It was ages, too, since she'd had time to go to a dog show. And she certainly didn't like being suspected of dognapping. Jenny had tried hard to ignore McCai's curious looks, his less than subtle questions. But his suspicious attitude was becoming more and more difficult for her to ignore.

"It's nice, isn't it?" McCai said from behind Jenny. "I look on the apartment as nothing more than a place to sleep. But the view..." His voice trailed off as he walked over and stood beside her at the railing, his shoulder brushing her arm. "It's spectacular."

Jenny felt that light caress and shivered. "I agree," she said softly.

McCai absorbed the slight quivering of her body into his being. He looked down at her. Odd, he thought fleetingly, had there always been those three tiny curls hugging her temple? Was that the ghost of a dimple in her cheek? And would there ever be a time when he wouldn't find something new and exciting about her?

"I definitely agree," Jenny repeated. "But then I'm prejudiced." Watching the emotions come and go on McCai's face reminded her of a huge collage of human feelings. Then suddenly, as if he were fearful someone might catch a glimpse of the real Jonah McCai, Jenny witnessed the closing of his features, leaving nothing but a face as unreadable as the facade of a towering building, a cold and impenetrable assemblage of mortar and stone—only in this instance the wall was a blend of skin and muscle and bone.

A warm, breathing human being.

A man.

A man Jenny was determined to expose as being far more gentle than he allowed people to know, a man who evoked the wildest sensual fantasies imaginable in her dreams both day and night . . .

Jenny turned back to her silent contemplation of the city below. By now she'd learned that McCai only revealed the other part of himself when he was ready. Thus far, she'd been unable to find that emotional hot button each person was supposed to possess. McCai had a unique way of controlling his own destiny.

"Are we going to spend an entire evening acting like polite strangers?" the instigator of her dark mood asked.

Dammit! His hands, which rested on the iron railing, turned into tight, hard fists. Never in his professional career—for the government or private—had he found himself in such an uncomfortable situation. How was it possible for him to desire a woman he counted as one of the suspects in his case? How was it possible for him to want to hold a woman like her in his arms, to want to kiss every inch of her, from her toes to her silky dark hair? How was it possible for one part of him to plot her downfall when the other part of him was determined to be her lover?

Yet even as he was going over those agonizing questions, McCai felt himself hardening, felt his body responding to the physical, the sensual side of the problem. Thief or not, he wanted Jenny Castle. Worse yet, he intended to have her.

McCai turned and rested his back against the railing, his arms braced on the top rung, his gaze centered on the angry line of Jenny's lips and the grim set of her features. She looked so innocent. "Are you going to pout at me forever, Jenny?"

Jenny forced herself to look at him, praying for the strength to keep her emotions in perspective. But was that ever possible with a man like McCai? Why couldn't she have met him under different circumstances? People met that way all the time. She knew they did. She had friends who had met their husbands or boyfriends in situations that were quite normal. In fact, she figured that a majority of people led calm, uneventful lives. Why couldn't she? Jenny wondered.

"Pouting isn't exactly what I'd call it."

"Oh?" he said easily. He dropped a quick kiss on her unsuspecting lips, then leaned one elbow against the railing, one hand lightly clasping the other, and regarded her with open curiosity. "What would you prefer to call this tension between us?"

"This tension, as you call it, is the result of your overly suspicious mind, McCai."

"Is that a fact?"

"Yes. For some reason, known only to you, you've decided that I'm closely associated with the underworld—head of the dognappers of America as it were."

The corners of McCai's mouth dimpled with annoyance. This wasn't the way he'd wanted to handle the problem. This evening was supposed to have been quiet and romantic—as much so as the situation would allow. "I'll admit there are...certain aspects of the case that aren't clear at the moment."

Suddenly Jenny clapped her hands several times in rapid succession. "Bravo, McCai!" she exclaimed in an exaggerated tone, the beaming smile on her lips not quite making it to her eyes. "You have a marvelous way with words. 'Certain aspects of the case that aren't clear at the moment.' That's brilliant. You should be with the State Department. May I assume those certain aspects will be clear in five minutes...ten minutes...or will it take an hour...an entire day?" By then she was square in front of McCai, her hands jammed on her hips, her eyes boring angrily into his.

"Why don't we discuss this another time?" McCai asked, trying to instill a calming influence. Was this petite, angry female glaring at him really the sweet, mild-mannered Jenny Castle?

"Correction. Why don't we be honest with each other for a change, McCai?" Jenny countered.

He frowned, his heavy, dark brows beetling to a black slash above his green eyes. "What do you want from me, Jenny?"

"The truth."

"I haven't been dishonest with you."

"You think not? I disagree, McCai. By your insinuations you've as good as said that I'm at the top of your list of suspects. I resent that."

And I wish it weren't true, McCai wanted to yell at her. But it was true, and he was positive he'd never felt more miserable in his entire life. "All right. I won't lie to you. I mentioned something about the suspects in this case the first time we met. Do you remember?"

"You told me lots of things."

"I told you then that everyone, including you, was a suspect. So far, that's still the case. And though it may certainly look that way to you, you alone aren't being singled out, Jenny. However, I am an investigator. It's all part of my job to examine each and every aspect of a case. I charge my clients a damn high fee, so they have every right to expect results. But there is one other thing you might consider."

"What's that?" Jenny asked suspiciously.

"If you aren't guilty, then there's nothing for you to worry about, is there?"

The sound of someone knocking on the door brought the fiery conversation to a halt.

As he pushed away from the railing, McCai also glanced at his watch. "That's our food." He hesitated for a moment, torn between his suspicions and what his heart was telling him. "Look," he said gruffly, "however this thing works out, I'll stand by you. We'll work it out together. Okay?" Without waiting for a reply or even expecting one, he swung on his heel and went to answer the door.

Jenny stared disbelieving at McCai's broad back as he disappeared through the French doors. Dear Lord! The man was well and truly bonkers!

She wanted to stamp her feet or perhaps throw something—preferably at Jonah McCai's head. She wanted to scream in frustration. Her only crime was being unlucky enough to have been in the vicinity when two of the dogs McCai was searching for disappeared.

Suddenly it occurred to Jenny that it would be impossible for her to sit down to dinner with a man who considered her a thief. She took a couple of determined steps toward the French doors, then just as quickly paused as McCai's last remark kept repeating itself in her mind.

The huge, overgrown pain in the behind had offered to stand by her. *How gallant,* she thought angrily. She closed her eyes briefly and shook her head. She couldn't decide what was more upsetting: his asinine inability to see that she wasn't guilty or that side of McCai she'd been so positive existed.

WHILE MCCAI WAS ADMITTING a young waiter with a punk hairstyle and showing him where to set up the table, Joey Tate was pacing the limited space of a kitchen in another part of town.

While Jenny contemplated her next move in the chess game of human emotions in which she and McCai were involved, Phyllis Gliden was preparing Joey's dinner, occasionally darting apprehensive looks at him.

Inviting him to dinner was her attempt to keep him from being so angry with her for losing Noah. She knew that if he ever found out she'd taken the dog to a vet, he'd kill her. But how could she have left poor little Noah lying there on the wet pavement? He'd been whimpering with pain, his dark eyes begging her to do something for him. Somehow she had to keep Joey from finding out.

"I still can't believe you did such a stupid thing after I warned you over and over to be careful," Joey said stonily for the umpteenth time to the crestfallen Phyllis.

"What did you say?" Phyllis asked, turning just as he finished speaking, and so lip-reading only the last few words.

Joey rolled his eyes upward in exasperation. Why was he surrounded with incompetents? Why, of all the people in the world, had he gotten himself involved with someone as pathetic as Phyllis Gliden?

"What did you say, Joey?" Phyllis repeated. Her face was a mess, and her eyes were even more swollen than they'd been the night before.

At the moment Phyllis's main concern was that Joey was going to fire her. He was moody and difficult at times, but at least he didn't ridicule her because of her handicap.

Hard, cold chills of fear scampered down her spine at even the thought of having to start looking for a new employer. Memories of her life before meeting Joey brought a fresh rush of tears streaming down her

cheek. She'd been crying almost nonstop since the
evening before, when she'd lost Noah.

"Why?" Joey yelled. "Why the hell did you deliberately do what I'd told you over and over not to do?"

"We...we didn't go far, Joey," she said in a barely
audible voice.

"'We didn't go far, Joey,'" he mimicked, his lips
curling in anger. "Out the front door was too damned
far, Phyllis. You disobeyed me, and now we don't
know if Noah's alive or dead."

Phyllis buried her face in her hands. "Please don't
say that," she sobbed. "Please."

For a moment Joey maintained a totally dispas-
sionate air as he watched the grieving Phyllis. But
slowly the depth of her feeling began to pull at his
heart. She was a dumb little klutz, he told himself, but
she was harmless. "For God's sake, stop that bawl-
ing," he snapped. He limped over and put an arm
around her shoulders. He pulled her hands away from
her face, then simply stared at her.

Phyllis's blue eyes were filled with trepidation as she
met Joey's cynical ones, her effort great as she sought
to keep her lips from trembling. "Are you going to fire
me?"

"No," Joey said roughly. "I'm not going to fire
you. I should, but I'm not." He patted her clumsily on
the shoulder, then made his way to the table and sat
down. "You'd better get back to your cooking."

And though she was still heartsick over the loss of
Noah, Phyllis was so relieved that her job was safe, she
threw herself into preparing the rest of the meal.

Joey, however, wasn't as easily pacified. The loss of Noah meant a change in certain plans, perhaps even a change in his departure date.

Unless . . . unless . . .

He clasped his hands together and stared out the window, chewing pensively at one corner of his mouth. The real estate firm interested in his uncle's property was still waiting to hear something positive.

Joey's eyes narrowed as he considered the different options for obtaining money that his fertile imagination was providing him with.

CHAPTER SEVEN

DAVID MOREAU STARED at Joey Tate as if he'd suddenly taken complete leave of his senses. "I can't believe you're asking me to do such a thing!" the vet exclaimed. "There's no reason at all for me to be inquiring about that dog."

"I'd say the fact that you could get five to ten years in the state pen should be incentive enough," was Joey's candid rejoinder. "You better start learning how to loosen up a little, pal, or life's going to be mighty uncomfortable in the days ahead. One would think professional courtesy would certainly allow you enough freedom to make discreet inquiries regarding the dog."

"And if I refuse?" Dr. Moreau said stubbornly.

"Then it's highly possible that at some point in the future the police will be knocking on your door."

"I refuse to involve myself further," the vet declared. "This entire situation is unethical."

This time it was Joey who stared incredulously. "Unethical?" he repeated. "Of course it's unethical, just as you are, you sniveling ass. Unethical to the tune of several thousand dollars that you were more than willing to take over the past eighteen months. And all you had to do was sign your name to a few health certificates. As long as things went smoothly you were more than willing to cooperate. But now that there's a slight hitch in the plans, you're ready to join the bird gang." Joey cast a quick, deprecatory glance around the less than tidy office. "You're not the most respected veterinarian in town, you know. If I were you, I'd do what was asked, and not make waves."

"You promised there wouldn't be any trouble," Moreau said nervously.

"Well, I'm not God, Moreau, so stop complaining. But I was hoping to ease some of our trouble by finding out if that dog was taken to a vet or if he died. All we're sure of at this point is that it was hit by a car. A certain person saw the accident, but was in a hurry and didn't have time to wait around and see the outcome."

Moreau shrugged, his expression grim. "I can't promise anything."

"Suit yourself," Joey told him.

WHILE JOEY AND DR. MOREAU were having their discussion, Jenny was attempting to make some headway in the pile of paperwork stacked on her desk. She picked up the latest bill from the plumber, who had worked at the Arbor first thing this morning.

The events of the evening before flashed before her eyes, from McCai's startled entry into the kitchen during the burst pipe episode to the waiter's knocking on the door of McCai's apartment with their food. So much had been said, so much had been felt by each of them.

Jenny wasn't so naive as to think she could walk away from Jonah McCai and never think of him again. If he were to suddenly leave there would be an enormous emptiness in her heart. Finally admitting to herself that she cared for McCai brought a momentary halt to Jenny's musing.

For all the good it was going to do her, Jenny might just as well have declared to the world that she was running for the presidency. It would make just about as much sense as becoming emotionally involved with Jonah McCai. From all she'd seen and heard about the man she'd so unwisely chosen to care for, she got the distinct impression he needed and used women with the same indifference he exercised when selecting a clean shirt for the day.

Jenny even went so far as to try to rationalize his suspicions of her. Knowing she was innocent had her wondering how he could be so blind. On the other hand, if she was going to try to understand McCai's position, then it was imperative that she be as objective as was humanly possible.

With that idea in mind, and given his years of experience dealing with people, Jenny could see how he might possibly regard her as a suspect. After all, she had been at dog shows in Texas when one dog was stolen and in New Orleans when another mysteriously disappeared from its handler's motel room. And one of her own dogs had been lost for a while. Add to that her involvement with the nursing home and the different dogs needed for the project there, and even a novice detective would have difficulty eliminating her, Jenny concluded.

She sighed, then slid farther down in her old-fashioned desk chair till her neck was resting against its back. Even finding Dulcie must have looked to McCai like part of a well-organized operation.

When Dolly's gray head appeared in the doorway, Jenny was dozing.

"Matilda Atwood is here, Jenny," Dolly said in a loud no-nonsense voice.

"Good gr—"

"Just go right in, Matilda," the cook-housekeeper interrupted, giving her a what-was-I-supposed-to-do look. "Nice day we're having, isn't it?"

"Indeed it is, Dolly," Matilda agreed as she entered the office, wearing a smile so friendly, Jenny knew at once the wisest thing she could do would be to jump out the window and run for cover before she found herself falling in with whatever Matilda suggested.

"So, Matilda, how are the plans coming along for the fete?" Jenny asked boldly as she waved her guest to a seat. Perhaps if she got her shots in first, she would be able to control the conversation and not be roped into anything.

"Wonderful, Jenny," the older woman told her. "As usual, everyone is being so supportive of the affair, and rightly so. We had a public relations firm do an impact study regarding the fete and its benefit toward the economy of Jefferson City. We were quite thrilled to learn exactly how much additional revenue was brought into the town through the society's efforts.'' She named a figure that surprised even Jenny. "Of course we didn't have to pay for the firm's services. Agatha Beauchamp's nephew owns the company, and he graciously provided us with that information for free. Wasn't that sweet of him?''

"Yes," Jenny said, nodding. Privately she was wishing Agatha Beauchamp's nephew had a suitable house for the tea and the ball. "It was very sweet of him," she agreed, then waited for the proverbial other shoe to drop!

"By the way, dear," Matilda began while she scrambled in the huge purse she always carried, "I have something for you." She finished her searching, then leaned forward and placed a check on the corner of the desk. "One item of business on the club's agenda last week was your bank note, with a reminder that the society failed to do as they'd agreed. If I do say so myself, I did a magnificent job of pleading your case."

Jenny, clearly surprised, reached for the check, smiling her thanks. "I really appreciate this, Matilda. Keeping this place going isn't easy."

"I know, dear," Matilda agreed. "Kathleen was always complaining about it, but of course, she had the money with which to keep it going."

"Precisely. But this," she said, indicating the check in her hand, "will certainly help."

"Good. Now, since we honored our end of the bargain, may we assume you will again allow us to hold the tea and ball here at the Arbor?"

The question was simply put. Jenny stared across at the round, almost cherubic face, the still-bright eyes regarding her so intently. Somehow Matilda reminded Jenny of her friends at the nursing home. She'd known Matilda all her life. She liked her. She was also thankful that Matilda was still physically and mentally capable of functioning on her own, and wasn't a resident in a place where, as McCai had said, people were just waiting to die.

"Of course, Matilda," Jenny said softly. "You caught me at a bad time the other day. I'm sorry if I was rude. I'd be happy to host the tea. But I'm afraid the society will have to be responsible for any damages."

"No problem," Matilda said firmly. "But this time I think we should do it a little differently. We also discussed placing a deposit with you prior to the events. How does that sound?"

"I think it's an excellent idea," Jenny agreed.

"Well, now that it's all settled, I must run. I'll call you for a time when you can meet with the caterer. I'm sure Kathleen is pleased, my dear," Matilda remarked as she walked out of the office.

Dolly wasted only a minute or two before presenting herself in the small office. "Does Kathleen being pleased with you mean that we've been rooked into hosting that shindig again?"

"Something like that."

"I'm not surprised. You've always been a sucker for a sob story."

"Am I to assume by that remark that the indefatigable Matilda was successful?" McCai asked from the doorway. "I passed her going out as I was coming in."

Jenny felt her heart lurch at the sound of his voice.

McCai's hungry gaze devoured the person seated behind the desk.

Jenny.

There was an early-morning freshness about her that made him jealous that he hadn't the slightest thing to do with how she looked. He didn't consider Jenny a beauty in the literal sense of the word. But there was an aura of sunshine about her, a special field of energy surrounding her, that had captured McCai as surely as if she'd found him hobbled in some wicked steel trap. Her special fragility left him wanting to hold her in his arms for an entire night—for many nights, then watch the day break, spreading its golden rays across Jenny's sleeping face. He wanted to kiss her into wakefulness, wanted to see passion and desire for him spring to her eyes as he began to make love to her.

Jenny inclined her head to one side, her eyes eagerly absorbing each and every square inch of McCai. She saw thick dark hair that looked to be still damp from the shower. The sprinkling of gray in his sideburns sparkled like silver. A tiny nick could be seen on his chin where he'd cut himself while shaving. His suit, as usual, was dark. The first two buttons of the white shirt were, as usual, undone, revealing the ebony crispness of hair covering his chest. Last night, when his shirt had been wet and plastered to his skin, Jenny had noted the pattern of growth that covered his chest, then spiraled to a provocative black wedge disappearing into the band of his pants.

She wondered what it would be like to explore the progress of that dark wedge? Her fingers curled into her palms, the tips of her oval nails biting into her skin. There was a quick tightening sensation in the lower part of her stomach—contracting, then relaxing, over and over again. Hollow, yet full.

"Eavesdropping already, McCai?" she replied. "It's only eight-thirty."

"Of course," McCai answered without hesitation. He walked into the room till he was standing beside Dolly. "I was hoping to be invited to eat some of Dolly's famous biscuits. I hear they're the best in the South."

"South, north, east and west," Dolly agreed unabashedly. She smiled her approval at McCai. "When you get through discussing your business with Jenny, come into the kitchen and I'll feed you." She looked him over from his expensive loafers to the tip of his head. "I'm not saying I can fill you up, mind you, but I can at least keep you from dying of starvation."

When they were alone, McCai walked to Jenny's side of the desk, then took a seat on one corner. He crossed his arms over his chest, tipped his head to one side and stared at her.

Jenny, not to be outdone by his cockiness, tried to stare him down. However, when her eyes started watering and stinging, she dropped them. Somehow she never seemed to make headway when trying to get the best of McCai. "What's on your mind this morning, McCai? Have you found some new evidence that will send me away for at least twenty years?"

"Are you aware that within a two-year period, the number of dogs shipped out of the country from this area has almost tripled?"

For a moment Jenny's face carried a totally blank expression. "Er...no. No, I'm not. What has that got to do with me or my kennel? I don't ship dogs out of the country. I do very little breeding because puppies take time, McCai. Time that I don't have." *What the devil was he up to now?*

"Not a thing that I know of," McCai said innocently, a flicker of a smile touching his lips. "By the way, I really like that tough stance you took with Matilda Atwood." He reached out and touched Jenny's chin with a gentle fist. "You really held your ground."

Jenny, tired of being the butt of his jokes, pushed back the chair and got to her feet. She began straightening the mess of papers on her desk. When her hand found the check Matilda had given her, she held it out toward McCai. "I was doing fine till she undermined my firm resolve with this. But even if the society hadn't paid the bill, it would have been difficult denying Matilda. I've always liked her."

"And just who will help you and Dolly with all the extra work that will have to be done for the occasion?" McCai asked. Damn it all! Jenny was either the best actor in the world or he was completely misjudging her. There hadn't been the slightest bit of change in her expression when he'd mentioned the dog exports. For once in his career McCai had found himself hoping that the evidence he had against a suspect proved to be nothing more than a series of bizarre coincidences.

"Gee, McCai," Jenny said innocently, "you actually seemed concerned for my welfare. How touching. Does this mean that you'll come visit me in the slammer?" She continued to watch him, her arms crossed under her breasts, her eyes twinkling with devilment. After he'd brought her home from his apartment last night, Jenny had decided that teasing McCai and trying to ignore his insinuations might be the best way to handle her attraction to him. Anything was worth a try.

"I don't usually visit the people I send to prison. But since your case is special, I'll try to work it into my busy schedule," McCai replied in a flat, unamused tone. He got to his feet, his much greater height making Jenny feel tiny and insignificant. "I think I'll go visit with Dolly. She's more fun to talk with than you are."

"Ha!" Jenny exclaimed to his departing back. "It's not conversation you're seeking, my high and mighty friend. You're here to fill up on Dolly's hot biscuits. Don't forget to try some of that new syrup. Mix it with butter, then sop it with a biscuit. It's delicious." She yelled the last few words as McCai disappeared from view.

Jenny continued putting papers in order on her desk, smiling to herself as she pictured the serious-minded McCai sopping biscuits in butter-streaked syrup. It was a shame no one had ever taken him in hand and taught him how to relax. Apparently all McCai's life had been spent with a definite purpose in mind. From what he'd told her, when he was a child his main purpose had been simply to survive. As an adult, his goal had been to succeed.

Survival and success.

Two words that very aptly described Jonah McCai. Yet they were two words that seemed so devoid of human emotion.

Jenny paused, her expression thoughtful. McCai needed to relax, didn't he? What if she were to arrange for him to do something she bet he'd never done in his entire life? Would he be angry? Would he demand that she stop her nonsense and let him get on with his business of proving she was the biggest dog thief in the Southwest?

WHILE JENNY WAS PLOTTING against Jonah McCai, Joey Tate was just finishing up his morning kennel chores. Since his first appointment at the studio wasn't until eleven, he, too, hoped to catch up on some paperwork.

Once seated at the rickety desk in one corner of the main room of the kennel, Joey unlocked a drawer, then removed a manila folder. The first matter of business was to check on the number of signed health

certificates he had left. He quickly counted them. Not
nearly enough.

Joey was still for a moment, staring into space, his
thoughts taken over with the problems at hand. Like
it or not, he would have to pay David Moreau another
visit. The vet was scared. That alone could cause ir-
reparable damage at any moment. Joey knew perfectly well that pushing the man too far could be
disastrous. But the health certificates were of the ut-
most importance. It would be too risky shipping the
dogs with bogus papers. All it would take for the authorities to be on him in a second was for one of the
dogs to become ill during shipping, and for a vet to be
called. With Moreau's name on the certificates, there
was no problem. Joey didn't want there to be a single
error, a single mix-up, that could cause the slightest
problem in the transactions. He wanted to sell the dogs
out of the country as he'd planned, collect his money,
then vanish.

He'd taken care of every single detail. He even had
a buyer for his kennel, ready to hand him the check
and take possession the minute Joey said the word. All
he needed was two or three weeks to complete the
shipping of the four dogs. They'd be his ticket to a
new and better life. He was being extra cautious, but
with the detective snooping around, Joey figured he
needed to take every precaution. On the other hand,
the questions the man had asked Moreau were strictly
routine. Joey evaluated the entire incident as nothing
important. The joker had asked his questions, con-
ducted a routine investigation and was probably gone.

But just to be on the safe side... Joey reached for the phone and dialed a number written in a thin leather-bound book that was also in the folder.

"This is Joey Tate. Is Mr. Tremont available?" he asked.

"Just a moment, please," a woman said briskly.

For a tiny space of time Joey felt his confidence soar. How many other men could boast of being put right through to a man as important as André Tremont? Someday, Joey thought, he was going to wield as much power as Tremont himself.

"All right, Joey, make it quick," Tremont said when he picked up the phone. "I've got an important meeting in fifteen minutes."

"Sure thing, Mr. Tremont," Joey agreed. "I thought I'd better tell you that I might not be able to come up with my usual...er...quota for the month." There was no way in the world Joey could tell André Tremont that a detective was in town investigating stolen show dogs without implicating himself.

"Listen, Joey," Tremont said in a cool, steely voice, "and listen close. In my organization, quotas are made to be kept. You've already been short once. If you can't keep your end of our bargain, then your usefulness to me is over. Are you telling me that your usefulness is over, Joey?"

Joey felt his palms begin to sweat. "Not at all, Mr. Tremont. It's just that I've had some personal problems, Mr. Tremont, that might slow me down a little bit this month."

"Problems, Joey? Do you need any help with these problems?"

"Er...no, sir. It's nothing I can't handle," Joey hastened to assure him. "It's just that I don't want people to become suspicious of me. I mean, if I'm seen in the different neighborhoods too often, then people might put two and two together and come up with four."

"People don't suspect cripples, Joey," André Tremont replied callously. "That's why I hired you. Now stop all this damned noise about staying out of sight and get to work. If all the people on my payroll were as skittish as you are, I'd be broke."

The line went dead, and Joey was left holding the receiver, the dial tone sounding like a huge bee buzzing in his ear.

Even though he didn't want to admit that his plan was running into problems, Joey was beginning to have some doubts. If he continued securing and selling dogs to André Tremont for resale to research labs, it was quite possible he would attract the attention of the local police. If he didn't continue working for Tremont, his life wasn't worth a penny.

He tried to convince himself that Tremont was correct when he said a cripple was the least likely person to be suspected of a crime. It was the first time in his life that Joey had ever felt his disfigurement to be an advantage. Though it never failed to infuriate Joey, he'd learned very young that people automatically assumed that since his body wasn't perfect, his brain was impaired as well. Initially elated after being approached by a member of André Tremont's organization and taken to see the boss, Joey suffered a sizable blow to his ego when he learned that it wasn't his superior mental capabilities that had brought him to Tremont's attention, but his limp and his facial disfigurement.

Well, Joey Tate wasn't through yet, he decided angrily. Not by a long shot. He still had four lovely dogs to dispose of. Perhaps four weeks would be long enough to wait. Any longer and he might lose his remaining chance for a new and different life.

CHAPTER EIGHT

THE FIRST THING McCai noticed when he turned onto the street where Jenny lived was the dark sedan. It was parked a ways down from the Arbor, but it had been in that same spot when he'd arrived at the guest house the first time that morning. He'd gone back to his place to change clothes as Jenny had asked him to do. McCai knew why the car was there, and he felt guilty.

He brought the Mercedes to a halt beside the sedan so abruptly that the person behind the steering wheel of the other car actually gave a start. Without stopping to consider his reason for doing so, McCai let down the window on the passenger side. He identified himself, then asked, "Am I correct in assuming that you're working for McCai Limited?"

The man, recognizing McCai, nodded. "Yes, you are."

"I'm taking over the surveillance of Ms Castle for the day. You can report back to James Baldwin and tell him that I relieved you."

"Sure thing, Mr. McCai."

As he drove toward the Arbor, McCai realized that the sight of the detective watching Jenny had made him fighting mad. *But you're the one who wanted her watched,* his conscience reminded him. *You're the one who can't make up your mind if Jenny is guilty or innocent.*

Jenny walked out onto the veranda of the Arbor at the same time McCai drove into the parking area. She took a seat in the old-fashioned swing, then leaned back and let her eyes feast on him.

He was wearing a navy-blue shirt with the sleeves cuffed back over his thick forearms, faded jeans and what appeared to be scruffy-toed boots. The instant Jenny saw how he was dressed, she knew exactly why he avoided wearing a tie. By his refusal to fall in line with what was supposed to be proper dress for a gentleman, McCai was making a statement. A statement of nonconformity. It added to the maverick image Jenny had of him, an image that set him apart from other men of her acquaintance. She also couldn't help but wonder if the maverick streak in McCai was responsible for her dissatisfaction with her own girl-next-door image.

Jenny was unaware of her eyes narrowing with sensual pleasure as she watched the easy, loose-limbed stride with which he moved. And though she wasn't sure any other man she knew executed that walk as effectively as he did, it seemed to her to be a walk peculiar to most tall men, accomplished with a fluidity of movement not usually found in men of less stature.

Watching him come toward her, Jenny hadn't the slightest problem imagining McCai living one hundred years ago—even one hundred and fifty—as a wild west lawman. He would have been a leader in any era. Men would have looked up to him and women would have fallen in love with him then as now. Just as she was afraid she was doing, she thought with a sinking heart. She knew McCai had a gentler side than usually seen by the world, but even with that to his credit, she wasn't foolish enough to count on that quality transforming him into the man she would live the rest of her life with.

"I'm delighted to see that you have something other than dark suits in your wardrobe, McCai," Jenny remarked as she watched him make his way across the wide veranda. She glanced down at the watch on her wrist. "You're also fifteen minutes early. A virtue, McCai, truly a virtue."

It was a lazy fall day that had begun with temperatures in the forties, but had warmed up to the high sixties or low seventies. Tempting weather...good fishing weather. The kind of weather that caused one to lose sight of the fact that during the night the temperature would dip into the thirties.

McCai paused, then leaned his shoulder against one of several round supporting columns placed at intervals along the sides and front of the Arbor. He crossed his arms over his chest and stood regarding Jenny with a mysterious gleam in his green eyes. She looked good in jeans, he thought. From what he could see, they fit her just right in all the right places. And the red sweatshirt wasn't bad, either, he decided.

"When a beautiful young lady tells me to go home and change into my working clothes, because she needs my help with something, then I take her at her word."

"Even if the beautiful—your words, not mine— young lady is suspected of being a thief?"

"Especially if the beautiful young lady is suspected of being a thief," McCai told her as he walked over to the swing. He started to sit down beside her, then paused, his body half bent. "Have you or your Aunt Kathleen ever had this contraption checked to see how stable it is?"

"I'll have you know this house was built from cypress and heart-of-pine lumber. Those bolts—" she looked upward to where the bottom halves of two eyebolts could be seen "—were installed years ago by one of my relatives."

"Well, I'm mighty proud of him, honey. I'm sure it was quite a chore drilling a hole in cypress. It's a hard wood," McCai said silkily. "But that doesn't mean dry rot hasn't set in."

Jenny looked upward and sighed. "The only dry rot round here has probably set in your brain, McCai." She turned her head and stared at him. "Sit. Relax, if that's possible. If the darn swing falls with you, you have my permission to sue me. I can't promise that you'll be able to collect, but you can sue."

"How reassuring," McCai said, chuckling. He slowly leaned back, then eased one arm behind her shoulders, resting the other hand on the arm of the swing. "You're such a soothing person to be around, Jenny," he told her with mock innocence. "Tell me, what's on the agenda for this afternoon? I canceled all sorts of important meetings to help you with this dire emergency.''

"Be patient, McCai. We're waiting for Dolly."

"Dolly? Is she helping us?" Somehow that knowledge left McCai feeling slightly down. Whatever the problem, he'd assumed only he and Jenny would be involved. He didn't want Dolly with them—he didn't want anyone with them. On the one hand he was almost afraid to push his investigation for fear of learning that his suspicions of Jenny were true. On the other hand, he was becoming almost compulsively protective of her. Lately, he'd been wondering if he should turn the case over to someone else in the firm.

"No," Jenny told him, regarding him stonily. "You're going to be entirely alone with me—at my mercy. Think you can handle it?"

McCai's face took on such a comically martyred expression that Jenny, in spite of being annoyed, was unable to keep from laughing. "Sure, if you promise not to ravish me the first chance you get," he told her.

"Gee, McCai, you've ruined my day," she muttered.

"I like your style, Jenny Castle," he said huskily. He made no move to touch her, yet in spite of the tension hanging over their relationship like some huge, dark cloud of doom, Jenny felt the caress of his voice smoothing the surface of her skin, as if he'd touched her.

Jenny couldn't help but wonder at the remark. He had serious doubts about her credibility, yet he liked her style.

"Meaning?" she asked boldly. It occurred to her—either in that second or because it had been in her subconscious all along—that she deeply resented the picture McCai must have of her. She reasoned that a man like him had known many women. That being the case, she seriously doubted he'd be impressed with her do-gooder image. Deep in her heart she wanted him to view her as an exciting woman—exciting in every sense of the word. But was she capable of projecting such an image? More important, was she capable of projecting it in such a way as to be convincing?

"Meaning I don't like this damn tension that's eating away at both of us." His large hand cupped her shoulder and dragged her against his chest. His chin came to rest on the top of her head and she felt strangely protected by the gesture. "I don't know you very well, honey," he said gruffly. The silkiness of her hair dragged against the emery side of McCai's beard, and he felt his body respond with a tightening in his thighs. "I suppose time is about the only thing that can help us out of this mess."

"What you're saying, McCai, is that you don't know me well enough to say you trust me, isn't it?" Much like a cat rubbing against its master, Jenny gently moved her head back and forth, relishing the feeling of being surrounded by him.

McCai heaved a deep, shuddering sigh and held her tighter, as if by that very act he could keep his suspicions and the rest of the world at bay. He wanted to absorb her into his being and never let her go. Neither of them seemed to notice or care that it was already

past noon, and that they were in plain view of the
street. "Something like that."

"You want to believe me, but the evidence won't go
away. Is that what's bothering you?"

"Yes."

"Have you decided what my motive is?"

"I think so."

"Would you mind sharing that secret with me?"

McCai shifted his head so that he could see her face,
but his arms retained their hold on her. "Even though
the circumstances are new to me personally, this certainly isn't the first time a situation like this has happened. But I always thought it happened to other
people. I prided myself on being strong enough to
carry justice through to the very end ... and all that.
Now, as to a motive. It's simple, really. *If* you were to
be involved," he said thoughtfully, "then the motive
would probably be money. It's possible that this
damned white elephant, as you call it—" he gestured
toward the front door of the Arbor "—has put you in
such a financial bind that you're desperate. But there's
also another scenario."

"Please, let's hear them all."

"You know dogs, and you have access to quality
animals the average person doesn't have. That could
be a very tempting situation for you as well as for
anyone else involved with showing and breeding
dogs."

"I'll admit both those ideas have merit, McCai,"
Jenny admitted. "But you don't have any concrete
proof yet, do you?" She had finally begun to realize

the weird sense of power she had over McCai. The re-
alization of her own seductiveness was heady...
bizarre.

Was being in the haven of his arms responsible for
her wishing she could exercise her newfound power
and lure him into the fantasy world she'd created in
her dreams? Was it the heavy, yet gentle, weight of his
hands on her? Was it the unquestioned acceptance that
when she was with McCai or in his arms she was safe
and wanted? Which of those things could it possibly
be? Jenny asked herself.

She didn't try to understand it, there wasn't time.
Understanding would come later, she hoped. In the
meantime, just knowing that some inexplicable link
existed between them was enough.

"I'll admit it's circumstantial," he agreed, nodding. He hoped and prayed it stayed that way, too.
"But that's the way most cases are built against a person. And because I believe in keeping my word to do
the best job I possibly can for my clients, I have little
choice but to see that the investigation continues."

"Well," Jenny began thoughtfully, "did you mean
what you said when you offered to help me if I needed
it?"

For a split second McCai thought his chest was
going to explode! "Yes," he said, barely able to
manage the word around the dryness in his throat.
"Why?" It was years since McCai had prayed. He'd
been a child then, praying to a God he knew little
about. But in that hairbreadth of space between his
two replies, he prayed with all his heart.

Jenny saw the light of panic dawning in McCai's eyes. Beneath her hand resting on his chest, she felt his body tense, felt the rapid thump-thumping of his heart. Her question had thrown him into shock.

"Why?" he repeated harshly.

"Be—because I think it's a very caring thing for you to have done. I still say you're a far nicer person than you want people to know. Is that all right? I mean—do you mind if I think you're a nice person?"

Relief coursed through McCai's veins like quicksilver. He stilled the natural response of pulling her more tightly against him. Even the thought of taking her mouth in a hard, demanding kiss was vetoed. There were no sexual overtones in their embrace. There was no need. For the moment simply holding Jenny in his arms was enough. But McCai knew that wouldn't always be the case.

"McCai?" Jenny murmured barely above a whisper. She was disappointed. From the moment he stepped out of his car, she'd wanted to kiss him. He hadn't seemed interested, and she hadn't wanted to be pushy. She felt cheated. "Did you hear what I said?"

"I heard." He removed his arm from behind her shoulders and relaxed against the swing. "How can I argue with a beautiful woman?" he asked with feigned innocence. "I know I'm a great guy, but it's nice to see that you have such excellent taste."

"You're also a conceited jerk," Jenny informed him without batting an eye. She stopped the gentle motion of the swing with the toe of her shoe, then stood and looked back down at his smirking face. "On your feet, McCai. We have things to do."

McCai did as she bade him, laughing. "I like to follow you, Jenny," he said, teasing. "I enjoy looking at your cute little behind. It moves just enough to be enticing, yet not so much as to make one seasick."

"It takes all kinds" was Jenny's only reply.

They entered the kitchen just as Dolly was closing the lid of a huge picnic basket. McCai's puzzled gaze went from Jenny to Dolly, then back to Jenny.

He nodded toward the basket. "What's that?"

"A picnic basket," Jenny answered.

"And?"

Jenny gave him a long considering look. He was helpless. "You and I are going on a picnic, McCai. Quite probably your first, and most likely your last. If tradition holds, there will be ants fighting us for their tiny cut of our lunch. We might even brush against poison oak, and we'll for sure hit a bramble bush or two. I'm giving you the same advice I did regarding the swing on the porch. If you don't have a good time, then sue me."

"Sue you?" Dolly repeated. "Why on earth would Mr. McCai want to sue you?"

"Because Mr. McCai has taken a solemn vow never to do a single thing that he will enjoy, Dolly," Jenny replied.

"Are there biscuits in there?" McCai asked Dolly, nodding toward the basket.

"Certainly there are biscuits in there," Dolly said, laughing. "They're so light and fluffy you'll have to tie a rope around them to keep them from floating away. And the chicken . . . why, it's fried as golden brown as a Rhode Island rooster. There's also potato salad, deviled eggs and a blueberry cobbler that tastes so good, it'll turn a sinner into a saint on the spot.''

Jenny, who'd been watching McCai's face during Dolly's recital of her menu, laughed. "I think you've just raised the stock in picnics at least a hundredfold, Dolly," she said, nodding toward McCai. "If the goofy-looking expression on his ugly mug is anything to go by, he'll most definitely enjoy himself."

"Only an insane person wouldn't jump at the chance to eat Dolly's cooking," McCai informed her. What he couldn't say was that Jenny didn't know how right she was about his never having been on a picnic.

Jenny picked up the container of lemonade and a black-and-red-plaid blanket. "Would you mind carrying the basket?" she asked McCai. She told Dolly where they were going, then followed McCai out the door.

"Wow! It's neat following you for a change, McCai," she continued in the same vein he'd used earlier. "You have a really cute tush . . . especially for such a big man. You have just the precise amount of motion. Not too little, and not so much that one gets seasick. Yes, sirree—watching the male tush is one of my favorite things to do."

Some thirty minutes later, and nine miles from the Arbor, McCai was following Jenny down a well-worn path through the woods, muttering a few choice oaths at the gnats darting around his eyes, and the tiny branches that insisted on attaching themselves to his shirt or his hair. Suddenly he and Jenny emerged into a tiny clearing on the bank of a fast-flowing creek.

McCai stopped beside her, his narrowed gaze focused on the setting. He saw a shallow stream of water with a bed of white and multicolored pebbles. Along the edges of the sloping banks were huge, moss-smeared rocks, and interspersed among them were large clumps of wild ferns growing in carefree abandon, their emerald fronds stretching upward toward the gleaming warmth of the sun. A huge willow tree jutted out over the water, its branches weaving and trailing wraithlike in the gentle breeze.

"Well?" Jenny asked after a few quiet moments, as she turned and looked and McCai. The expression on his face stopped her dead in her tracks! His eyes, intriguing at any time, had turned a deep, glowing emerald. His lips were drawn into a tight, straight line, and his features were like chiseled stone.

What in heaven's name was the matter with him? she wondered. Back at the Arbor she'd noticed that he offered few comments about the outing she'd thought would be such a success. She'd honestly thought it was just McCai, being his usual cranky self. Now she wasn't so certain. Had she inadvertently stumbled into an area of painful memories that should never have been disturbed?

"McCai? Are you all right?"

"I'm fine," he answered in short, flinty tones.

Rather than continue to stare at him, Jenny spread the blanket beneath the branches of a large oak tree.

"Why don't you put the basket here," she said casually. He did as she suggested, then walked to the edge of the creek and stared into its clear depths.

Jenny followed him, wanting to reach out to him, but holding back for fear of his rebuffing her. "I'm sorry," she eventually murmured. "I really thought you'd enjoy a picnic."

McCai looked down at her worried face, then reached out and began drawing her into his arms. One hand cupped the side of her face, pressing it into his chest. His other arm held her body against his. "Don't be sorry," he whispered against her hair. "Please... don't ever be sorry."

How could he tell her that the little things they'd shared during their short acquaintance meant more to him than he cared to admit? That Dolly's fussing over him, and Jenny's taking him down a peg or two when he was "ornery," as she termed it, gave him a brief glimpse of what it could be like if he had a family?

Jenny shifted slightly in his arm. McCai let her get comfortable, then caught her close again. At the moment he needed her. He needed the warmth of her, he needed the sunshine in his life that she brought with her. But most of all he needed to know that she was not involved in the case he was investigating. Worrying over what he would find each time he examined a new clue was driving him mad.

"McCai?"

"Mmm?"

"Are you angry?"

"No." How could he be angry when she'd gone to such trouble for him? The women he knew weren't interested in doing something for nothing. They didn't put themselves out for anyone.

"Are you hungry?"

"Yes. Both ways."

"Both?" Jenny asked, then gasped when he turned her so that she was fully facing him and placed both his hands on her hips. He caught her tightly against him and the evidence of his arousal.

Jenny tried to move back; McCaie refused to let her. He smiled at the light tinge of pink that heightened her cheeks. "Don't be shy with me, Jenny. And don't be embarrassed by the most natural occurrence in the world."

"Listen, McCai," she said, trying for a casual tone, "standing in a man's arms in the middle of the day while he's fully aroused is rather new to me."

"Oh?" he said dryly. "Do you usually stand in his arms in the middle of the night when he's aroused?"

"Don't be deliberately obtuse," Jenny said quietly. "You know perfectly well what I mean."

McCai chuckled. Jenny heard the sound deep in his chest and felt the reverberations reaching out to her own body. She refused to look an inch higher or lower than his chest. But even there, the dark hair showing in the opening of his shirt had Jenny longing to touch him. "I have a question to ask you, Jenny Castle."

"Shoot."

"How many men have you gone to bed with?"

"This is the eighties, McCai. Women have all sorts of rights these days, or haven't you heard?"

"How many?" he persisted.

"One."

"How long ago?"

Jenny frowned, trying to remember exactly how long it was since she'd decided she'd see what all the fuss was about. She'd been a freshman at Louisiana State University when she had sex with Arthur Lewis, a junior. Immediately afterward she'd made up her mind that she and Arthur had to have been missing some vital information concerning that most intimate act between two people. Since then, there hadn't been anyone she considered qualified to fill the gap in her sexual education.

"Seven . . . almost eight years ago."

McCai's mouth twitched at the corners. "It must have been a very memorable occasion to have sustained you all these years."

Jenny responded with a well-aimed kick to his shin. She pushed out of his arms and stalked back to the blanket. "Go suck an egg, McCai!"

She wouldn't speak to the filthy-minded swine ever again, she kept telling herself over and over as they helped themselves to Dolly's lunch. But each time she looked up, she found McCai's eyes on her. She could almost see tiny devils of mischief dancing in their depths. His dedicated study was her undoing. In a far shorter time than she cared to think about, she found herself laughing and talking as if nothing at all had happened.

When the last biscuit had been eaten, they dropped back on the blanket replete, their eyes closed, sighing contentedly.

JENNY WAS DREAMING. She had to be dreaming. Why else would she be feeling warm, heavy hands gliding over her stomach and breasts? Why else would she feel the slightest pressure of sensuous lips tasting hers, then moving on to tempt and tease the side of her neck, the tip of her ear?

A familiar fragrance caused her nose to twitch. It was outdoorsy...male...completely male. It smelled like McCai. McCai.

McCai!

Jenny's eyes flew open and looked straight into McCai's controlled gaze. He was lying beside her, his upper body braced on one elbow while his other rested on the curve of her hip.

"Y-you startled me," she stammered, then caught her breath in her throat. She felt his hand move, then sensed the edge of her sweatshirt being raised.

It hadn't been a dream at all.

"Lift your arms," McCai told her. When she did, he whisked the shirt over her head and freed her arms of the long sleeves, then dropped it on the blanket.

The front clasp of her bra was found and dealt with so quickly and smoothly that Jenny wondered fleetingly if McCai devoted a few minutes each day to improving that particular technique.

The impudent thrust of her breasts, their rose-pink nipples stiff and erect, caused McCai to take a sharp deep breath and hold it. For a moment his head dropped back on his shoulders and his body tensed. His eyes closed and his lips were drawn tight against his teeth as if he were in deep pain.

Every damned thing about her suited him! Everything. Yet...

"McCai," Jenny whispered. She knew instinctively that he was trying to distance himself from her, trying to avoid any further involvement. Jenny eased her fingers into his shirt and held them there against the warm, vibrant skin.

Contact. Any kind of solid contact. She was trying desperately to maintain a link with him, yet not totally understanding what it was she was fighting.

"Shh," he answered, knowing he was defeated even before he started, "it's all right. It's all right," he repeated, then kissed her.

The kiss was hard, almost savage, the buttons of his shirt biting into her tender skin. Each of them were hungry for the taste of the other, hungry and indifferent to pain. Flesh bit into teeth, breath was forgotten till the pressure in their lungs forced them apart.

McCai lifted his head as his hand palmed a creamy, pink-tipped orb. He teased the nipple with his thumb, stroking the sensitive tip back and forth, over and over again. From time to time his lips replaced his thumb, going from breast to breast and then her lips.

Three points of sensitivity beyond her wildest imagination! Jenny moved against his hands and lips shamelessly. She arched her slender body, then let it fall back against the blanket... sated, yet unfulfilled.

Her body was hot. It was burning, ready to burst into flames. She'd never felt this way before. It was new, it was painful, and it was so excruciatingly exciting she was finding it very hard not to cry out.

McCai watched the writhing motion of her body and felt the blood rushing anew to his thighs, engorging his manhood with renewed desire. He understood the dam of passion waiting to burst inside Jenny. "Don't fight it," he whispered. "No one can see us. Let it come, honey, let it come," he whispered. He caught her hand then and carried it below his waist to the proof of his arousal, throbbing with heat and desire.

Jenny cupped the hardened bulge for a moment, then fumbled for the opening of his jeans. She wanted him next to her, without barriers of any kind separating them. McCai understood the urgency controlling her, pushing her, and helped her.

His jeans, her jeans.

His shirt and briefs, her briefs.

Their clothes added a colorful splash to the beige and browns of late fall.

McCai's dark skin contrasted sharply with the honey color of Jenny's. He knelt between her legs, then placed a hand on either side of her, his eyes moving over every inch of her.

"Why am I not surprised by the way you look?" he asked huskily, his gaze committing to memory the curves and lines of her body. It was a while since he'd been with a woman, yet he knew that his brief abstinence had nothing to do with his lack of control. From what Jenny had told him earlier, he guessed her one and only encounter with sex hadn't been at all what she expected. He wanted this time to be different. He wanted it to be perfect.

"You're psychic?" Jenny suggested in a sultry voice, her hands reaching out, trailing seductively over his chest and stomach. Though the sun shone brightly, her passion-drugged eyes were dark and luminous.

"Yeah, psychic," McCai murmured, smiling devilishly. "Would you think me psychic if I did this to you?" he asked, his lips and tongue leaving a glistening trail from beneath her breasts, over her waist and stomach, to the sensitive bud of her femininity hidden in that soft mysterious cleft.

Jenny's hips rose to meet the teasing thrust, her hands clutching at his head, her fingers tangling in his hair. She felt a hot, spiraling hunger growing in her, but was unable to feed it. Her eyes closed tightly against the turmoil inside her body. She was hot and cold, wistful and ecstatic. She thrashed her head wildly from side to side as she sought to regain some semblance of control.

Suddenly McCai caught Jenny tightly into his arms, tested himself against her so as to warn her, then entered her, quickly and firmly.

Small. Tight. Hot. Sweet . . . unbelievably sweet! Those few words kept going round and round in his head till they became a single thought, controlling his mind.

Jenny knew she was raking McCai's back with her nails, but she couldn't stop herself. He was hard, velvety hard, and he was filling her. Gorging her on the most wonderful feeling she'd ever known.

Their movements were frenzied at first, then slowly tapered into a calmer rhythm that gave them time to savor each other rather than greedily snatch bits of pleasure.

When they felt the inevitable rush of climax, McCai cradled Jenny's face with his hands.

"Look at me," he muttered harshly, trying to hang on to what they had for one single millisecond longer. He wanted to share every instant with her...every ounce of feeling.

She obeyed, and when she stared into his eyes she knew for certain that they were indeed one...as close at that precise moment as two people ever can be.

CHAPTER NINE

"HOW WERE THE BISCUITS?" Dolly asked Jenny as they unpacked the picnic basket.

"I should think that not a crumb of leftover food would indicate that everything was delicious—as usual," Jenny said, chuckling. "Many more meals like that one and I'll be on a very strict diet."

Dolly laughed and shook her head. "Sure, and I'm Marilyn Monroe. By the way, I'm glad to see you going out more with that nice Mr. McCai. I knew if you were patient, he would get over the silly notion that you had anything to do with stealing dogs."

"Think so?" Jenny asked.

The housekeeper looked at her sharply. "Do you mean . . .'"

"Indeed I do. I'm still at the head of the list. But at least it's giving him some bad moments." She reached for a plump red apple and sank her teeth into it. "But he did offer to stand by me if I needed him."

"Well, I never!"

"Neither have I," Jenny agreed. "But then, I haven't spent most of my life chasing thieves and murderers, either. I honestly think McCai has devoted so much time trying to figure out the criminal mind, he's lost track of what makes normal people tick. He's convinced he has tons of circumstantial evidence against me.''

''I hope my biscuits give him severe indigestion,'' Dolly said grimly.

She'd worked for Kathleen O'Reilly for close to fifteen years. After ownership of the Arbor changed hands, Dolly had simply transferred her devotion and support to Jenny. When she first heard that Jonah McCai considered Jenny a suspect, Dolly had been shocked. Now, however, having learned that he was still of the same mind, and eating her biscuits to boot, Dolly was ready to fight! She'd looked after her ''family'' for too many years to allow some outsider to besmirch their good name.

''Don't let it bother you, Dolly,'' Jenny said soothingly, seeing the red stain in the housekeeper's cheeks and the angry set of her jaw. She patted the older woman on the shoulder, then got to her feet. ''You know perfectly well that with your blood pressure, you shouldn't get upset.

''If you hear a noise, don't panic, it's McCai. He's using the telephone in my office. I'm going to grab a quick shower, then try to finish the bookkeeping I started this morning. By the way, there's a kennel club meeting tonight, so I'll be out for a couple of hours.''

When Jenny passed the section of hallway that led to the front of the house, she fully intended going straight past it toward her own quarters. But the sound of her name spoken by McCai caused her to pause. She was perfectly aware that eavesdroppers weren't supposed to hear good things about themselves, but she doubted McCai would be so crass as to talk about her while using her own phone.

However, she had heard her name, hadn't she? She eased closer to the door, her sock feet making no noise at all on the wood floors.

"That's fine, James," she heard McCai say. "By the way, I've decided to handle Jenny Castle's surveillance during the day. That detective you put on the job can take care of the nights."

Surely she'd heard wrong, Jenny told herself. Was McCai talking about a detective watching her?

"No, no. There was no problem. I just want to handle it a little differently," McCai said.

She heard the receiver being replaced, followed by determined footsteps walking across the room.

Jenny was frozen to the spot!

McCai had actually held her in his arms and made love to her, knowing all the while that as soon as they returned to Jefferson City, he or his private sleuth would begin following her again.

It couldn't be true. No. A thousand times no, she cried out in silent agony. But no amount of wishing or denying what she'd heard could erase the rough timbre of McCai's voice when he'd been talking to the faceless James.

As the footsteps drew nearer, Jenny trembled. She crossed her arms beneath her breasts, her palms tightly cupping her elbows. For a brief moment she was tempted to turn and run as far as her legs would carry her—anything rather than face McCai.

She didn't want to have to look at him and remember what a total and complete fool she'd been. Yes, she thought dejectedly, running might certainly prove to be far less painful. But even as she was trying to convince herself of that, she knew she wouldn't. It simply wasn't her style.

Her eyes were riveted to the doorway, her heart pounding like a huge drum inside her chest. Her trembling hands were clenched into tight fists, her nails biting into clammy palms. But as the moment of confrontation drew near, Jenny was unaware of anything except feeling sick at heart. That and the mind-numbing implications of McCai's conversation.

The first thing McCai saw when he gained the doorway was Jenny's face.

She knew!

Dammit to hell! She knew. He must have been talking louder than he thought. A feeling of sick helplessness rose in McCai's throat. Before his very eyes Jenny was distancing herself from him, and there wasn't a damned thing he could do to stop her.

Earlier there had been pink in her cheeks. Her eyes had been glowing, her lips swollen from his kisses.

Now she was white as a sheet. He saw pain and disillusionment on her face.

"Someone else doing another survey, McCai?" she asked quietly, amazed at how steady her voice was. This morning he'd told her the man in the car he'd stopped and talked with was conducting a survey. Thinking back, she was amazed how easily he'd lied.

McCai worried the inner side of his bottom lip with the edges of his teeth while he stared thoughtfully at her. Silence, profound and painful, hovered between them.

Jenny wondered if he'd even heard her.

McCai wished he could rewrite the past half hour and dynamite the damn phone!

"Will you please listen to my explanation?" he eventually asked in measured tones.

Well, at least he hadn't insulted her by trying to deny anything, Jenny thought. But an explanation? Did she really want an explanation? "I don't think so, McCai."

For one of the few times in his adult life, McCai found himself at a loss for words. By the look in Jenny's eyes, he knew that nothing he said was going to make one iota of difference in the way she was feeling. She felt betrayed, tricked, and if he were honest with himself, he couldn't blame her. He tucked his hands in his back pockets, then stared down at the floor, then down the hall, then out the window behind Jenny. Anywhere but into the god-awful pain on her face.

"I think you should leave now, McCai," Jenny told him.

"Jenny, please—" He reached out a hand to touch her, but drew it back when she stepped aside to avoid his touch.

"No," she said, shaking her head. "Don't...please. Today has been a huge mistake in several ways."

"No, it wasn't!" McCai said roughly. He couldn't leave now. If he did, he knew in his very soul there would never be another chance for him with Jenny. He ran a hand through his hair in frustration. "I care for you, you have to know that. I'm not a damned machine. I can't turn my feelings off and on at the flip of a switch."

"Oh, I don't know about that, McCai. Judging by your performance today, I'd say you do that quite well," Jenny said grimly. "You remind me of the chameleons I used to get such a kick out of watching when I was a little girl. Just as they're able to change colors, you seem equally adept at changing characters, and quite convincingly at that. I'm sure you'll excuse me if I don't see you out."

Jenny turned quickly before he could see the tears welling in her eyes. She walked the few feet down the hall to the section of the Arbor set aside for her personal use. She entered the sitting room, then closed the door and leaned back against it. She took a deep, trembling breath as tears overflowed and eased down her cheeks.

Jenny wasn't certain how long she stood leaning against the door. But gradually she became aware of the familiar sounds of the house. A guest asking Dolly about a certain historical landmark a few miles out of town, a couple inquiring about extending their reservations for two more days, the occasional barking of the dogs. She raised a tentative hand to her cheeks, her fingertips brushing against the tracks of her tears.

She had no idea when she'd stopped crying. But her hands, pressed between her hips and the door, were tingling, so she'd obviously been standing in that same position ever since she came into the room. Her gaze touched on the familiar surroundings of the sitting room. At least nothing had changed here. How tempting it was to simply lock the door and stay inside for weeks and weeks. Or at least until her heart healed.

How long did it take for a broken heart to mend? Jenny wondered. Perhaps there was some magic potion known only to people suffering from that particular malady.

But just as as she'd decided earlier against running away, Jenny knew she wouldn't closet herself away in her room like some Victorian maiden. Nor would she wallow in self-pity.

"It'll hurt. It'll hurt like hell," she murmured around the huge knot that lodged in her throat the moment she tried to talk. "But I'll get through it." Then Jenny walked briskly toward her bedroom and adjoining bath. As she went along, she left a trail of clothing behind. In the bathroom, she purposefully avoided looking into the large square mirror about the vanity counter. She wasn't interested in facing the biggest fool of the century. Certainly not until she washed Jonah McCai's touch from her skin.

WHEN MCCAI LEFT the Arbor, he drove to his apartment. Without turning on a light, he poured himself a stiff drink of Scotch and then stretched out on the sofa.

He'd broken one of the cardinal rules of investigative work by allowing himself to become involved with a suspect. But not just any suspect.

Jenny Castle.

Jenny had become more than just another name on a list of people to be investigated. She'd taken on an identity. An identity that refused to allow McCai to categorize her. She'd became a warm, loving person. With her sunny disposition and her laughter, she'd worked her way into McCai's tough heart.

He took a sip of the Scotch, inhaled deeply, then let the breath out noisily, a sad smile tugging at his lips. Not only was she all those things, she had him making simple mistakes even a junior private investigator wouldn't have made.

His miserable mood was briefly interrupted when Nate called and said he was sending over some very interesting information regarding the case. He asked McCai to meet him later for a drink, but the invitation was refused.

Somehow, after talking with Nate, McCai suddenly knew there was only one way he could possibly get any peace of mind. He swung his feet to the floor, stood, then walked into the bedroom. He picked up the phone and punched in a number, tucking the tail of his shirt into his pants as he waited for the party to answer. "James. Sorry to bother you at home, but I want you to let your man know that I'll be watching Jenny Castle tonight."

"Er...all night?" James asked, clearly taken aback.

"All night," McCai said again. "I haven't worked surveillance in years. It'll be nice for a change. Besides, I have a special interest in this case, and I might as well work it from all angles."

"How long will it take you to get in place?"

"Give me an hour," McCai replied, then dropped the receiver in its cradle.

As Jonah McCai hung up the phone in his posh apartment, Phyllis Gliden stood staring at the veterinary clinic where she'd taken Noah. She'd been standing there for quite some time, and more than once she'd tried to make herself walk across the street, enter the building and simply ask if the dog had lived or died. She had also told herself, more than once, that it was best to let the matter drop. Joey would get really angry if she were to visit the vet's office, she reasoned. She just knew he would.

But she kept her lonely vigil, watching the front door of the clinc and chewing indecisively at one corner of her lower lip.

Poor Noah.

Phyllis knew what it meant to be alone. Hadn't she been alone for most of her life? Even growing up in the foster homes where she'd spent most of her childhood, she had been alone. Oh, there had been people around, she thought, but because her hearing was impaired, her communication with them had been limited. None of the foster families seemed to want any more, so she'd become resigned to a way of life she didn't care for, but was helpless to change.

Even after she graduated from college, thanks to a grant from a private foundation that sponsored the disabled, she had led a very lonely life. Until she met Joey and his dogs, and Noah. Joey and his animals had opened up a new world for her. They'd given her a reason for getting up in the morning. Keeping a dam in whelp, then looking after the puppies for Joey made her feel needed.

Now Noah was either hurt and lonely in the building across the street, Phyllis told herself, or he was dead. And it was all her fault, because she hadn't listened when Joey told her to keep the dog in her backyard.

The vet must be busy with an emergency, she reasoned, because it was almost nine-thirty and she could see through his window a little boy sitting in the waiting room, reading a magazine.

How would it hurt if she walked over and asked one or two discreet questions? What would it matter? After all, Joey said he'd already settled with the customer who owned Noah. And ever since she'd known him, hadn't Joey also said that there was a certain element of risk involved in operating a boarding kennel? Phyllis assumed that was why she'd gotten to keep Noah at her place. Joey had told her that Noah's owner, a close friend of his, was away for several months and he'd requested that the dog live in a family atmosphere. Phyllis thought it awfully nice of Joey to take such pains with his friend's dog. But no, she quickly corrected herself, continuing to berate herself, Joey hadn't taken chances with the terrier.

But she had. She'd taken stupid chances.

Breathing deeply, Phyllis squared her thin shoulders and stepped off the curb.

IT WAS CLOSE to ten-fifteen when Jenny returned to the Arbor from New Orleans and the Severn Oaks Kennel Club meeting. There had been a number of things to discuss, including the theft of one member's pet boxer three days before. Jenny had cautioned everyone to keep a close watch on their animals. Apparently the dognappings had started up again.

She'd no sooner walked into the kitchen, when the phone rang. Jenny hurried to answer before it woke Dolly. "Hello?"

"Jenny. Thank goodness!" exclaimed Marge Williams, the nursing home director. "I was hoping I'd find you at home."

"I just walked in, Marge. What can I do for you?"

"It's Edna Davis."

"Edna?" Jenny repeated, her heart jumping into her throat. "Has something happened to her?"

"It's her heart. The doctor is concerned that she's not responding to her medication. Frankly, Jenny, I don't expect her to pull through."

"Oh, Marge," Jenny cried softly. "Not Edna. She's one of my favorites. I know I shouldn't say that, but she is. Is there any way I can help?"

"Maybe...at least I hope so. Edna keeps calling for someone named Mildred. When one of the nurses asked her daughter who Mildred was, the daughter hadn't the slightest idea. It dawned on me after dinner this evening that since the two of you are so close, she might have mentioned someone by that name. I wouldn't have bothered you, but apparently not seeing this Mildred, whoever she is, is creating a great deal of stress for Edna."

"Well, I'm delighted that you called, and you can stop looking," Jenny said gently. "Mildred is the little beagle she plays with."

"Can you possibly bring the dog to her?"

"Now?" Jenny asked. "Are you sure the doctor or her daughter won't mind? I mean ... some people aren't as fond of pets as we are."

"They won't mind, and yes, I want you to bring Mildred over now," Marge said firmly. "I think it's time we prove how beneficial the dogs are to the patients, rather than just making claims. We've kept daily records on each of the patients in your program, and after your visits their state of mind as well as their vital signs—are remarkable. If Edna's vital signs improve with the appearance of Mildred the way I think they will, then that will go a long way toward persuading the powers-that-be to fund the program."

"Give me thirty minutes. Okay?"

"Fine. And thanks, Jenny. I hate to ask you to go to this trouble, but it does seem to be a desperate situation."

Jenny quickly wrote a short note for Dolly, then quietly slipped out the door.

What a temperature change, she thought, shivering as she made her way from the house to the kennel building. She pulled the collar of her jacket closer around her neck, remembering the warmth of the sunshine that had shone down on her and McCai while they picnicked...and while they made love...and while they sat and talked and reveled in the newness of what they'd shared. Somehow it seemed appropriate that, as in their relationship and the brutal finality of it, with the ending of the day had come the rain, causing the temperature to drop.

A few minutes later Mildred, sitting in her crate on the passenger seat of the van, watched her mistress with sleepy-eyed curiosity. She gave a huge yawn that earned a chuckle from Jenny.

"I know, sweetie, I know," Jenny said softly. She took one hand from the steering wheel, eased it through the stainless steel opening and chucked the beagle under the chin, then rubbed her satiny ears. "We're doing this for your friend, Edna. For her and all the others, Mildred." Jenny frowned, then sniffed. "I wish I'd had time to give you a quick bath, but—"

Though her personal aroma might not have pleased the masses, Mildred wasn't aware that she didn't smell like a million dollars. Her tail was wagging like crazy, and if she could have smiled, Jenny knew she would have done so. That was one reason she'd found beagles to be a good breed to take to the nursing home. Their personalities made them perfect for the affection showered on them by the patients.

It suddenly occurred to Jenny that it was probably just such harmony between the elderly and the dogs that was making the program so successful. Neither of them expected more from the other than they were able to give; neither of them bothered putting on an act. They were what they were, and they accepted one another without reservations.

Why couldn't people treat one another with the same consideration? Jenny wondered.

When she entered the nursing home and began walking down the long corridor toward Edna's room, Jenny was aware of an air of urgency she'd never noticed during the day. Perhaps its cause was the sounds coming from some of the patients confined to their beds—weak, trembling moans that bespoke the suffering of body and mind far more clearly than words.

Jenny shivered. She hated to admit it, even to herself, but she much preferred to visit the home during the day. Death and suffering were exposed less harshly in daylight than in the frightening uncertainty of darkness.

She stopped outside Edna's room, not sure whether to go on in or knock. The decision was made for her when the door suddenly opened and Marie Gordon stepped out into the corridor.

"Jenny," she said warmly, "how nice of you to come. And this must be Mildred," she remarked as she reached out and stroked the beagle's head. "Marge seems to think this little girl is going to help Mother rest a little easier."

"So do I, Marie," Jenny added. "We've seen some really remarkable interchanges between the patients here and the animals. I also have several really good articles on the subject that you might be interested in reading."

"If your Mildred will help my mother," Marie said, sighing, "then I'll gladly read your articles."

"Do you know where Marge is?" Jenny asked, just as she saw the director hurrying down the corridor toward them.

"Sorry I wasn't here to meet you," Marge said in a rushed voice, one hand patting Jenny on the shoulder, while the other one absently rubbed Mildred's head. She glanced from Marie Gordon to Jenny. "Shall we go in?"

CHAPTER TEN

JENNY STEPPED OUT into the corridor and gently
closed the door behind her. She turned toward the exit
at the far end, then froze in her tracks!

"What are you doing here?" she asked, her loud
whisper sounding harsh in the nighttime quiet of the
nursing home.

McCai, his features grim and uncompromising,
pushed away from the wall directly across from Edna
Davis's room. He walked the few feet to where Jenny
was standing, then reached out and cupped her elbow
firmly. "We'll talk outside. I'd rather not discuss it
here."

"There's nothing to talk about," Jenny said stiffly.

"Okay," McCai said silkily, retaining his hold on
her arm, "if that's what you want, I'll be glad to talk
here. Right here," he emphasized with a wave of his
hand. "Right smack in the middle of the hallway,
where anybody that happens along can hear us talking about you being a suspect in the dognapping case,
about our making lo—"

"Stop it!" Jenny cried. She turned and began
walking beside him then, her lips pressed together in
a thin line of disapproval, her shoulders rigid with self-

control. "For the life of me, McCai, I can't think of a single thing we have to discuss."

"Then you're either the silliest person in the world, or you're the most uncaring," he countered. "No two people can share what we have today and not be affected. I know I was, and I think you were as well. I can't walk away and pretend our lovemaking never happened. Of course, as you've pointed out to me in the past, I'm a realist. In that cozy little dreamworld you inhabit, everything is always perfect, and people act like characters at the end of a fairy tale. That's about as far from reality as life can get. Maybe it's time you faced some cold, hard facts about life, Jenny. It's not always perfect, but you make the best of it and go on."

"Don't be a deliberate ass, McCai," Jenny said angrily. How dare he presume to lecture her on her faults, or insinuate that the only reason for the gulf between them was her pettiness. "Learning, just after we've made love, that you have detectives watching my every move doesn't mean I'm uncaring or silly, McCai."

"You most certainly are when you refuse to listen to reason," McCai said. Dammit! he thought. She was acting like a Missouri mule. He felt like shaking her.

"What's there to say?" she taunted him. "You're convinced that I'm a crook, a thief. I should think that's simple enough."

McCai remained silent as he held open the door for her. The moment they were outside, however, Jenny felt the heavy weight of his wide hands on her shoulders, and then he swung her around to face him. "All right," he said roughly. "I'll admit the evidence at this point shows you in a more unfavorable light than others, but that doesn't mean I'm about to handcuff you and drag you off to jail. We have other leads that we're checking out, and we'll continue to do so till we find the answer."

"And in the meantime?" Jenny asked.

"In the meantime I would like for us to keep seeing each other." She was so terribly angry with him, McCai was thinking, yet he'd never seen her looking more beautiful.

"You want me to keep on seeing you?" she asked, disbelieving.

"Is that such a horrible thing to do? I've watched you be generous to others, Jenny. Am I such a terrible person that you think I have no redeeming qualities?"

"You ask a lot of a person, McCai," Jenny said. "In fact, it's probably more than I'm capable of giving."

"I don't think so," he said, shaking his head. "I just think that for the first time in your life you've found yourself in a position that can't be corrected with a smile or a good deed. Nor am I going to allow you to ignore me. If you don't see me willingly, then I'll let someone else handle the investigation and I'll sit outside your house twenty-four hours a day."

And Jenny was afraid he might do that very thing. "It won't be easy, McCai," she freely admitted. And it wouldn't be, she told herself. She didn't know of a single person who enjoyed being played for a fool.

McCai continued to press his point. "You're blaming me, Jenny, instead of looking at circumstances. I could resent you just as much, but I don't."

"You? It seems to me you came out of this mess smelling like a rose. Why on earth should you resent me? What have I done to you?"

"Because of you, I've broken rules. Once or twice in my lifetime, breaking rules could have gotten me killed. It would get an employee fired from McCai Limited just like that." He held up his right hand and snapped his fingers. "Because of you, I almost feel I should withdraw from the case."

"Considering how rigid you are when it comes to your precious rules and regulations, I'm sure that's a difficult position for you to be in. And if you're trying to make me feel guilty, then you can stop, because I don't," Jenny said honestly. "I didn't ask you to come into my life with your crazy accusations, and I refuse to take the blame for any difficulties you might be having. Instead, I think I'll offer you some of your own advice. You've lived so long in a world where crime has been the dominating factor, you've let it warp your thinking. To paraphrase you, McCai, get real and grow up."

McCai knew a fear far greater than any he'd ever experienced. The other times when he'd been this afraid had involved the risk of losing his life. In a way that had been far simpler. Once he'd accepted that death wasn't something reserved for *other* people that

it was as close to him—in his particular profession—
as eating, he quit worrying. Back then he hadn't had
anyone or anything to live for. During the first dan-
gerous months of his career with the government he'd
resigned himself to his own demise.

Ahh...but the danger looking him square in the eye
now, he thought, was entirely different. Now he was
faced with the permanent loss of Jenny from his life,
with having to go on and function without her.

Suddenly McCai reached for her. He tugged her
tightly against his chest, his arms binding her to him.
Jenny resisted being this close to him just as she had
when he forced her to walk beside him. But her efforts were in vain. McCai was just as determined and
far superior in strength.

He slipped two strong fingers beneath her chin and
forced her head up. "Look at me, Jenny," he said
gruffly.

Jenny did, and immediately wished she'd continued staring at the tips of her running shoes. In addition to his rough-hewn features, she saw despair
reflected in his eyes. Despair mixed with...was it anger?

"I can't walk away from you," he said flatly.
"Don't ask me to explain why I find that impossible
to do, because I don't have an answer that's even remotely sensible."

"Then don't ask me to let it be business as usual,
McCai," Jenny told him. "Hearing you on the phone
this afternoon made our lovemaking seem cheap to

me. Now, instead of making love, I feel like it was nothing more than just plain sex."

"Don't you dare say that!" he exclaimed in a voice barely under control. "What we shared was wonderful. And it was shared, understand? It was beautiful. Sex is an act between two people who are interested only in their individual gratification. There's no comparison."

For a long moment they stared into each other's eyes, neither of them seeing a solution to their problem, nor a way to stop the aching of their hearts.

McCai broke the spell by dipping his head as he muttered an oath, and taking Jenny's soft lips in a hard, rough kiss that was hurting but strangely fulfilling at the same moment.

Hard kiss.

Gentle hands.

Thundering heartbeats.

The same pattern as their relationship, Jenny was thinking between the sweet surge of desire flowing in slumbering waves over her body.

McCai knew that if it were humanly possible, he'd absorb Jenny into his being and keep her with him always.

Did that mean he was falling in love with her? he wondered.

Certainly not, he answered just as quickly. He cared for her, that was all. He definitely didn't need something as betraying as love in his life.

He lifted his head and studied every detail of Jenny's face. "Funny," he said gently. "I don't think I've ever noticed the difference in the taste of a kiss."

"Taste?" Jenny asked, puzzled by the remark. What was he talking about?

"You. You taste sweet. Every time I kiss you, it tastes like you've just eaten a peach."

"I detest peaches," Jenny said stubbornly. "They make me break out in a rash."

"Nevertheless, your mouth tastes like a peach," McCai told her, grinning at her obstinacy. He pushed back a reluctant curl from her forehead, one lingering finger softly tracing her hairline. "And I know you liked the kiss, Jenny. Your response was beautiful."

Jenny refrained from answering. What was the point? She stepped out of the warmth of his arms, then tugged her jacket back into place. "I...I have to get home. Dolly will be worried about me."

"I'll follow you home."

"There's no need."

"I know," McCai told her. "You're a big girl and all that garbage. But you also happen to be a woman out late at night. That being the case, I'll see that you get home safely."

"Believe it or not, McCai, I didn't run into a single burglar, thief or murderer on my way over here."

"Very cute, Jenny. Do you ever bother to read anything in the newspaper other than the comics?"

Jenny ungraciously allowed herself to be escorted to where the van was parked. She took the keys out of her jacket pocket, unlocked the door, then looked at the stern-faced man at her elbow. "I do hope you consider it safe for me to drive back to the Arbor? Or would you rather have one of the detectives chauffeur me? By the way," she remarked, craning her neck in order to see around McCai's large person for a better look at the parking area and the street beyond, "where's my bodyguard? When I was eavesdropping on your conversation today, I got the impression that I was so notorious I was to have the best of the best."

"Oh, you do have the best, Ms Castle," McCai said evenly.

"Oh?"

"Yes."

"Then where is he?" she asked pointedly.

"You're looking at him."

Jenny's startled gaze collided with McCai's enigmatic one. "But you said—"

"Precisely, Ms Castle," he murmured as he nodded. "Now, shall we get started?"

"But—"

"Later, Jenny," McCai interrupted. All the while they were talking, he'd been urging her into the van. Now he made sure she fastened the seat belt and instructed her to lock the doors.

While driving back to the Arbor, Jenny was intensely aware of the twin headlights of McCai's car visible in the rearview mirror. He didn't exactly tailgate, she thought, but he certainly stayed close enough to annoy her.

She touched her lips with the tips of her fingers and thought of the kiss they'd shared. Even though, at the moment, she was devastated by what he'd done, her feelings for him hadn't vanished into thin air just because of his actions. Like him, she couldn't put their relationship out of her mind and walk away without a backward glance She winced when her finger found a particularly tender spot, and wondered if his lip would be sore in the morning. Would it be just another scar to remind her of her encounter with Jonah McCai, an encounter she'd lost without ever really knowing why?

When she reached the Arbor, Jenny followed her usual habit of parking the van on the concrete apron in front of the kennel. She glanced into the side mirror for some sign of McCai, but didn't see him. Had he merely followed her home, then gone on somewhere else?

Just as she opened the door, McCai appeared.

"You need to have the air in the right rear tire checked. It's low," he said calmly.

"Thank you. I'll take care of it tomorrow," she answered, then put her hand in his outstretched one and let him help her from the high seat of the van. McCai held her hand until she was standing beside him, and even then he seemed reluctant to let it go.

Very much the gentleman, Jenny thought grimly. How touching. She glanced up at him then and noticed his head tipped attentively to one side. "Is something wrong?"

"Your dogs," he told her, nodding toward the kennel building a few yards away, a frown creasing his brow. "I've never heard them do that much barking before."

"Now that you mention it, neither have I, unless something was bothering them."

A few minutes later Jenny, with McCai at her side, stood puzzled, staring at the opened gates of two of the outside runs.

"I don't believe this," she said finally, as the shock began to wear off. "They sawed the chain," she muttered angrily. "They actually stood here in front of God and anybody that happened to pass by and took the time to saw the darn chain!"

"It wasn't difficult to do, honey. The chains aren't that big," McCai said thoughtfully, noting that each of the runs was similarly equipped with the chain and a large metal snap on the end. "Did you check everything inside? Are any of the dogs missing?"

Jenny, who had carefully searched the runs while McCai examined the chains, shook her head and sighed. "Other than the jimmied lock on the back door and this one, everybody's present and accounted for. But I'm convinced that's only because we surprised them before they had time to complete the job."

"I think you're probably right. Why don't you check everything inside again, while I have another look around out here," he told her. "Maybe we'll get lucky and find something. At this point, anything would be helpful. And if I were you, I'd leave these outside lights on. At least for the next few nights."

Jenny went to do as he'd suggested, muttering under her breath about dishonest people preying on society. She removed the food pans from each of the inside runs, did another head count on the dogs and double-checked the windows. "By the way, McCai," she yelled with perverse pleasure, "if you'd been watching the house instead of trailing me to the nursing home, none of this would have happened, you know."

Jenny smirked when McCai didn't respond. Just like a man. When they screwed up, they chose to remain as silent as a tomb. But let it be the other way around, and the whole world knew.

"For your information, Ms Castle, though the Arbor is a grande dame among houses, we aren't the least bit interested in watching it," he said evenly. "Do either of the college kids who work for you walk with a limp?"

"What?" Jenny asked incredulously. "Don't tell me you think they're responsible. Honestly, McCai! First me, now my help. Don't you ever stop and think before you make such rash accusations?"

A pained expression crossed McCai's face. "It would be interesting to see just how you'd go about explaining that statement. Care to try?" he asked with maddening calm. He walked over to the desk where Jenny was trying each drawer to make sure that the lock hadn't been tampered with.

She watched his progress out of the corner of her eye, praying he would keep his distance. She suddenly felt shy in his presence, probably as a result of their kiss in the parking lot. Not very original, she admitted, but it was how she felt nevertheless.

"It just seemed to fit," Jenny offered rather lamely, gesturing with her hands, then rubbing her damp palms against her slacks-clad thighs.

"Meaning?" McCai persisted. He was watching her like a hawk. She was fidgety and that pleased him. Their shared intimacy was proving to be more difficult for her to handle than he'd thought. That fact amused McCai, yet at the same time it made him feel strangely protective.

"You jumped to the wrong conclusion where I'm concerned, so when you mentioned the kennel help, it seemed to fit."

"Have I honestly jumped to the wrong conclusion where you're concerned, Jenny?" McCai asked.

Suddenly the room became so quiet one could have heard a pin drop. Even the dogs, sensing the tension between the two people, were quiet, their eyes never leaving McCai and Jenny.

"Yes, McCai," Jenny said softly. "You have. I don't care what kind of evidence you have, nor how much it points toward me, I have never taken anyone's dog. And if that isn't enough, I lost Dulcie, not to mention this little fiasco."

"You have a point," he conceded grudgingly. On the one hand it was embarrassing to think that he could have misread a situation as badly as he had this one. On the other hand, it was highly unlikely that anyone would break into her kennel if she was as involved in the case as he'd thought.

"I bet saying those words almost choked you, didn't it, McCai?" Jenny asked, grinning in spite of herself.

"It's against your principles to admit you could possibly be wrong in judging a person, isn't it?"

"Now wait a minute," McCai told her. "I merely said you had a point. And you do. And I promise to keep a very open mind where you're concerned... er... regarding the case."

"McCai," Jenny said sweetly, "without a doubt, you are the biggest ass I've ever met, seen or heard of! Now," she added haughtily, "if you'll be so kind as to remove your detestable carcass from my property, I'd like to lock up." McCai's deep, infuriating chuckle had Jenny gritting her teeth till her jaw ached.

"By the way, what took you to the nursing home so late?" he asked while waiting for her to lock the door.

"Edna Davis," Jenny said, then realized that the surprise of seeing McCai at the nursing home and then the attempted break-in at the kennel had erased Edna from her mind. "She has an inoperable heart condition, and right now she's not doing so well. In fact, she's very ill. She kept asking for the dog I take to see her, so her doctor and Marge wanted to see if her seeing the animal would help."

"Did it?"

"I don't know," Jenny told him. "She barely recognized me when I got there, but when I put Mildred down beside her, she became very quiet." She looked at him and shrugged. "What can I say? I felt I was in the way, so I didn't stay long."

"I'm sorry she's not doing well," McCai replied. "When I first went with you to the nursing home, I could see that you and she were great friends. Maybe

Mildred will be able to do what modern medicine can't." He dropped an arm around her shoulders and pulled her close to his side. "Come on, let's go see if Dolly happened to leave any coffee in that pot she always keeps going."

"I don't recall asking you in for coffee, McCai," Jenny said, though she knew for all the good it would do, she could just as easily not have spoken. He seemed to have a hide as thick as a rhinoceros's.

"But knowing what a sensitive and caring person you are," McCai began, "I'm sure that was nothing but an oversight due to your extreme concern for Edna Davis."

Jenny regarded him with a look so expressive that McCai threw back his head and roared with laughter. "In a pig's eye!"

"Seriously now," he continued, when he could speak without laughing, "wouldn't it be nice to sit out on the front porch in that antique swing of yours and talk?"

McCai knew she was worried about her friend, not to mention the kennel break-in. He could see it in her face, in her eyes, he could hear it in her voice. He could also sense her distrust and he knew she was unsure of herself in his presence. For the first time in his entire life McCai found himself concerned about how someone else felt toward him. Would he be able to break through that wall of uncertainty or had she been completely driven away by what she'd overheard him saying to James?

"It . . . would be nice," Jenny admitted cautiously. "But would it—"

"Then do that," McCai interrupted her. "Stop trying to analyze why it would feel good, just know that it will, and stop there. You're under a lot of strain. And even sunshine girls have to break down and admit to being normal sometime."

"Have you ever resented being tagged a certain way?" she asked curiously. They had reached the house by then. Jenny handed the keys to McCai, who unlocked the door, then stood aside for her to enter the large kitchen.

"I don't know that it's ever been done in my particular case. Even if it ever has, no one's had the nerve to tell me. Why?"

"I feel like everyone expects me to always be smiling, to never think an unkind thought or perform an unkind deed. There are times when I'm tempted to do something really bad just to show the world that they don't know the real me."

McCai reached out and ruffled her hair. "Stop worrying about what people expect and be yourself. But I've got a sneaky feeling that you really are all those things you just mentioned."

"You're not scoring any Brownie points, McCai," Jenny told him, frowning. She walked over to the sink and began washing her hands. "Please," she said, nodding toward the adjoining sink, "wash up here or use the half bath through there," indicating a door off the kitchen.

While Jenny fixed a fresh pot of coffee, McCai washed up at the kitchen sink. "I think you should call the police in the morning," he told her as he dried his hands on paper towels. "That kind of damage was done by someone very determined and very methodical. My gut feeling is that they were going to steal your dogs. I hardly think they'd go to all that trouble just for crates or feeding pans."

"For once we're in agreement," Jenny said, then told him about the kennel club member who recently lost a dog. "Do you think I should call the police tonight?"

"Not really. It's unlikely there will be a crowd of people walking over the place," McCai replied. He copied her stance against the counter edge, far closer than Jenny would have preferred, much, much closer. "The local police force, though small, seems competent enough. They've gone out of their way here and in New Orleans to help me."

"What did you mean when you asked if one of my staff had a limp?" Jenny asked, hoping the tremor in her voice would go unnoticed. McCai smelled like the outdoors after a spring shower—spicy and woodsy.

"There are several footprints that have a strange, dragging pattern on the right. They're around the back door. Be sure to point that out to the police in the morning." He didn't bother telling her that he'd already had a background check done on the young men who helped out at the kennel.

His arm brushed hers.

Jenny took air into her lungs like a drowning person, then turned and began taking down brightly colored mugs. Her hands were shaking pitifully, and she prayed he wouldn't notice.

"I'll remember."

He thought her a thief. Yet he was the only man she'd ever met who made her forget everything but the touch of his hands on her body.

McCai felt the tension holding Jenny in its merciless grip and hated himself for being the cause of her unhappiness. He wanted to take her in his arms and assure her that everything would be all right. But he didn't. Instead, he took a firm grim on his emotions. *Don't be an ass,* a tiny cautionary voice told him. *Don't push her... don't crowd her. Be a friend, give her a shoulder to cry on if need be, but don't even think of trying to play the part of the lover tonight.*

Heedless, he reached out for her anyway. He caught her hands and guided them to his shoulders, then clasped her waist and turned her to face him. "Jenny, sweetheart, relax. Okay?" At her jerky nod, he went on. "This hasn't been the best day you've ever had, but even so, don't let it get you down. Things will work out, I promise. Edna will get better and the police will probably find whoever it was who broke into your kennel."

"And you, McCai?" she asked softly. "What about you? Will you still distrust me a week from now... a month from now?" There were tears in her eyes, large, glistening tears that tore at McCai's heart.

"Ahh... Jenny," he whispered roughly. With infinite tenderness he folded her into his arms, his chin coming to rest on her shiny hair. "You'll be cleared, Jenny Castle, and don't you worry."

But in McCai's heart, he wasn't nearly as positive. There was new evidence on his desk that was giving him some really bad moments. Evidence that could possibly cast Jenny in an even worse light.

CHAPTER ELEVEN

"WHAT DO YOU MAKE OF IT?" James Baldwin asked as he leaned back in the desk chair, his hands clasped behind his head.

"Convenient as hell," McCai said wearily, "but for who?" He tossed the stapled pages of the report onto the desk, then rose to his feet and walked over to the window. He knew the text by heart; he'd been carrying it around in his mind since receiving it from Nate last night.

Edna Davis. Tom Harper. Emily Dupree. Evelyn Morrison.

Each of those names was included in Nate's packet. Each of those names was listed as a patient at the nursing home where Jenny visited several times a week, and each was credited with having shipped dogs to Mexico within the past eighteen months.

"I didn't make the connection till last night, when I was waiting for Jenny at the nursing home. Then it hit me."

James studied the grim profile of his friend and colleague for several unsure moments, finding himself at a loss for words. "May I impose upon our years of friendship and ask you a very personal question?"

McCai lifted his hands indifferently. "Why not?"

"Are you in love with Jenny Castle?"

"I refuse to answer on the grounds that it would sure as hell tend to incriminate me, James. Anything else?"

"I'm...sorry. Do you want someone else to handle the case?"

"No!" The one word exploded from McCai's lips at the same time he whirled around to face James. For a moment even he looked puzzled by his outburst. "Er...no," he said and shook his head. "I'll stay on the case."

"Then may I make another suggestion?"

"Shoot."

"Sometimes we can become so involved in something, we can't make rational decisions. The forest and the trees stuff—you're familiar with the metaphor. That could be the case with you and Ms Castle."

"Could be," McCai admitted, "but I sure as hell can't let it go now."

"All right," James said quickly. "That's no problem. Even with your involvement, you're professional enough to ask for help if you need it. My other suggestion is, let me have the file for the day. Give me time enough to go over it, to study it and see what I can make of it."

"I know what you're saying makes sense. It really does," McCai answered. He began pacing about the office, his features dark. "Who the hell am I trying to kid, James? If one of our employees had handled a

ase the way I've handled this one, he'd have been
ired."

"Well, I think the difference between the amateur
nd the professional lies in the ability to see that,
McCai. And we both know that you're not an ama-
eur."

"Perhaps not yesterday or tomorrow. But for today, I'm a dud."

"What about it?" James asked, holding up the file.

McCai shrugged. "Why not? It certainly can't
urt."

McCai was positive he'd never felt so frustrated in
his entire life. Last night when he left Jenny, he'd been
stricken with a deep sense of foreboding that refused
to leave him. After the information arrived by mes-
senger from Nate, he'd gotten only a couple of hours'
leep and then he'd dressed and driven to the office.
Once there, he began going over the case, including the
newest information from Nate, searching for the tiniest bit of evidence that didn't point directly toward
Jenny.

He walked slowly to the door, then paused and
looked back at James. "Needless to say, background
checks are being run on the closest relatives of each of
those names on that list. If Nate calls, buzz me on the
beeper and I'll get right back to him."

"Will do," James murmured without looking up,
already engrossed in the file that had incriminated
Jenny.

ACROSS TOWN, Joey Tate was gripping the receiver :
tightly his knuckles were white. The dogs were bar
ing, and he was having a difficult time hearing. "Wh.
do you mean you can't risk being involved a
longer?" he asked angrily.

"Just that," David Moreau told him. "It's gettir
too risky. I want my money and I want out, Joey."

"When it's finished you'll get out, and not a mi
ute sooner," Joey told him. Moreau had been threa
ening for months to pull out of the operation, but no
his mind seemed made up. Joey wasn't dumb. F
knew how to read people; he'd had to know in ord
to survive. "I'll need at least ten more health certi
cates."

"Cash only. You can pick them up this afternoo
around three-thirty," Moreau told him.

Joey dropped the receiver into place, then leane
forward on the desk. A sharp sensation of fear washe
over him. In his mind's eye he could envision tl
dream he'd cherished for so long slipping from h
grasp.

That simply couldn't happen. He couldn't allow
to happen.

He dropped into the rickety chair, then reached fo
the calculator in his shirt pocket. After a few minut
of quick arithmetic, he leaned back in his chair ar
stared thoughtfully into space.

Money.

He was still short of the amount he needed. Rathe
he amended, the amount he considered necessary t
enable him to afford his coveted life-style. Losir

Noah and Moreau's help were two major setbacks. Now he would have to pull from his reserves. Perhaps it might be a good idea for him to make his final move sooner than he'd planned.

THE GRASS WAS STILL DAMP with dew the next morning when Jenny showed Joseph Atwood the damage done to her property the night before.

"Why didn't you call us last night, Jenny?"

"Because it was after midnight when I got home and discovered what had happened, Joseph. I didn't want flashing lights disturbing my neighbors, not to mention my guests."

"Hmm."

That one sound irritated Jenny just about as much as everything else about Joseph irritated her. "No one has been here, so you don't have to worry about anything having been disturbed. By the way," she said as she walked around to the back door, "there are some footprints here that might interest you."

"Hmm," Joseph murmured again, then squatted beside the deepest print for a better look. "Looks like this person has a problem. Could be a cripple. Interesting."

Jenny waited for Joseph's final conversational brick to fall. When it didn't, she closed her eyes for a moment and gave a brief thanks.

"Hmm."

Jenny's eyes opened and she glared at the heavens, then turned and started back into the kennel.

"Er...Jenny?"

"Yes?"

"Would you mind getting that briefcase out of the back seat of the squad car? I need to make a plaster cast of this print."

"Not at all," she answered, forcing herself to keep calm, then walked the short distance to where the black-and-white vehicle, complete with blue lights on top, was parked. She couldn't help but wonder if he was going to ask her to mix the materials for the cast?

In addition to the chief of police and various other law enforcement personnel, there were at least eight or nine uniformed members of the Jefferson City police department. How could she have been so lucky as to have gotten Joseph Atwood for her investigator?

"Why me, Lord," she muttered. "What terrible deed have I committed that would cause you to send the plague of Joseph Atwood down upon me? You know I've despised him since childhood."

"Prayers so early in the morning, Ms Castle? May one be so bold as to assume the day has gotten off to a bad start?"

Jenny's head swiveled around like a puppet's set on a wooden pole. "It's going steadily downhill, McCai," she remarked dryly, then reached in for the briefcase.

"Let me help," he offered solicitously, struggling to hide his amusement at the less than pleased look in her eyes when she saw him. Even when she was angry, he thought she was beautiful. "I can see you've been prompt in enlisting the help of the local gendarmes."

"Reading something into that, McCai?" Jenny snapped, refusing to allow her gaze to linger on him or to let the scent of his cologne throw her off stride. "Does that make me more guilty this morning than last night?"

"Not at all, Ms Castle. I think it's very sensible."

"Well, miracles do happen occasionally," she said in hopes of annoying him. "Come meet one of Jefferson City's finest. I've disliked him for most of my life, but if he finds out who tried to break into my kennel, I'll be forced to alter my opinion—perhaps."

"Come now, Jenny," McCai returned innocently, "let's not be overly generous with our praise. It could go to the man's head."

"Go suck an egg, McCai," Jenny murmured in a less-than-flattering undertone as they approached Joseph, who was on his knees, gently brushing away debris from the footprint in the soft dirt.

"This should be an excellent one, Jen," Joseph remarked. "Yes, sirree, a really excellent one."

"Joseph, this is Jonah McCai. Mr. McCai is a private investigator from Dallas. He's here working on a case," Jenny said as she introduced the two men. "You met Joseph's mother, McCai, the day you arrived in Jefferson City. Remember Matilda Atwood?"

"Certainly," McCai said, nodding. "A charming woman. I hope the Fall Fete is coming along nicely."

Joseph rose to his feet. "According to her it will be the best one yet."

Jenny watched the two men shake hands, noting how the normally robust Joseph paled in comparison to McCai. She realized that neither made an overt effort to outdo the other. They exchanged nothing more than the obligatory handshake in acknowledgment of a normal introduction. But it was simply there—McCai the dominant one, with an aura of authority emanating from him that had Joseph Atwood immediately falling all over himself with explanations of what he was doing, and why.

"I'll need some water to mix with this powder, Jenny," Joseph told her as the three of them walked into the kennel. "Oh, I also found this. It might prove useful," he added, opening his hand to reveal a curved piece of metal resting against his palm.

McCai reached for the shiny item and held it up. He looked at Jenny and grinned. "Care to guess?"

"I haven't—Could it be part of a spur?" she asked rather hesitantly.

"Not bad, Jenny. Offhand I'd say it's the heel plate from some sort of brace," McCai offered after examining the strip of metal. He looked back at the indentation in the ground. "That would account for the unevenness of that print. Did you notice that?" he asked Joseph.

"Yes, I did. They came down heavy on the outside of the right foot. Which leads me to think that the right leg has to be shorter than the other, hence the brace, making the foot heavier and causing it to drag."

"Makes sense," McCai agreed, still studying what he thought to be the heel piece. He pointed to the six-digit number engraved on the inner side of the metal. "This is a good place to start," he told Joseph. "Will you be able to do anything on this today or would you mind some help?''

"Naturally we'll check it out," he said, looking at Jenny and shrugging apologetically, "but our resources are limited. We usually have to take something like that—" he nodded at the object in McCai's hand "—to New Orleans or send it to the state crime lab. Either way, it'll take a while longer than it really should."

"What would you say to my having this checked out by my firm?" McCai asked. "I can have a team of experts on it within hours."

"Hmm," Joseph murmured thoughtfully, causing Jenny to want to pull out her hair. "I haven't listed it in my report yet, so if I don't mention a particular curved metal strip and if it isn't in my possession, then technically I don't know anything about it, do I?"

"No, you don't," McCai agreed. "Let's also make another impression of that footprint. If the numbers aren't as easy to check out as we think, then we might have to go another route."

Again the two shook hands, and Jenny was amused at how quickly men could strike a bargain. She'd found women, on the other hand, more likely to discuss each and every tiny detail for hours or sometimes days.

After Joseph made two impressions of the footprint and left, with the promise to let McCai know if the New Orleans police or the state crime lab had a matching one, Jenny invited McCai in for coffee.

"From what I've seen on TV, surveillance work is tiring," she remarked with feigned innocence as she placed butter, a basket of still-warm biscuits and a small brown crock of strawberry jam on the table. She poured each of them a cup of coffee, then sat down opposite him, watching him dispose of a biscuit with surprising quickness. "I'm going to list you as a dependent on my income tax this year, McCai."

"I'm trying to clear your good name," he retaliated with a grin that caused his eyes to sparkle. "I'm even doing the work of the police to see that not a stone is left unturned in your defense."

"I'm impressed," she said flatly, "I think." And in spite of his joking mood, Jenny knew he was sincere. "This is my day to go to the nursing home. Care to join me? You made quite an impression on Mr. Harper."

"How is he?"

"Okay," Jenny said thoughtfully, then told him about the conversation she'd interrupted between Mr. Harper and his nephew. "If looks could kill, I'd be dead by now."

"From what Mr. Harper told me, he could have stayed home after his stroke if the nephew had helped at all."

"That's a pity," Jenny said softly.

"Did you say you met the nephew?"

"No," Jenny told him. "They both shot out of the room so fast all I saw was a badly scarred face."

"I'll have to remember to ask Mr. Harper about him. Have you heard anything about Mrs. Davis this morning?" McCai asked.

Jenny reached for a biscuit, broke it open, then spread butter and jam on it. "I called first thing. Marge says there seems to be some improvement. Edna knows where she is, and is making sense when she talks. Last night she alternated speaking gibberish and begging for Mildred."

"Do they attribute this slight improvement to Mildred?"

"Well," Jenny said slowly, "it's a thought. Actually though, it's more that the dog was a calming device. Until we put Mildred in her arms, she was delirious and thrashing around in the bed. However, once she became aware that the dog was there, she settled into a deep, peaceful sleep. They didn't change or increase her medicine, so..."

"So this could help in getting funding for the program. Right?"

"Hopefully. Even the budget I first proposed has been cut to the bone in hopes the governor's committee studying it will give it their approval."

"Are there funds available for such a program or will they have to be generated?" McCai asked.

"The way I understand it, the money is available under some specific grant for aid to the elderly. Of course each program is viewed alone, and has to be approved by the committee I just mentioned."

"Does it have to be finally approved by the legislature?"

"I don't think so. We've been led to believe that the committee has the power to allocate those funds. And from what we've heard, they're a hard-nosed group."

"Well, at least you know they aren't wasting your money," McCai reminded her.

"This is true, but I also want to know that they're as thorough with everyone else. I strenuously object to having my pet project become an example of what not to fund," Jenny remarked. She glanced out the window next to the table and waved.

McCai followed her gaze and saw the kennel help starting to exercise the dogs. "How long has that kid worked for you?"

"More than a year, McCai," Jenny answered. "His name is Frank, and no, I'm not suspicious of him in any way."

"That's nice," McCai said smoothly. "A person should be able to trust the people who work for them. Will I have time to make a phone call before we go to the nursing home?"

"Sure," Jenny said, nodding as they both got to their feet. She waved toward the wall phone beside the fridge. "Help yourself. But there is one thing I'm curious about, McCai."

"What's that?" he asked, holding the receiver in one hand, his other one poised over the dial face.

"Rather than follow me, have you decided to simply stay with me all day?"

"Something like that. Any objections?" he asked. He punched in a 1 and then entered his office number in New Orleans.

"No," Jenny replied, uttering the lie without hesitating. Actually, she was thinking how unnerving it was going to be having him underfoot all day. Her feelings for McCai ran deep, yet their situation was as close to impossible as any she could ever imagine. It was difficult for her to pretend everything was normal when she knew it wasn't that way at all. She wondered if he was having similar problems.

"McCai Limited," a cool, pleasant voice sounded in McCai's ear. "May I help you?"

"This is Jonah McCai, Wendy. Let me speak with James Baldwin."

"Certainly, Mr. McCai," the receptionist said quickly.

"I asked for the whole day to study this file, McCai," James said a moment or two later. "It's only nine-thirty."

"This will give you something else to ponder," McCai replied, then filled him in on the strip of metal Joseph Atwood had found behind the kennel. After reciting the number, he went on, "I know it's going to take some digging, James, but send that information out to the Dallas and Chicago offices. And get in touch with local manufacturers. I'd start with the major companies that supply braces, then work your way down."

"Do you see a connection between the attempted break-in, Jenny Castle and the dognappings?" James asked.

"I'm not sure," McCai told him. "But I have a feeling this might give us the break we've been needing."

"Is it a good or bad feeling where your friend is concerned?" James had learned long ago that in detective work hunches were an invaluable tool.

McCai let his gaze rest on Jenny, who was putting the cups into the dishwasher. "I'm not sure... which in itself could be good."

"Well, let me be the bearer of some good news for a change," James began.

"Shoot."

"A veterinarian by the name of Richard LeJeune called a few minutes ago. He said he really needed to speak with you. Something about that wire fox terrier and the young woman who brought him in."

"Is he in his office?" McCai asked quickly.

"Said he'd be there till around eleven-thirty. Here's his number."

"Thanks, James. Talk with you later." McCai broke the connection, then tried the vet's number. By the time he got LeJeune on the phone, Jenny was standing in the middle of the kitchen floor with her purse and keys in her hand, tapping her foot impatiently.

McCai placed his palm over the mouthpiece. "Five minutes," he said softly. "Promise," he added when he saw the impatient set of her mouth. "Dr. LeJeune," he said suddenly, turning so that he was facing away from Jenny. "Jonah McCai. My office said you were looking for me."

Jenny listened to the one-sided conversation for a moment or two, then walked outside and headed toward the kennel. After her experience the day before, she wasn't too interested in eavesdropping. But the name Richard LeJeune was familiar. In fact, a friend of hers who raised Dalmatians used him as her vet. Jenny wondered what on earth Dr. LeJeune had to do with the case.

WHILE JENNY WAS TRYING to figure out Richard LeJeune's involvement in the dognapping case, Phyllis Gliden was on her way to Joey's studio to pick up the weekly checks and bills.

There was a lightness to her step this morning. A lightness brought about by happiness.

Last night she'd seen Noah. Of course, she congratulated herself, she hadn't dared to call him by name. That would have been dumb. She had to remember to cover her tracks very carefully.

The visit with Noah wasn't a long one—not even five minutes. But it had been enough for her to see that he was his usual perky self, and doing just fine. Except that one of his poor little back legs was all bundled up in a heavy cast that made his movements stiff and awkward. But when he saw her, he struggled to his feet, his upright tail moving from side to side as if it had a tiny motor inside. Tears had blinded her eyes for a moment.

He hadn't died, Phyllis told herself, he hadn't died, and that was what counted. She held her fingers

against her cheek. She could still feel the roughness of
his whiskers when he licked her skin.

Yes, she thought, Noah was doing fine. Just fine.

Her problem now was deciding whether or not to
keep on visiting him. If Joey were to ever find out, he
would kill her or at least frighten her half to death.

AS PHYLLIS SOUGHT to keep her secret from Joey,
Jenny was getting a certain sense of satisfaction in
seeing the always bandbox-fresh McCai perspiring as
he removed ten crates from the back of the van and
carried them to the large recreation room of the nursing home. She'd been surprised when he agreed to
come with her.

"Set that small crate on top of that large one," she
instructed him as he brought in the last one.

"How many dogs do you usually carry to a show?"
McCai asked.

"Three, sometimes four. Why?"

"Do you take someone with you to help?"

"Occasionally I travel with friends. It's not so bad
money-wise, but there really isn't enough space in a
van by the time everyone packs their grooming equip-
ment and their clothes. Why?"

"Because those crates are heavy," McCai said
bluntly.

"Yes, I kind of noticed you perspiring," Jenny remarked, tongue in cheek.

"And I'm sure it tickled you to death," he told her,
watching her like a hawk. "I wonder why?"

Jenny was embarrassed. She hadn't thought of being called on to explain her amusement at seeing McCai out of what she assumed to be his element. "You must be imagining things, McCai," she replied, and knew that she hadn't fooled him in the least.

"There's another entirely different side of me, Jenny, that you're still in the dark about."

She met his mocking gaze squarely. "I've seen two sides of you, McCai. The professional and the lover. Which would you prefer to be?"

"Why not Jonah McCai, the ordinary man?"

"Is there a difference?"

"Very definitely."

"Will I ever know that man?"

"Oh, yes. One way or the other."

"Jenny!" Marge Williams exclaimed as she entered the room behind McCai. "I wasn't expecting you till after lunch." She came closer, her curious gaze lingering on the good-looking man helping Jenny.

"I called this morning and cleared the time change with your recreational director. Is there some problem?"

"Not at all. We're glad to have you any time. By the way, Edna has shown marked improvement since last night. And Mildred has done nothing but eat and sleep."

Jenny was relieved the dog was adapting so well and said so. She introduced Marge to McCai, then watched with a rueful glint in her eye as he charmed the socks off Marge.

"It's so nice of you to give Jenny a hand, Mr. McCai," Marge said. "She's really made a difference in quite a few lives here."

And in mine, McCai wanted to add before Marge walked off, but didn't. He was watching Jenny, and he could have sworn he saw a flicker of jealousy in her gaze. However, it vanished so quickly he decided he must have been mistaken.

"Let's start handing out the dogs, McCai," Jenny told him. "We've kept our friends waiting long enough."

McCai looked over his shoulder and saw a semicircle of elderly people sitting in their chairs, their attention on the dogs in the crates. For a moment he felt uncomfortable as he stared at the wrinkled faces.

They were simply sitting.

They weren't demanding attention or becoming loud.

They were simply waiting.

For a moment McCai felt annoyed. When he was talking with Jenny and Marge, it hadn't occurred to him that the patients were being deprived of a few minutes of their enjoyment. He was angry with himself and them. Why hadn't they said something? Why had they sat so quietly? Why? he asked himself. Why?

It was a question that kept coming to mind as he and Jenny carried each of the dogs to its adopted owner. It kept coming to mind as he was introduced to the old, expectant men and women, as he grasped and shook the hands that age had slackened and time had altered. It came to mind as hand after hand, bent and crippled with arthritis, caught at his arm or tugged at his shirtsleeve or even tapped him on the leg, or as a not-so-steady voice hailed him with, "Hey, young fella."

When McCai finally reached Tom Harper, he found the old man gently smoothing the shiny coat of the golden retriever puppy and watching McCai with a frown on his face.

"I thought you told me you were some kind of highfalutin detective?" Tom said accusingly as they shook hands.

McCai pulled up a chair and sat down. "I am," he assured Tom. "I'm just helping Ms Castle this morning."

"Are you sweet on her?" Tom asked bluntly.

"Could be," McCai said honestly, finding it remarkably easy to talk with the man.

"Have you popped the question?"

"Er...you mean, asked her to marry me?"

"Certainly."

"No," McCai said, shaking his head. "We haven't gotten that far yet."

"Listen, son," Tom began. "Don't wait too long. A good woman is hard to find these days. You don't have to know someone for years to know that you love 'em. Why, I only knew my Mary for two weeks when we wed. We'd been married for fifty-five years when she died."

"Fifty-five years," McCai said slowly. "That's a long time, Mr. Harper."

"Oh, call me Tom. You want to know a little secret, McCai?"

McCai leaned closer. "What's that?"

"Those fifty-five years were the shortest ones of my life."

"Has your nephew been to visit you lately?" McCai asked, not sure just how much he should encourage Tom to reminisce. He remembered Jenny saying something about the old man having cried on one of her visits.

"Yeah, he's been here. Wants me to sell some of my land."

"Is that what you want, Tom?"

"No!" he said forcefully. "I'm not crazy, McCai. I know exactly what Joey wants. Some big development company was trying to get their hands on that property before I ever came in here. By now, they've probably approached Joey and waved a few dollars under his nose. It won't hurt him to earn his own way."

"What does Joey do?"

"He's involved in several things, but mainly he's a photographer. A good one, too."

"Do you still own your home, Tom?"

"I sure do," the old man declared. "A nice brick house right in the middle of forty-five acres of prime land. And I pay my own way here, too. I'm not a charity case. My aim, McCai, is to get well enough to go home to die. I suppose they're nice enough here, but I want to be back with my Mary. She's everywhere at home. No matter where I look, I see her."

He leaned back in his chair and stared out the window behind McCai, his hands resting on the sleeping puppy. "Why, I can even hear her talking to me sometimes. I've even seen her a time or two. My neighbors, they'll come get me and take me to visit Mary's grave. But here..." He shook his gray head slowly, his faded blue eyes watery with tears. "Here, McCai, I can't seem to find her. I'm dying with grief. I want to go home."

"Maybe," McCai said slowly as he got to his feet, "maybe you'll get to do that before long, Tom. If I were you, I wouldn't give up hope."

"Can you help me, McCai? Can you do that for Mary and me?"

McCai looked around him. He saw the old, the hopeless and, in many cases, the dying. He looked back at Tom Harper and in those old eyes, he saw a mighty warrior. A proud warrior.

Such a warrior was deserving of some happiness in his final days, wasn't he?

"If it's humanly possible, Ed, I'll see that you get back to your house in the middle of your forty-five acres. If it isn't harmful to your health."

Tom held out his hand. "In my day a handshake was as binding as a signed contract."

McCai grasped the thinner hand. "It still is, Tom."

EDNA WAS SLEEPING. A gentle smile stole across Jenny's lips as she stood by the bedside of the old woman. Mildred, lying lazily in the crook of a thin arm, eyed her young mistress but made no effort to move. It was almost as if the beagle knew that her mission was to give Edna the strength to fight, the will to live in spite of a heart that was slowly winding down its life-sustaining cycle.

Jenny was saddened to see her friend—always so radiant, always so full of life—lying still as death. She wanted to push back the beckoning hand urging Edna from this world.

But there was nothing she could do, Jenny reasoned. Edna's future was in the hands of a power mightier than man.

There was nothing to do but wait.

There was nothing to do but pray.

CHAPTER TWELVE

"THANKS FOR HELPING ME, McCai," Jenny said as they stacked the last of the crates in one corner of the kennel.

"My pleasure," he told her, smiling. "I've been thinking, Jenny, you've really taken on a load with this project."

"Shame on you, McCai," she chided him. "I thought you enjoyed visiting with Tom Harper."

"This has nothing to do with visiting Tom—which I do enjoy. I've even dropped by a couple of times on my own and played a game of checkers with him. You didn't know about that, did you?"

"No, I didn't. That was very thoughtful of you."

"It wasn't thoughtful, honey," McCai protested. "I promised the old guy, and I didn't want to break my word. But let's get back to this project you're pushing."

"I may have to get someone to help me later on, but right now I don't feel I can do that."

"Why not?"

"Because the good the program does is too valuable to endanger. That being the case, it's imperative that the committee see a smoothly run operation. And since I'm the one who started it, I feel I have to continue with it, at least till it's off the ground. Once it's established, then we'll recruit additional help.''

''And you really believe in this program, hmm?''

''McCai, it isn't necessarily what I believe. There are documented facts to back up my theory. There have been any number of scientific studies done by various groups. Almost without fail, all of them agree that there are numerous benefits from the bonding that takes place between the elderly and a dog—or any kind of pet. And it's not the elderly, but children . . . even people with emotional problems. The animal—or pet—isn't judgmental. It simply accepts a person, McCai,'' Jenny said, smiling. ''Acceptance, that's the key word. For in the long run, isn't that what we all want?''

''That's an interesting concept.''

''I agree. It's also interesting that by petting or talking to a dog, some patients have had their blood pressure and anxiety levels lowered. Children with emotional problems who've been unresponsive, even with their therapist, responded beautifully when they were given a chance to pet a dog. I won't bore you with more facts, but be assured that it does work.''

''Believe me, I'm not bored. But like a lot of other people, I've never even thought about the subject.'' As they walked toward the door, McCai looked back over his shoulder at the run, where Mildred was eating. ''Do you plan on taking her back to the nursing home later today?''

"Not unless they call. If Edna needs Mildred, all they have to do is call me," Jenny told him.

"Well, it's about time," Dolly remarked when they entered the kitchen. It was filled with the aroma of freshly made coffee. The older woman cast a suspicious glance McCai's way, then waved Jenny and McCai to the table, where sandwiches and cups of the hot brew were waiting.

"You must be psychic, Dolly," Jenny answered, smiling, then gave the housekeeper a quick hug of thanks. "Give us a few minutes to wash up and I'm sure there won't be a crumb left on that plate."

McCai was the first to return to the kitchen. Dolly placed slices of freshly baked pound cake on the table, then removed the plastic wrap from the plates of sandwiches.

"Caught any dognappers this morning?" she asked bluntly as she moved about the kitchen.

"'Fraid not," McCai answered. He leaned his shoulder against the wall and stared at the elderly woman.

"And you're not about to find any here either" was her curt rejoinder. She turned on the faucet in the sink, then picked up a small brush and began scrubbing vegetables. "Thinking you would is the dumbest thing I've ever heard of in my entire life."

"Okay, Dolly," McCai said patiently. "Why don't you tell me why you're ready to part my skull with a meat cleaver?"

Dolly turned off the water. She picked up a towel, then turned and stared angrily at McCai as she dried her hands. "I've known Jenny Castle since she was knee-high to a grasshopper, mister. She's about as apt to go traipsing around the country stealing dogs as I am." Dolly continued to stare at him coldly. "Do you consider me the sort of person who would steal dogs?"

McCai spread his hands, palms up. "Not in the least."

"Then why Jenny?"

He smiled at the belligerent question. "This is a very complex case, Dolly. In fact, I'd say it's the most annoying one I've ever encountered. There isn't anything run-of-the-mill about it. Nothing."

"And that made you decide to honor Jenny by accusing her?" Dolly demanded to know.

"Please," McCai said gruffly. "Set your mind at ease. I have not accused Jenny. Though I will tell you that there have been a number of incidents that have caused me to suspect her."

"You have the nerve to stand here in her own house and admit to that?" the housekeeper asked disbelieving.

"Would you want me to lie and say that I haven't the slightest idea what you're talking about?"

"No," Dolly murmured grudgingly, "I suppose not."

"Whether or not you believe me, I'm just as interested in finding the real culprit as you are," McCai assured her. He suddenly wondered just when he'd begun thinking of someone else as being the thief rather than Jenny.

"I suppose that's better than nothing," Dolly said stiffly.

"Then it's all right to eat the sandwiches?" McCai asked. "You didn't lace them with arsenic?"

Dolly returned his teasing look with a deadly serious one. "Don't give me ideas, Mr. McCai."

"Dolly, I'm shocked! I thought you and I were friends."

"We'll discuss the progress of our friendship when you clear Jenny's good name, and not a minute before. Now," she said decisively as Jenny chose that moment to return to the kitchen, "you'd best eat. The caterer will be here shortly to talk about the Fall Fete tea."

Jenny was aware of the tension between Dolly and their guest, but since neither offered an explanation, she thought it best to let the matter drop.

She reached for a sandwich. "Care to sit in on the catering session, McCai?" she asked pertly. "You never know when that kind of information will come in handy."

McCai regarded her steadily across the table. She looked tired. He knew for a fact that it had been close to two o'clock when she got to bed. He also knew how early she got up to take care of her dogs. That hadn't left too much time for sleeping. "I have a better suggestion."

"Oh?"

"Why don't you see the caterer, then take some time out for yourself and grab a nap?"

"Concerned for my health, McCai? What's the matter? Are you afraid I won't be healthy enough to stand trial?"

McCai looked down at his plate for a moment, his lips pressed together tightly. He raised his head and looked hard at Jenny. "I don't particularly care for your brand of humor, Ms Castle," he snapped. He pushed back his chair, then rose to his feet. "Thanks for the lunch, Dolly," he said to the housekeeper. "The food was delicious. The conversation was ... interesting. Good day, ladies."

Jenny sat in stunned silence, the sound of McCai's firm footsteps growing fainter as he went through the dining room, the main entrance hall and out the front door.

"Well, well," she finally said to a watchful Dolly. "I wonder what brought that on?"

"Must have been something he ate," Dolly said innocently.

"THIS IS JONAH McCAI, Joseph. My office said you called me." McCai was seated at the desk in his office, his heels crossed and propped on one corner.

"Thought you'd want to know that the New Orleans Police Department had an exact match of the footprint found behind Jenny Castle's kennel."

McCai's feet hit the floor as he sat upright in his chair. "Tell me more," he said.

"I figured you'd ask me that, so I had a friend of mine do a little checking. There was a pet shop burglary about two and one-half years ago. Couple of cats, two or three dogs and one or two other small animals were taken, but no money. There had been several other complaints around that time about cats being stolen, but no arrest was ever made, so nothing was done about it. In the pet shop job, however, they did pretty much agree at the time—based on expert knowledge—that the person was a male. Something to do with a male's center of gravity being different from a female's—thus creating a different stance and stride, plus the weight and build of the brace pointed toward the wearer being a man. My friend also said there've been other recent inquiries regarding the number of missing pets reported. Would that have been your agency?"

"It could easily have been. Many times we're able to come up with leads in really tough cases by feeding all sorts of information into our computer bank. Unfortunately, in this particular instance, about all we've been able to come up with is that there is a person or persons out there who either dislikes dogs—and probably cats as well—or is stealing them for resale to labs or other markets."

"What's your personal feeling, McCai?" Joseph asked. "By the way, my chief told me to cooperate with you fully. He appreciated your dropping by when you began your investigation. In some instances, just because we're a small-town operation, the big-city guys tend to ignore our existence. But to get back to my question, what do you really think?"

"My gut feeling is that it's a twofold operation. Possibly research labs *and* selling top-quality dogs out of the country."

"Hmm," Joseph murmured. "Very interesting."

"Thanks for the information, Joseph. If you run across anything else, I'd appreciate hearing from you."

Some time later, while McCai was sitting at a red light, silently cursing the congested traffic, he remembered the remark he'd made earlier to Dolly about Jenny's innocence, and his thoughts at the time. Why had he suddenly begun to feel that Jenny wasn't responsible for the thefts?

PHYLLIS GLIDEN RAISED her arms above her head and stretched, then looked at her watch. Three-thirty. She'd been working since seven o'clock that morning, with only a short break for lunch.

She sat very still for a moment, excitement spreading throughout her body.

All day long her thoughts had been with Noah. She wanted to see him. But did she dare take the chance? Would visiting the dog for the second time cast suspicion on the story she'd invented, that she was nothing more than a passerby who'd happened to see the accident?

Phyllis got to her feet and began straightening her desk. Hurting Joey or causing him the slightest problem was the furthest thing from her mind. Yet she loved Noah. He'd even slept at the foot of her bed.

Phyllis pressed her hands to her cheeks. What should she do?

Almost of their own volition, her steps carried her into her bedroom, where she freshened her makeup, touched her hands to her hair, then turned without looking directly into her eyes reflected in the mirror.

She paused in the living room only long enough to pick up her sensible black purse, making sure she had her keys. Then she moved quickly across the room and out the front door.

Never once did her steps falter until she reached the corner directly across from the veterinary clinic. Then the pangs of self-doubt reemerged, causing her palms to become wet with perspiration and crazy pains of fear to fill her chest.

Before she could lose the false courage she'd managed to dredge up, Phyllis stepped off the curb. She took one hesitant step forward, then another and another, till she was darting and weaving her way through the heavy traffic, oblivious to the strident sounds of horns blaring or the angry yells from frustrated motorists bringing their automobiles to screeching halts to avoid hitting her.

WHILE PHYLLIS WAS DEALING with her conscience, Jenny ended her meeting with a caterer. She closed the door, then leaned against it, her thoughts immediately returning to McCai.

"I still can't believe it," she said in a soft undertone. "I still can't believe it." In spite of himself, he was beginning to believe in her. Jenny knew it. He hadn't come right out and said it, but she knew. She crossed her arms over her breasts, her palms cupping her shoulders and hugged herself.

McCai was beginning to trust her.

Jenny didn't know what had happened to cause even his slightest change of heart toward her, but it was there. She'd seen it in his eyes when he looked at her. More important, she'd felt it when he kissed her on their return from the nursing home.

"You're making me want to chuck this whole damn mess and take you away to a very special place. A place where I can make love to you for hours on end without anyone bothering us," he'd whispered against her lips.

Jenny had pulled back from him then, her expression wary as she studied the strong features she'd come to know as well as her own. "What's happened to you, McCai? Last night—even this morning, you were still making rumblings that had me pegged as your number-one suspect. Has something happened that I don't know about?"

He hadn't answered her for several moments. Instead, he'd simply stared, his forefinger tracing the outline of her lips, then lingering on the still swollen, still sensitive, spot he'd caused the night before. "I don't have an answer, Jenny," he'd told her. "It may sound corny as hell, but it's the truth. Just let what happens happen. Don't try to figure it out." He'd dropped a quick kiss on the tip of her nose, then returned to the van for another dog.

Now Jenny was left to wonder if his almost tentative change of heart would mean a significant change in their relationship. Or was the change in light of new information regarding the case, information that would make McCai return to Dallas sooner than she'd thought?

Not being one to dwell on matters over which she had little or no control, Jenny decided it was time for her to go to the attic and start getting the Christmas decorations together.

She found Dolly in one of the guest rooms, inspecting the lace curtains on the tester bed. Because of thoughtful handling and care, the lace was still in excellent condition, except for one or two tiny tears Jenny had found the last time she'd dusted the bed.

"Think you can fix it so that it won't show?" she asked Dolly.

"Probably," the housekeeper answered. "But let's make sure we don't rent this room to anyone with children anymore."

"Good suggestion. I'm on my way to the attic, Dolly. If you want me, just yell. By the way, do you need anything from the store for breakfast before I get started?"

Dolly shook her head. "I don't think so. I'm making picnic lunches for both guests tomorrow, but I have everything I need. But one of us should go to the store in the morning. Chickens are on sale. And since we advertise fried chicken and hot biscuits, we need an endless supply."

"Will do," Jenny remarked, then she went upstairs and spent the next couple of hours sorting through decorations. When she was through, she happened to glance out the tiny round window nearest her and was surprised to see that it was dark. Just as she started to turn away from the window, she caught the head-lights of McCai's Mercedes.

A sharp thrill of excitement shot through Jenny. He'd said he would call, but she hadn't expected him to come back again. She remained at the window long enough to see McCai get out of the car and start to-ward the front door. Jenny quickly left the attic. She was halfway down the stairs when she heard the front door open and close.

Jenny paused, feeling an urge to watch McCai unobserved. She stood poised on the stairs, one foot resting on the step behind her, one hand on the rail-ing, the other at her side.

McCai hesitated in the wide front hall, feeling a prickly sensation of being watched. So many of the antebellum houses in the South were famous for stories of some love affair that ended tragically. Did the Arbor have such a history?

He started to walk into the sitting room, but he stopped. Again he sensed something not quite right. Too many times in the past that same feeling had stopped him from walking into a bullet or a knife or worse. Without knowing it, McCai looked up, straight into Jenny's face.

The sight of her, her hair like a dark cloud and its soft disarray framing her pretty face, caused McCai to inhale so swiftly that the air tore through the passages of his chest like a two-edged sword. She was still dressed as she'd been that morning, in the same loose-fitting sweats and scruffy shoes.

Slowly, deliberately, McCai began walking toward the mahogany staircase, his green eyes never wavering from the blue ones watching his every move.

On the first step he exhaled roughly.

On the second he wondered fleetingly how he would handle leaving New Orleans and Jefferson City and not seeing Jenny every day.

On the third one he seriously doubted his sanity for having gotten involved with her in the first place.

On the fourth one Jenny blocked his progress, just as her presence in his life had blocked him from thinking rationally.

He put his hands on her waist.

She put her hands on his shoulders.

They stared into each other's eyes, trying to see into the future. A future that promised happiness overshadowed with fear, passion undermined by uncertainty.

McCai eased her toward him till her breasts were pressed flat against his upper chest, till her thighs were pressed against his lower torso. His hands moved to her neck then, his fingers cupping her nape, his thumbs supporting the line of her jaw. His lips touched hers so gently, so lightly, Jenny wondered if she'd imagined it. But she knew she wasn't imagining it when those same magic lips teased the side of her throat, then took the tip of her ear into his mouth and gently sucked.

McCai drew back, his gaze narrowed against the desire gripping him, the proof of his arousal pressing against Jenny's thighs. "Let's go to my place," he murmured against her throat.

"I need to shower and change clothes," she protested lamely.

"Grab a change of clothes," he said, his lambent gaze sending her pulses leaping with the need to feel him around her, in her. "I promise, I have plenty of water at my apartment."

Jenny knew she was going to do as he suggested. Yet for one brief moment, some inner voice warned her to be careful. Could she truly trust her heart to the man holding her in his arms?

"What's wrong?" McCai asked, feeling the shiver that ran across her skin.

"It's nothing, really," she said after a moment, then placed her hand in his and followed him down the stairs. But in her heart, the doubt remained.

CHAPTER THIRTEEN

SENSUOUS LIPS TEASED, traveling up a slim, shapely thigh, past hip and trim waist. Progress was delayed by impudent nipples crowning two small breasts, before the tempting journey was once again resumed.

"Mmm...."

"Am I to take it that you like that?"

"Well...maybe."

"Does that mean I'm to continue?"

"If you insist."

"Oh, I insist. I definitely insist."

For a while the only sound was from the tiny needles of water rushing from the shower head to impact against the flesh of the man and woman standing in the shower. An occasional "ah" or an "oh" was uttered in a slow, sleepy tone or a soft, throaty chuckle.

Arms and hands. Touching...caressing.

Mouths meeting, lips tasting, tongues curling around each other, igniting fires of desire.

Heart to heart.

Soul to soul.

"Turn around," McCai said to Jenny. She did as he told her, her swollen nipples brushing against his hair-covered chest. That slightest friction brought an awareness of growing excitement.

He saw her flinch, then quickly close her eyes and suck in a deep gulp of air. His dark head bent to the two pink tips where his tongue sheltered first one and then the other, laving them with the sweet, hot fire that was slowly consuming every inch of her. "Does that make it better?" he whispered.

"Y-yes," she said in a slow disjointed fashion. "So much better. But how did you know?"

"I could say I had a vision," he told her teasingly, his breath cool against her heated skin, "or I could confess and say that I saw you flinch when your breasts brushed against my chest. Which would you prefer?"

"Both, I think," she said boldly.

"Then that's exactly the way we'll leave it," he said decisively.

He ran large, firm hands over her body from shoulder to midthigh.

Slowly...gently.

When his fingers invaded the tender cleft of her femininity, protected by the shadowy darkness of tightly formed curls, and teased the tiny bud of arousal, he felt her hips suddenly arch firmly against his and heard her soft whimpers.

His finger left its teasing and found the core of her being. He entered her, feeling the satiny sheath, fiery and moist around him, holding him.

"Please..." Jenny whispered, her forehead pressed against the wide chest, her head turning from side to side against that solid wall of human flesh. She was poised on the brink of an explosion, her insides tensed, her senses alive with desire.

McCai reached into the very depths of his soul to sustain the control that was slowly being taken out of his hands. He held his body rigid, containing his breath deep in his chest for what seemed like an eternity.

"Put your arms round my neck," he said finally, huskily, his hands cupping her buttocks and kneading the firm flesh. He lifted her. "Now your legs," he whispered, "lock them around my hips."

His voice was hypnotic, bidding Jenny to do his will and then robbing her of the slightest thought of resistance. When she felt the hardened proof of his manhood pressing against her, her legs tightened convulsively around his hips.

He began to enter her then, as slowly and determinedly as his hands had caressed her body earlier.

Again she was caught in the inescapable bonds of passion, the explosion coming closer and closer to its peak. She grasped frantically at his shoulders, her head falling back as she tried to deal with the tidal wave of awareness washing over her from head to toe. "Ohh . . ." The deep, harsh sound burst from within her and issued softly from her parted lips.

McCai held her, one strong hand cradling the back of her head with infinite tenderness, the other arm secure around her waist. He smiled at the look of ecstasy on Jenny's face. A heart-shaped face that was beautiful. A face with smoky, blue-gray eyes, thick,

dark brows slanted slightly upward at the outer edges
and a mouth he never tired of kissing. A face that was
at that precise moment transformed by complete and
total passion.

McCai knew exactly what she was feeling. That
same helplessness was the prelude to the incredible
high slowly encompassing his own body. He moved
deeper inside her . . . deeper till they were truly one.

Flesh to flesh. Breath to breath.

Time and thoughts became blurred as the lovers responded to the needs of their bodies. The tempo of the
rhythm changed as frequently as the wind heralding a
storm, their emotions enduring a battering just as
strong, but entirely different.

As JENNY TURNED from placing a pan of sizzling bacon back in the oven, she found her way blocked by
McCai.

"If you want to pass, then you have to pay a fine."

Jenny looked him over for a moment, grinning in
spite of herself at the brevity of his costume. Actually, the towel was large enough, but the ends
weren't tightly tucked and it looked to be in danger of
falling to the floor any minute.

"It's indecent to parade around nude," she chided
him, then leaned forward and gave him a quick peck
on the cheek.

"Oh no," McCai said swiftly, grabbing her before
she could duck out of his way. "Kiss me properly."

Jenny leaned into him, letting her body meld into
the curve of his, becoming the aggressor as she kissed

him hard and long. When she pulled back that time there were no complaints.

"Better?"

"Much better." He looked down at her, at the way her nipples tented the front of his shirt and felt a warmth in his thighs. He turned reluctantly back to tending the eggs he was scrambling. "I never knew my shirt could look so sexy."

"I'm sure you say that to all the women who borrow your clothing." It was a dumb remark, one Jenny regretted the moment it was out of her mouth. She picked up the plates and napkins, then walked over to the table.

"You are the first and only woman to wear that shirt," McCai returned in the same teasing vein, though he was well aware of her embarrassment. He watched her out of the corner of his eye as she set the table, finding her presence as soothing as slowly sipping brandy.

"I hope you aren't going to be slow with the toast, woman," he said in mock sternness. "These eggs will be ready in about one minute. You do know that I run a very tight ship when it comes to kitchen detail, don't you?"

"Of course," Jenny replied airily.

"Is that disrespect I'm hearing in your voice?"

"Certainly not. How can you ask such a thing?"

Jenny was relieved by his teasing. The awkward moment had passed.

Soon the meal was on the table. Jenny couldn't remember ever having eaten eggs, bacon and toast by candlelight with soft soulful music in the background, but it was something she hoped she would do again ... with McCai.

"May I inject a note of seriousness into this setting by asking about the case?" Jenny asked after McCai returned to the table from putting a new tape into the player.

"What do you want to know?" he asked cautiously.

Jenny watched him closely, trying to gauge his thoughts by his reaction to her question, but as usual, McCai was as unreadable as a sphinx. "I guess I'm a bit weary of the entire situation." She looked down at her plate, then back at him. "I honestly thought at first that it would all be sorted out within a few days and we'd have a big laugh about it, or that you'd solve the case and go back to Texas. But neither of those things have happened. Is there something else that you aren't telling me?"

McCai picked up the coffeepot to his right and refilled each of their cups. His dark brows were drawn together across the bridge of his nose, his wide brow furrowed as he thought over her remarks. "I suppose it's best if we do get it behind us. But remember," he warned her, "whatever we discuss is confidential. Okay?"

"No problem," Jenny agreed, then listened, at times incredulously, while McCai touched on each area that had caused him to wonder about her involvement in the case, repeating the things he'd told her earlier.

"I realize some of the things I've mentioned might sound petty to you, honey, but I learned the hard way long ago that it's never wise to assume what a person will or won't do."

"And now?" she asked curiously, still amazed to hear that some of her normal day-to-day activities had been misconstrued as covert. "Have I been toppled from the head of the list of suspects?"

"I think so."

"Please, give me reasons. Rebuild my ego by heaping words of praise on my head, you rat."

"Several reasons," McCai told her, chuckling, "plus a gut feeling that you're innocent."

"The reasons first, please. We'll deal with gut feelings in a moment."

"Pushy baggage, aren't you?" McCai remarked teasingly. He took a sip of coffee, then began to tell her about his conversation with Joseph Atwood.

"You're kidding!" Jenny exclaimed. "They actually found another footprint?"

"I'm not kidding," he said, grinning, "and they did."

"Okay," Jenny said, feeling better and better the more they talked. "You told me there were several reasons. What else is there?" McCai stared at her till Jenny began to feel uncomfortable. What was he thinking about? she wondered uneasily.

"What would you say if I were to tell you that Edna Davis, Tom Harper and several other patients at the nursing home are listed as having exported dogs during the past eighteen months?"

"I'd say that's the most ridiculous thing I've ever heard. Some of them are in wheelchairs and the others are barely able to walk."

"I agree, but it's true, nonetheless. I have copies of the transactions."

"And you?" Jenny asked. "What do you think about it?"

"I've seen you at the nursing home, Jenny," McCai said gruffly. "There's no way in the world you'd do anything to hurt any of those people."

"Is that all? Is that the only reason you think I'm not guilty?"

"No," he said softly, his gaze never wavering. "I've held you in my arms and made love to you twice, honey. Trust me when I say that a man can tell a lot about a woman in...certain moments of passion, and vice versa."

"Thank you, McCai."

"No," he quickly corrected her. "Thank you."

The moment threatened to become another embarrassing one, and Jenny didn't want that. "Tomorrow I'm suppose to go over to a friend's kennel and pick up two new dogs for the nursing home program. Why don't you come with me?"

"It's really not necessary," McCai told her. "I've already told you that I trust you."

"It would make me feel better," she explained. "I don't want there to be a single doubt in your mind about where I get the dogs that I use."

"Then I'll certainly go." He took a piece of toast from the rack, buttered it and spread it with jam. "Here—" he held it to her mouth "—try this."

"I'm really not that hungry."

"That's obvious," he said, frowning. "I slave over a hot stove to fix you gourmet scrambled eggs, and you barely taste them. I'm not sure my ego can stand such a put-down."

"I don't think I'm going to forget this evening for a long time, McCai."

"Neither will I, honey," he murmured as he watched her teeth bite into the toast, then saw the pink tip of her tongue pass over the surface of her lips to remove the sticky sweetness. That gesture was as erotic as any he'd seen, McCai thought. He wanted to feel her tongue running over the surface of his lips, over other parts of his body as well.

Suddenly he pushed back his chair and then stepped to her side and lifted her into his arms. "I don't think this is an evening either of us will forget for the rest of our lives," he told her as he left the kitchen and carried her back to the king-size bed in his bedroom.

THOUGH HIS EXCITEMENT stemmed from an entirely different source than lovemaking, Joey Tate knew, as he watched the flight leave the New Orleans airport, that he was only days from flying to the tiny coastal paradise in Mexico.

He really hadn't wanted to let the standard poodle go for the price he had, but things weren't going as he'd planned. Cutting the price of the dog by five hundred dollars irked him, but he had had little choice.

Joey glanced at the papers in his hand, and at the name he'd used this time. Tom Harper. Wouldn't Uncle Tom be surprised if he knew he'd just shipped another dog to Mexico? Joey laughed. A hardened gleam shone in his eyes as he continued to stare at the paper. If the old man had cooperated and sold that land, then things could have been handled differently, much differently. But, Joey rationalized, that was life.

IT WAS TEN MINUTES past eight the next morning when the doorbell sounded at the neat, well-kept bungalow in the quiet neighborhood.

Phyllis, sitting at the kitchen table eating her breakfast, saw the red light next to the wall phone begin to flash. She quickly rose to her feet and hurried to the door.

What could Joey want so early? It had to be Joey, for she rarely had any other visitors. Being deaf caused her to lead an isolated life.

Rather than check through the peephole as she usually did, Phyllis opened the door.

"Ma'am," the short, stocky man in a brown suit murmured, nodding his head at the same time. She saw his mouth moving, but he wasn't looking directly at her, and Phyllis hadn't the slightest idea what he was saying.

She glanced helplessly at the tall, broad-shouldered man with him. He had dark hair and the most intense green eyes she'd ever seen. She felt as if he knew every single thing she'd done in her entire life. His careful scrutiny made her want to run and hide.

Phyllis saw the tall man tell his companion that he thought she was deaf—as if he had read her mind!

"I'm sorry," the first man replied, this time turning and looking directly at Phyllis.

"That's quite all right," she said nervously. "I . . . I should have told you."

"I'm Detective Spencer of the NOPD, Ms Gliden," he told her, holding out his identification for her to see. And this—" he indicated his companion "—is Jonah McCai, a private investigator. If you don't mind, we'd like to ask you a few questions about a dog you've been visiting at Dr. Richard LeJeune's veterinary clinic."

Phyllis felt unable to swallow. She gripped the edge of the door with one hand, the other one clenched into a tight fist. "I really don't think there's much I can tell you about him," she managed to say despite the absolute terror building within her.

Dear God! The police and a private investigator. If word got out that Joey didn't care for his dogs, it would ruin his business. Worse still, if Joey found out what she'd done, he'd kill her.

"Would you mind answering a few questions, Ms Gliden?" McCai asked. "I promise we won't take more than a very few minutes of your time."

Unless she wanted to create a scene and no telling what kind of suspicion, Phyllis knew she had no choice but to do as they asked. She stepped back and waved them in, praying all the while that Joey wouldn't decide to drop by.

"Exactly what line of work are you in, Ms Gliden?" McCai asked after they were all seated in the living room. Through an oval opening he could see into what he assumed was the dining area. At the moment, however, it looked as if it had been turned into an office.

"I'm an accountant," Phyllis said softly. "I keep books for several small businesses. It pays the bills, and allows me time to study. I plan on taking the C.P.A. exam in a few months."

"I'm sure you'll do well," McCai said courteously. "Ms Gliden, on the night of the accident, how did you happen to be the one to take the wire fox terrier to Dr. LeJeune's office?"

Phyllis glanced down at her clasped hands, then back toward McCai. "I . . . I was out for a walk. Suddenly I noticed a group of people standing by the curb looking down. When I got closer and saw that it was a dog, and he'd been hit by a car, I became furious. Not one of those people offered to help the animal. Not a single one."

"But you did," McCai reminded her. "That was a very nice thing to do."

"Thank you," Phyllis murmured, embarrassed. "I remembered the vet's clinic a couple of blocks farther along the street. So I picked up the dog and carried him to Dr. LeJeune's. Other than visiting him a couple of times, I'm afraid that's all there is to it. Did I do something wrong?"

"Not at all," Detective Spencer assured her. "We have reason to believe that the car that hit the dog might have been involved in a robbery. We were hoping you might have actually seen the accident and could give us a description of it."

"I'm sorry," Phyllis said, shaking her head. "As I said, when I got to him, the dog was lying on the pavement. I didn't see anything of the actual accident."

"Do you have a dog, Ms Gliden?" McCai asked.

"No. But I do hope to get one someday."

"Well," the detective said, looking from McCai to Phyllis, "I believe that about answers our questions." He and McCai rose to their feet. "Thank you, Ms Gliden, for seeing us. And if you do happen to remember anything else you think we might be able to use, call me at this number." He took a card from the inside pocket of his jacket and handed it to Phyllis. "If I'm not in, whoever answers will know where to reach me."

"Ms Gliden," McCai murmured, and handed her his card also.

"Well?" Detective Spencer murmured the moment he and McCai were alone. "What do you think?"

"Oh, I think she was telling the truth...to a point," McCai replied. "I really do. However, that doesn't mean she told us everything."

"Ah, so you also think the young lady left out something, mmm? Such as the clerk in the convenience store seeing a young woman fitting Ms Gliden's description walking a terrier just like the one hit by a car?''

''Something like that,'' McCai muttered. ''She's certainly not wealthy, so where the hell did she get a dog like that? And that dog or some other dog has been in her home.''

''Oh?'' the detective asked, grinning. ''How do you know? Did you get hair on your trousers?''

''I might have,'' McCai said ruefully. ''But more important, I saw a toy bone. The same kind I buy for my dog. I stepped on it when I sat down on the sofa.'' He sat staring at the house they'd just left. ''Why would someone want a dog's bone if they don't have a dog?''

''Indeed. By the way,'' Spencer remarked, ''I think you made a smart move having the veterinary clinic watched. Unfortunately, we don't have the manpower for something so isolated. It'll be interesting to see what this meeting with Ms Gliden leads us to.''

LATER THAT MORNING, McCai was seated in the passenger seat of Jenny's van. He'd gone straight to the Arbor from Phyllis Gliden's house. ''This really isn't necessary,'' he said as they moved at a snail's pace in the heavy traffic en route to New Orleans. ''I told you last night that I believe you.'' He turned in the seat so that he could see her better. ''Have you forgotten?''

''No,'' Jenny said, shaking her head. ''I haven't forgotten. But it won't hurt for you to get some idea of what I was talking about. For example, I'm picking up two ten-month-old puppies this morning. As I told you, without friends helping me, I could never buy the dogs needed for my program.''

"I realize that now, honey," McCai admitted.

"You're positive you no longer suspect me?"

"Would it make you feel better if I were to tell you that one of the dogs that was stolen has been found here in New Orleans?"

"You're kidding!" Jenny exclaimed, finding it difficult to watch her driving and look at McCai. "Is that where you've been this morning?"

"Yes. One of the detectives we've worked with before went with me to pay a visit to a certain young lady." He then told her the story, but omitted Phyllis Gliden's name.

"That's incredible," Jenny murmured. "You know, I remember you telling me that you came to New Orleans because of the dogs that disappeared here. You played a hunch and it worked for you. You do know that terrier is in the running for the President's Award, don't you?"

"Sounds very nice. But exactly what is the President's Award?"

"It's given each year to the top dog, along with a check for five thousand dollars. It's a very prestigious award. What a pity the owners can't be told that you've found their dog. And frankly, I think there's more going on here than just the theft of a few show dogs."

"You mean the stealing-dogs-for-research angle?"

"Yes. I also think doggy people are more aware of that angle than the average person. And if you stop with the terrier, then the thieves can keep right on with their dirty business.''

''My sentiments exactly.''

''But I still hate it that the owners can't be told.''

''They'll know soon enough. In the meantime, the dog is being well taken care of. The important thing is to catch the person responsible.''

''You're right. But if you don't think the terrier was taken by the woman you saw this morning, how do you figure she's involved?'' Jenny asked curiously as they turned onto a tree-lined street, then into the second driveway.

''Ever heard of a pawn, Jenny?''

''Of course. And I even play a fairly decent game of chess. Care to try me sometime, McCai?''

He met her smiling gaze and held it. ''Honey, I'd love to try you—any time.''

CHAPTER FOURTEEN

"I KNOW IT'S terribly short notice, and very rude, dear. But Dad and I have been wanting to go on a short cruise during the holidays for ages, and this seems the perfect time. You're not to worry, though, we'll definitely be with you at Christmas."

"Don't worry, Mom, I understand. Have a nice time, and please give Dad my love. Bye."

"Bad news?" Dolly asked when Jenny hung up the phone. She was taking two pumpkin pies out of the oven, and the kitchen held the aroma of cinnamon and nutmeg.

"My parents have decided to join two other couples for a cruise. They invited me, but I really didn't want to go," Jenny told her.

"They pretty much do their own thing, don't they?" Dolly asked. She'd known the elder Castles since Jenny was a little girl, and she often thought she'd never known two people less equipped emotionally to be parents than they were. She knew for sure that the main reason Kathleen had left the Arbor to Jenny was her hope that it would add some stability to Jenny's life, some chance at having a permanent home.

"Yes, they do," Jenny admitted, staring out the window for a moment. She was used to her parents off-the-wall life-style, but this time it was different. She'd wanted them to meet McCai. "But then, they've always lived as they pleased. I suppose that's one reason it was so easy for me to move out. There was no friction between us, it was simply that I enjoyed one way of doing things and they enjoyed another. At times I wish it could be different, but it isn't." She turned back to Dolly. "So, give me something to do."

"Start peeling fruit for the Waldorf salad," the housekeeper said, nodding toward the worktable. "You do realize that without your parents coming we're going to be eating turkey for days and days?"

"I do," Jenny remarked stoically. "Perhaps McCai will want to take a doggie bag home with him. By the way, did he call while I was at the market?"

"No. Was he supposed to?"

"No. But I haven't heard from him in nearly two days. I thought he might have called." Yet why should he? Jenny asked herself as she picked up a rosy-red apple and slipped the edge of the knife under the skin. Just because they'd made love twice didn't mean he had to check in with her every hour.

After peeling the fruit and adding Dolly's mixture that kept it from turning dark, she covered the bowl with plastic wrap, then placed it in the fridge. She took a couple of steps toward the door, then paused.

"Thanks, Dolly."

The housekeeper glanced up, then turned her attention back to the corn bread she was mixing for the dressing. "All of us need to feel wanted at times. Don't ever be ashamed to admit that."

Jenny retraced her steps and dropped a kiss on the housekeeper's cheek. "Happy Thanksgiving, Dolly."

"Happy Thanksgiving, honey."

Jenny began decorating the public rooms in a mood that was, if not totally content, then certainly much improved over what it had been when she'd finished talking on the phone to her mother. Getting the house ready for the holidays was exactly what she needed to make her feel better.

She wondered if it was the simple act of creating something beautiful that boosted a person's spirits. With the holly and pine cones, bright greens and reds touched with silver and brass, the Arbor took on an added glow from the day after Thanksgiving till after Christmas. There was an air of expectancy, an air of happiness in the atmosphere that turned old Scrooges into docile teddy bears. Jenny loved every minute of the holiday season.

The time she spent reworking some of the decorative arrangements before placing them throughout the rooms went quickly. When that was done, she brought in the stepladder from the garage so that she could begin hanging what seemed like miles of garlands. But even though she felt a growing sense of accomplishment from decorating, Jenny couldn't keep her mind off McCai.

Attempting to keep herself from caring about him more than she already did was proving to be difficult. She didn't even have the excuse of telling herself he was leading her on. He wasn't. In fact he'd been painfully honest with her from the very beginning. She had to respect him for that.

She paused to adjust the piece of wire on one end of a garland, then strained to reach a tiny nail that had been left in the molding.

"Darn!" she muttered when her fingertips fell short of their mark by a mere fraction of an inch. She moved closer to the edge of the top rung, her arm stretched as far as possible.

She stretched . . . then stretched a tiny bit more.

There, she silently congratulated herself, she'd done it.

Suddenly she heard a loud creaking noise, and the ladder lurched to her right. Jenny realized she'd lost her footing. The fact that she was going to fall flashed through her mind, but there was little she could do to keep her body from slamming against the floor.

As if by magic an arm encircled her waist, snatching her against a hard body with such force the breath rushed from her lungs with a whooshing sound. She was held in that position for an electrified moment, then slowly eased to the floor.

Jenny looked up then, slowly, dazedly, and found herself staring into McCai's frozen features.

"Of course you do realize that you could have broken your neck," he said with icy calm, one hand gripping her upper arm, the other one settling the ladder. When that was done, he turned the still-stunned Jenny to face him. "Hasn't anyone ever pointed out to you a few simple safety precautions in the use of a ladder?'' he demanded, his voice becoming louder with each word. "You...do...not...stand on the top rung. Ever!'' he yelled.

"I...I know that, and I'm sorry," Jenny murmured, only just beginning to recover from the scare.

"You should be," McCai said. "I can't believe you'd do something so careless. If I hadn't just happened to walk in, you'd probably be lying there right now with a concussion or worse." He was still swallowing the sour taste that had rushed from his throat to his mouth when he'd seen the ladder tilt, and Jenny begin to fall.

"All right already," Jenny replied. "I said I'm sorry. Please let it drop." She wanted to yell at him, too, but not in anger. She wanted to tell him to take her in his arms and kiss away the scare.

"Let it drop?" he asked as if she'd just told him to go take a stroll on the moon. "Let it drop? You almost killed yourself because of some thoughtless mistake, and you tell me to let it drop?"

"I'm strongly hinting that you do that very thing, Jonah McCai."

"And if I don't?"

"Then I suggest that you turn around and walk right back through that door," she told him, pointing toward the front entrance. There were twin dots of color in her cheeks, and McCai didn't have to guess at her mood. "I do appreciate you saving me from a nasty fall. But I do not appreciate you standing there like a very angry moose, yelling at me. Furthermore, *I will not stand for it*."

"What on earth is going on in here?" Dolly Yates asked from the doorway leading into the hall. "Have you two forgotten that we have guests? It sounds like you should choose weapons and meet under the oaks at sunrise."

McCai ran a hand through his dark hair and looked away, his expression still grim.

Jenny chewed one corner of her bottom lip, feeling like the chump of the year for having been caught like a ten-year-old. "Er...I was too high on the ladder and almost fell," she said quietly. "Lucky for me McCai came in when he did."

"Oh," Dolly murmured thoughtfully, looking from one to the other. "How nice. There's a pecan pie waiting in the kitchen when you're through in here," she remarked, then turned and left the room.

They looked at each other. Jenny opened her mouth to speak just as McCai did. They both grinned sheepishly and looked away.

"I'm sorry," she said simply.

"So am I," he answered. He bent and kissed her quick and hard, then removed his jacket and threw it across a love seat covered in green brocade that had belonged to Jenny's great-great-grandmother. "You direct, and I'll finish the garland. Even with an extra-tall ladder, twelve-foot ceilings are a little out of your reach."

For a moment Jenny was tempted to decline his high-handed order. But who was she kidding? she asked herself. If McCai suddenly decided he wanted to cut a hole in the roof, she was terribly afraid she would get the saw for him.

They talked while they worked and Jenny knew she would never forget this evening. They spoke briefly about their childhoods, and about Jenny's parents waiting so late to say they weren't coming.

"Are you terribly disappointed?" he asked.

"Not real—" she began, then paused. "Actually, I am. I was looking forward to seeing them. But, as Mother said, they've been wanting to go on a cruise for ages. We'll be together Christmas, so that won't be too far off."

McCai didn't comment. Privately he was thinking her parents were obviously uncaring as hell. If he had children, he thought, nothing short of a major illness or death would keep him away from them on a holiday. But who was he kidding? It wasn't very likely he'd ever find himself in that position. A family meant commitment, and deep in his heart McCai was terrified of that word.

The conversation drifted to the dognapping case, and the way it had progressed so rapidly in the past two or three days.

"Isn't that rather unusual?" Jenny asked.

"Not really. In fact, it's more the norm. Most cases either start off with a bang, then fizzle out at the end, or vice versa. And once a case starts unraveling, as this one is doing now, then it has a way of exploding."

Jenny was silent after that, her fingers methodically straightening and fluffing the Scotch pine garland while her mind dealt with an entirely different problem. If the case was going to be settled as soon as McCai seemed to think, then her time with him would be even less than she'd counted on. How would she handle his leaving?

Jenny heard the telephone ringing in the background, but ignored it.

"Have you spoken with your friend Nate recently?" she asked McCai.

"A couple of days ago. Why?"

"He sounds like an interesting character. Does he have family in New Orleans?"

"Nate's like me," McCai said lightly. "He's alone."

"Oh. In that case, do you think he'd like to join us for Thanksgiving dinner?"

"The old reprobate might at that. When I'm through here, I'll give him a ring."

"Problems, Jenny," Dolly announced as she entered the room practically at a run. "That was the nursing home on the phone. Edna Davis isn't doing well at all, plus she's begging for her dog again. Her daughter wants to know if you'd please bring Mildred to her mother."

"Of course," Jenny replied softly. She dropped the garland, then headed for the back door.

McCai was off the ladder in a split second, catching up with her before she reached the hallway. He dropped a reassuring arm across her shoulders. "I'm going with you."

"I'd appreciate it," she said. She knew there was no point in trying to explain how she was feeling at the moment.

He knew.

He knew and he wanted to be with her.

They were almost to the kennel when Jenny paused, her head tilted to one side, a look of disbelief on her face.

McCai looked sharply at the building in front of them, and the dogs that were in the outside runs. He glanced back at Jenny. "What's wrong?"

"The gate on that far run is open," she told him. "I was the last one in the kennel, and I distinctly remember checking the gates on each run—inside and out. At least I thought I did."

"How many dogs were in that run?"

"Three beagles," she told him with a sinking heart, "including Mildred."

They made their way to the empty run, then stood staring at the catch, which was snapped, but not in the proper slot. With the slightest push against the gate, the beagles had been able to walk out of the run. It took only a few minutes to discover where the dogs had scratched their getaway hole beneath the outer chain-link fence.

"I don't believe this," Jenny said desperately. "It's only happened to me one other time," she murmured.

"It can't be helped," McCai told her. He turned and put his arms around her and hugged her. "It simply can't be helped, so stop blaming yourself. We'll just call the nursing home and tell them what's happened."

"I don't think I can do that."

"Do you want to go and look for Mildred and her entourage?"

"Beagles are scent hounds, McCai. Once they get their noses to the ground there's no stopping them. Mildred and her friends could be miles from here by now. They're all wearing identification tags, so hopefully they'll be returned."

"Were there any distinctive markings on Mildred that set her apart from other beagles?" he asked after a thoughtful pause.

"No," Jenny said slowly. "In fact, she was rather ordinary to everyone but Edna. Why?"

"Do you have another beagle?"

"No," she said ruefully. "The others are accompanying Mildred on her quest for freedom."

"Do any of your friends have a beagle that we could use in Mildred's place?"

"I doubt—" Jenny began, then paused, a smile touching her lips. "McCai, you're a genius," she cried, throwing her arms around him and hugging him. "A flaming genius!" She grabbed his hand, pulling him along with her. "Let's go."

It was close to an hour later when Jenny entered the dimly lit room at the nursing home and placed a docile beagle beside the restless Edna Davis.

"M-Mildred," the white-haired woman kept murmuring, her head turning from side to side. "Why won't they bring Mildred to me?"

"Mildred's with you now, Edna," Jenny said softly. She lifted the limp, veined hand and laid it on the dog's head. "See, Edna? It's Mildred. Your very own Mildred."

"Thank you so much," Marie Gordon whispered, then squeezed Jenny's hand. "I'm sure some people would say we're silly to let the dog be with her, but if it gives her peace, then why not?" They moved away from the bed. "As you can see, we've been unable to keep her quiet. That bed was straightened just a few minutes ago. And the rails," Marie murmured, tears filling her eyes. "I know how she hates those things, Jenny, but we don't have any other choice."

"You need to get some rest."

"I'm afraid to leave," Marie told her. "If she becomes rational, I want to be here for her. I know she felt thrown away when I moved her here, but I couldn't manage."

Jenny's heart went out to the tired-looking woman standing beside her. She put her arms around Marie and hugged her. "Something happened earlier this evening that really upset me, Marie. A friend was with me at the time. He put his arms around me and told me to stop blaming myself. You've been as supporting as Edna would let you be, and you're a loving daughter. So stop punishing yourself because of what you see happening to her."

Marie wiped at her eyes with a crumpled tissue, then patted Jenny's hand. "You're too young to be so sensible," she said softly. "Thanks for caring. By the way, I have an old school friend who's a member of the legislature. I'll be seeing him soon, and I plan on filling him in on the program you've started with your animals.''

"Thanks," Jenny said. "I'll be going now. Call me if I can help in any way." She slipped quietly from the room, closing the door behind her.

McCAI, NATE JONES and two guests staying at the Arbor joined Dolly and Jenny for Thanksgiving dinner. Nate and Jenny hit it off from the moment they were introduced. When Nate left—with enough food from Dolly to tide him over till the next day—it was with a promise that Jenny would make McCai bring her to see Nate's place in New Orleans's French Quarter.

The bed-and-breakfast guests excused themselves after dinner and went to their suite for a nap, but Jenny and McCai helped Dolly clean up.

As the three of them were going back and forth between the kitchen and the dining room, Jenny wondered how many other people had ever seen McCai carrying a tray of dirty dishes, or wet and with smudges of grime on his face and clothes after stopping a leak in a burst pipe. How many times had he loaded dogs into a van and unloaded them again for the sole purpose of brightening the day of a few elderly people? She thought, too, about him perched on a tall ladder, cursing under his breath when the Christmas garland he was trying to hang wouldn't cooperate.

Suddenly her path was blocked by the disturbing man of her thoughts. She looked into his eyes and knew that she was as much in love as she would ever be in her entire life.

"What's so funny?" McCai asked when Jenny broke into a grin. Somewhere Dolly had unearthed a hideous flowered apron, complete with bib, that partly covered the expensive white shirt and dark pants. He should have looked ridiculous, but he didn't, Jenny thought. He was devastating, as usual.

"Well," she said teasingly, cocking her head first one way and then the other to get a better look at his attire, "I was enjoying a very private moment, McCai. That is, until I got a look at you."

McCai bent and kissed her, then slapped her on her behind. "There's a lot to be said for private moments, Ms Castle," he whispered in her ear as Dolly walked past them, her sharp eyes not missing a thing.

The evening literally flew by, or so it seemed to Jenny. Dolly went to bed after her kitchen was restored to its usual neat state. McCai and Jenny pulled pillows from the sofa in her sitting room and stretched out on the thick rug before the crackling fire he'd built earlier.

"How much longer do you think it'll be before the case is wrapped up?" she asked, breaking a thoughtful silence. She was sitting between his legs, her back against his chest. His arms were around her, and Jenny knew in her soul that she could stay as she was for the rest of eternity.

"With the way things are moving now, it could be any day," McCai answered. He knew what prompted the question. He heard the dread in her voice, and he

felt like a rat. His feelings for Jenny were deep, so deep
he didn't understand them himself.

"What then, McCai? Where will you go?"

"The daughter of an old client of mine has disappeared. I've looked over the case, and it's interesting."

"And where will it take you?" She was playing with
his hand, lacing her fingers through his and then
slowly pulling them away. She looked down at their
hands, the flickering fire casting a rosy glow over their
skin.

"England . . . Scotland."

"So far," Jenny whispered, feeling the pain of the
separation already.

"What about you?" McCai tried for a semblance
of balance. He wanted to take her in his arms and
make love to her. But guilt held his emotions at bay,
guilt because he was breaking her heart, guilt because
for the first time in his life he'd found something good
and decent, but didn't know how to accept it. There
had never before been a Jenny Castle in his life.

"I suppose I'll be tied up with the tea for the fete,
then Christmas. After my program is approved, I
think I'll enter some dog shows. Several people have
asked me to handle their dogs for them. Maybe I'll
start doing that more."

"What about this place?" he asked. The thought of
her driving from show to show late at night when she
was tired didn't set well with McCai, but he refrained
from commenting. He didn't have the right to tell her
what to do with her life.

"I'll only be gone on weekends. We can hire some-one to come in then and help Dolly." Jenny knew he didn't like what he was hearing, but he was too darned stubborn to say anything.

"I see," McCai murmured, his tone cool and dis-tant. "When will your friend be coming back from his stint with the National Guard?"

Now what on earth brought that up? Jenny won-dered. "Any day now. I'm sure he'll be home for the fete. Hopefully you'll get to meet him before you leave."

"I can hardly wait."

They were silent then, both caught up in their thoughts. Hurting thoughts. Lonely thoughts.

CHAPTER FIFTEEN

McCai drank the last sip of coffee in the plastic foam cup, then tossed it into the wastebasket. His attention was focused on information in the dognapping case that seemed to have materialized overnight—information that had eluded him at first. Now, finally, McCai could foresee an end soon to his business in New Orleans.

He studied the report from his company's Mexican operative, which confirmed that the poodle recently shipped had a microchip implanted in the right ear. McCai then looked over a list of small companies obtained for him by his secretary. Those facts, combined with what he'd gotten from Nate, supplied three damned good clues.

At the moment McCai was still playing with the puzzle, but more and more often a certain name was showing up. It was all coming together. McCai was confident of that now. The feeling he always got when he was about to move in on a suspect was slowly uncoiling in the pit of his stomach.

The hunter closing in on his prey.

McCai sat back in his chair, his wrists clasped behind his head. So why the hell wasn't he happy? Why wasn't there the familiar sense of accomplishment?

He got up and walked over to the window and stared down at the city, awakening to a new day. He saw a white van stop at a corner, and a bundle of newspapers tossed from the vehicle to the pavement beside a street vendor's stand. From the other direction came a huge machine at a snail's pace, inhaling debris and leaving a clean path in its wake. There were joggers out in numbers, sweatbands in place, running shoes pounding the pavement; they reminded him of robots as they strove to balance with exercise the amount of food they'd eaten the day before.

McCai flexed his muscles and stretched. It was still early. A quick glance at his watch indicated it was 5:45. He'd been at the office since five.

Jenny would be up in fifteen minutes.

Jenny.

Common sense told McCai that thoughts of Jenny Castle would be with him forever. He'd formed habits where she was concerned, something he'd never done with another woman. He'd grown accustomed to seeing her each day, to laughing with her over little things, to sensing when the phone rang that it would be her, to hearing a song and thinking of her.

Grown accustomed.

Two very quaint words. Two very unfeeling words, in his opinion. Words that didn't come close to expressing how he felt when he thought of Jenny.

Grown accustomed hardly covered the gut-wrenching, heart-lurching sensations that grabbed him each time he saw her or heard her voice, or the flame-hot river of desire her soft touch awakened in him.

He turned from the window and looked back at his desk.

Work.

Work, the panacea that healed all.

Slowly he walked back to the chair and sat down. If he worked hard enough, he would be able to force Jenny from his thoughts.

"Jeanette said for me to come on in," James Baldwin remarked two hours later as he entered McCai's office, then closed the door behind him. "What's up?"

McCai reached for the material he'd been studying, then handed it to James. "I think this is what we've been waiting for."

James whistled under his breath as he quickly glanced over the information. "That makes two dogs recovered. And this Joey Tate," he said, scanning the pages more slowly, "isn't he Tom Harper's nephew? Oh, wait," he muttered. "I see now that he is."

"One and the same."

"He owns a photographic studio. According to your notations here, I assume he's into more than photography."

McCai grinned, then pushed another sheet of paper across the desk. "Now meet Joey Tate, kennel owner. And if I'm not completely wrong, frequent

exporter of dogs to Mexico and dognapper extraor-
dinare.''

"But it's all supposition at this point."

"This is so. But isn't it odd that of all the close relatives of the nursing home patients, Mr. Tate is the
only one involved with dogs? And isn't it odd that
Phyllis Gliden, Joey Tate's accountant, just happened to come upon the terrier when it was hit by a
car? And isn't it odd that Tom Harper—elderly, fee-
ble Tom Harper—just happened to ship a dog to
Mexico with a microchip in its ear that identifies it as
one insured by our client?''

"What are your plans now?"

"I'm greedy," McCai remarked. "I don't want to
stop just part of Tate's operation, James, I want to
stop him altogether. I think our friend Joey should be
allowed to carry out his plans, don't you?''

AT THAT PRECISE MOMENT Phyllis Gliden didn't share
McCai's optimism. She was still in her robe and pa-
jamas, staring at the two large crates in her guest bedroom.

"Joey," she said anxiously, turning and hurrying
behind him like a small, worried hen, "I don't have
room for three dogs." She also wanted to add that she
didn't want the responsibility. She was terrified something would happen to one of them as it had with
Noah. And what if she was visited again by those two
men? She hadn't enjoyed that experience one little bit.
She expected them to reappear any minute and demand to know why she'd lied to them.

"For goodness' sake, Phyllis," Joey snapped as he carried in the last crate and set it in line with the others. "It'll only be for a few days. Probably not more than four or five. Is that too much to ask of a friend?"

"Of course not, Joey," she murmured faintly. "I'm sorry."

"That's better," he said crossly. He was up to his ears in problems, and she was going on about keeping three dogs for four or five lousy days. Wasn't there anybody in the whole world he could count on?

"Now listen carefully," he said sternly as he knelt in front of the crates. He removed two five-pound bags of dry food from one crate, then reached over and took several cans from another crate. "Each dog gets one-quarter of a can of meat mixed with two cups of dry food. Feed them around four o'clock in the afternoon. That will give them plenty of time to exercise before bedtime. Oh, here," he added, reaching inside the nearest crate and pulling out a bucket. "Put this outside in the shade and keep it filled with water."

While Joey was explaining the feeding routine, Phyllis was wondering why the whole scenario with the dogs was making her nervous. Worse still was Joey's erratic behavior. Why was she having to keep so many of his dogs lately when he had a huge kennel?

His grouchy attitude was making her jittery. And when she got jittery she made mistakes. Stupid, silly mistakes. She didn't function well under stress, and any time she had a confrontation with Joey, she felt stressed out.

"I—I think I can handle that."

Joey rolled his eyes. "'I think I can handle that,'" he mimicked in a sneering voice. "Jeez, woman! Why don't you get real! Don't you ever get tired of playing the role of a stupid broad? Of acting and hiding like a timid rabbit?" he asked angrily.

"I'm not stupid, and I don't hide, Joey," Phyllis responded in a rare show of spirit.

"You don't?" he asked mockingly. "You don't call the way you seclude yourself in this house hiding? You don't call the way you work hiding? If you weren't afraid of your own shadow, you'd be out in the real world, showing other deaf people how they can adapt in spite of their handicap. But no, not you. You hide behind these walls and pretend everything is fine. Well, it isn't fine, Phyllis," he shouted. "Nothing is fine. The whole damned world stinks. Got that? So why the hell don't you grow up and face facts?"

Phyllis stared at him, her anger and humiliation so great she was speechless.

"There's no need to pout," Joey said callously. "You know what I said is the truth." He got to his feet, then reached out and clumsily patted her on the arm. "You need to break out of your shell, kid, live a little. Get yourself a boyfriend."

Phyllis hardly moved during the time it took Joey to finish getting his dogs settled. She was angry and hurt that he would dare mention her personal life. Didn't he realize how excruciatingly painful it had been for her to get as far as she had?

"I won't be able to keep the dogs more than a week, Joey," she surprised herself and him by saying.

"Oh my," he replied cuttingly. "You're a regular Miss Hoity-Toity, aren't you? What's the matter, Phyllis? Did I hit a nerve?"

"A week, Joey," she repeated, swallowing to hide the nervousness that was drawing every ounce of moisture from her mouth and throat.

"All right!" he yelled, the scar on his face turning a dull red. "A week. In the meantime I just might decide to find myself another bookkeeper, Ms Gliden. How would you like that, huh?"

"Wh-whatever you think's best, Joey."

He gave her a narrowed glance, then brushed past her. She felt the thumping of his uneven step as it progressed through the house and out the front door. He revved the engine in his van, then peeled off down the street. Phyllis breathed a sigh of relief.

Lately there had been something about Joey that was scary. He'd always been moody and quick to fly off the handle, but he'd never been cruel to her . . . till today. Phyllis thought back over the set of books she kept for him, but she couldn't remember anything out of the ordinary. He wasn't wealthy, but he was certainly making enough with his boarding kennel and his photography business to afford him a moderately comfortable life, and he was always prompt in paying her.

But she felt there was something else bothering him. Something that was changing him from kind and moody to mean and uncaring. She wondered what it was.

In the kitchen of the Arbor Jenny gently replaced the telephone receiver and then looked across at Dolly. "Edna died about twenty minutes ago."

"Oh, honey, I'm sorry," Dolly said gruffly.

Jenny nodded, not trusting herself to speak.

"If you can look upon the good Lord taking her as a blessing," Dolly spoke again after a brief pause, "then I wish you would. From what you told me about her, her quality of life had been steadily deteriorating."

"It had been," Jenny agreed, though she wanted to discount the logic and demand that Edna be given another chance. She pulled out a chair and sat down at the worktable, feeling suddenly drained of all energy. "And I do agree with you, Dolly. Edna is probably much better off."

"But that doesn't keep it from hurting, does it?"

"No."

"Nor should it. I've often thought that in grieving we grow. Perhaps that sounds silly to you, but it's what I think."

"Unfortunately, Dolly, you've always made perfect sense to me, even when I didn't want you to do so." Jenny stood, her hands automatically reaching behind her and tucking her blouse into the waistband of her slacks. "I know there's a mountain of work to be done here, but I think I'd like to be alone."

"Get your keys and go, child. Go someplace that's special, someplace where the memories are good."

"I know just the place. If you need me, I'll be at the old mill creek."

All during the drive Jenny refused to let the tears come. Instead, she let her thoughts dwell on the program with the dogs that had brought so much happiness to Edna. It wouldn't be the same at the nursing home without seeing her friend's smiling face, her words of encouragement and her feisty comments.

It wouldn't be the same at all. In fact, Jenny found herself wondering whether she even wanted to continue with the program.

When she reached the creek, she sat down on an old stump. She drew her knees beneath her chin and wrapped her arms around them, letting the tranquility of the setting wash over her. Eventually she stared at the stream.

The movement of the water over the sand and pebbles in its path reminded her of the cycle of life, its movement against the backdrop of the universe. People were born, they grew to adulthood and then they died. That was the usual pattern. Edna had followed the usual pattern, Jenny reasoned. And during that cycle she'd touched many lives with her caring.

Jenny cried then.

Deep, silent tears ran unheeded down her cheeks. She cried for her own loss of Edna. She cried for the feeling of guilt Marie Gordon was carrying. And finally she cried for the pain McCai was causing her. Unfortunately, when the crying was done, Jenny didn't feel the sense of release she was supposed to experience. Instead, she had a terrible headache.

She remained by the creek till the hunger pangs in her stomach reminded her that she'd left the house without breakfast and that it was way past noon.

But just before she eased the van onto the main road, she stopped and looked back in the direction of the tiny creek. In her heart she'd buried Edna. Oh, she'd go to the funeral, and offer the proper words of condolence. But she'd put her friend to rest by the little stream. In the spring the banks along the creek would be bursting into new life with the brilliant color of wildflowers. She'd come back, and she'd think of Edna.

THE DAY OF THE FUNERAL came quickly, or so it seemed to Jenny. She'd gone straight from Thanksgiving into thinking of Christmas shopping. Also weighing on her mind was getting the Arbor ready for the tea. It seemed the funeral was only a brief break in the season's hustle and bustle for her to pay her respects to her old friend.

"Don't feel like that," Marie Gordon told her when Jenny commented on her thoughts. It was the day of the funeral and they were walking away from the grave, slowly making their way to the waiting cars. The weather was overcast and cold. Such a bitter contrast to Edna's sunny nature, Jenny thought. "Mother would have been the first to tell you that life not only must, it does, go on."

"I suppose so," Jenny murmured.

"If you don't mind, Jenny," Marie said, "I'd like for us to keep in touch. And I meant what I said about your program for the elderly. I intend to talk to my friend in the legislature."

Jenny looked back over her shoulder at the stands of flowers surrounding the grave, and at the funeral director's employees in dark suits, waiting for the mourners to leave so they could get on with their jobs.

Rush, rush. Hurry, hurry. Mortuary personnel needed to get one funeral over with so they could hurry somewhere else and offer their services to another group of mourners, she thought fleetingly. For some reason that annoyed her. "I don't know, Marie. I'm not so sure I'll continue with the program."

Marie smiled gently and patted Jenny's hand. "You'll change your mind. You have that very special empathy with the elderly. It's a rare gift, cherish it. Talk with Marge, tell her how you feel. Perhaps someone else can fill in for you for a few weeks."

They said their goodbyes, then went their separate ways—Marie to the car provided by the mortuary, Jenny to the Mercedes where McCai was waiting. He was leaning against the fender, his arms crossed over his chest, his gaze never leaving her slender figure.

When she paused a foot or two away from him, he slipped an arm around her shoulders, squeezed it for a moment, then opened the door and seated her in the car. Instead of stepping back, though, he rested one arm along the top of the seat, the other on the dash. His face was only inches from Jenny's.

They looked into each other's eyes and saw glimpses of a future neither of them wanted to acknowledge.

Jenny saw an empty heart...a love, not unlike a lonely flower springing up unexpectedly from a hairline crack in a rocky slope, destined to die from lack of care without ever having had a chance to survive.

McCai saw a bleak and lonely life, and a fleeting, wraithlike figure, slim and beautiful, but with an expression so sad it broke his heart.

"I'm sorry," he said huskily, his breath warm on her cold cheek.

"I know," she answered, understanding the two-edged significance of the remark. Probably not today, she thought, but soon...soon...

She closed her eyes when McCai cupped the line of her jaw with his palm, letting her cheek rest against the strength she felt there. She would always think of strength when remembering McCai.

The days following the funeral were busy ones for Jenny and McCai, but somehow they managed to go out to dinner several times, they visited Nate, and once McCai spent an entire afternoon helping move furniture in preparation for the tea. Jenny knew their time together was fast running out, but she was determined not to dwell on the day when he would be gone for good.

Apparently McCai shared her opinion because he, too, refused to discuss anything remotely related to his leaving and returning to Dallas. Instead, they laughed, joked and at times shared thoughts and ideas. He remembered how frustrated he'd been at first when the case seemed to be going nowhere. Now he almost wished he could reverse the speed at which progress was being made.

When McCai told Jenny that Tom Harper was returning to his own house, she was surprised. "But how? I mean...who will look after him?" She'd taken Marie Gordon's advice and let Phil handle the nursing home project for a few days. But Phil hadn't mentioned that Mr. Harper was leaving the nursing home.

"A housekeeper has been hired, and his neighbors are very anxious to help out in any way they can. Tom said his nephew wasn't too happy with the idea, but that's life," McCai told her. "The man can afford to pay someone to look after him, so why not?"

"Why not indeed?" Jenny said, smiling.

The next day, at McCai's insistence, she went with him to see Tom in his home. They got there just as Joey Tate was leaving. As he passed them in his van, Jenny remembered him as the young man she'd heard arguing with Tom at the nursing home and reminded McCai of the incident.

McCai didn't comment. He'd deliberately not told Jenny all the details of the investigation, or that Joey Tate was the prime suspect.

Jenny found it hard to believe that the neat elderly gentleman who greeted them and invited them into his home was the same scowling, unkempt person she'd known in the nursing home. In a way, she reasoned, Tom's chance for happiness—no matter how brief—helped ease the pain of losing Edna.

AFTER TAKING JENNY back to the Arbor, McCai paid Phyllis Gliden another visit.

"Oh dear...er...Mr. McCai," Phyllis said in a rush the instant she clapped eyes on her visitor. Oh, Lord! The man facing her had the most unyielding features she'd ever seen. Just the sight of him got her so rattled she didn't have the slightest idea what she was saying. "Have my neighbors complained? Are the dogs bothering them? Oh dear!" she murmured, actually wringing her hands. "I told Joey this wasn't going to work. I know there's a city ordinance stating how many dogs a person can keep in their home, but Joey wouldn't listen."

"Why don't you tell me all about it, Ms Gliden?" McCai said soothingly as he stepped inside and closed the door. "Perhaps talking about it will help."

McCai stayed only a short while inside the little house, but when he came out, he looked pleased.

After McCai's departure, however, Phyllis was stricken with guilt. She stayed at the window till his car disappeared around the corner, then stepped back, her thoughts in turmoil.

Jonah McCai must have had a reason for stopping by to see her, but he hadn't said what it was, and she hadn't thought to ask.

JOEY HEARD THE PHONE ringing and reached for it.

But a heavy fist was quicker, smashing against his wrist and pinning it to the desk. A soft whimper escaped Joey's lips.

He closed his eyes and dropped his forehead, wet with perspiration, against the surface of the desk. Tiny red dots exploded behind his eyelids, while a most excruciating pain shot up his arm like a orange-hot flame slowly consuming his flesh.

"Did you hear what I said, Joey?" André Tremont asked. He was standing by the runs, idly petting one of Joey's latest finds. "Two months in a row you've had only half the number of dogs you're supposed to come up with. That's twice, Joey. Twice you've been behind in your quota. I can't have that. Do you understand?"

"Y-yes," Joey struggled to answer through clenched teeth. The fist bore down mercilessly on his wrist. "Yes, Mr. Tremont," he quickly amended. At a signal from Tremont, the man administering Joey's punishment stepped back.

"The grapevine has it that there's a private investigator in town by the name of Jonah McCai. I've had him checked out, Joey, and he's good. In fact, he's the best. He's asking questions about certain show dogs that have been taken. And for some strange reason, Joey, your name just keeps popping up," Tremont continued. "Now I have to ask myself why a P.I. would come snooping around in this particular area of the country looking for stolen show dogs? It would make me very happy if you would assure me that you aren't stealing expensive show dogs, Joey?"

Joey slowly raised himself upright, his left hand cradling his injured wrist, his stomach churning with fear, his body in pain. "No, sir." He managed to stay on his feet, terrified that if he sat down, the huge man at his side would attack him again.

"That's what I was hoping you would say. You see, Joey, picking up stray dogs here and there, then selling them to research labs is a nice little sideline. It brings in a tidy sum. However, stealing expensive pooches is another matter. That angers their owners and leads to all sorts of problems. Problems I don't want to have to deal with. I have a number of business interests, Joey. So it stands to reason that I wouldn't want any of my people doing anything that would cause the authorities to launch an investigation into my affairs, would I?"

"No, sir."

"It's amazing how much we think alike, isn't it, Joey?" Tremont said pleasantly. He brushed an imaginary speck of dust off the sleeve of his dark suit. "I really do think you've learned a valuable lesson today, Joey, don't you?"

"Yes."

"Good." Tremont turned and made a slight motion with his right hand. The man standing beside Joey, and another one standing just inside the kennel, walked outside. Tremont looked at Joey for several spine-tingling moments. "I'll kill a man for double-crossing me. You've had two chances, Joey. Don't let there be a third time. Remember that." He turned then, and walked out the door.

Joey remained frozen until he heard the car drive away, then he collapsed in the chair. He hated himself for cowering like a cornered animal. But survival had been uppermost in his mind. Survival and, he hoped, a chance to escape.

André knew something.

Joey felt as if his life wasn't worth two cents. Rumor had it that André made only one visit to a recalcitrant employee. His next move was to act. That was all well and good for Mr. André Tremont, but Joey decided he didn't plan on being around when it came time for Tremont to act.

It was a good thing he'd followed his hunch and moved those three dogs over to Phyllis's house. Otherwise, he'd have been dead by now. That was a cold, hard fact, but one Joey had to face.

He remained slumped in the chair for what seemed like an eternity. When he finally did stir, he knew there was only one avenue of escape open to him.

His legs were still shaky when he stood, the world spinning crazily. He waited till his head was clear, then made his way outside to his van.

Joey was so deep in thought over the pain in his arm, and the changes taking place in his life, that he failed to notice the van parked across the street, the workman in khaki-colored coveralls with the utility belt strapped to his hips standing at the back of the vehicle and the gray sedan that fell in behind Joey's van when it left the kennel, then dropped back several car lengths.

AT TEN MINUTES TO FOUR McCai took a break and called Jenny. He asked her out to dinner, but she surprised him by declining.

"Other plans?" he asked, knowing full well she was trying to widen the gulf that had been slowly growing between them.

"As a matter of fact I do. Ed Bayliss is home. He called this morning and asked me to go out with him."

"I see," McCai said icily. "I hope you have a lovely time." He quietly replaced the receiver, then picked up the empty soft drink can sitting on his desk. He wondered what Ed Bayliss looked like? Was he handsome? Was there something between him and Jenny, perhaps a first-love relationship that Ed was trying to rekindle?

The phone rang and he reached for it eagerly. "McCai."

"That visit Tremont paid Joey has galvanized him into action. It looks like Joey's on his way to the airport," Spencer announced. "I'll pick you up."

"I'll be ready," McCai agreed. "By the way, that mysterious piece of metal we found outside Jenny Castle's kennel was the heel plate from a leg brace. Joey Tate recently ordered just such a replacement part for his brace."

An hour later, McCai shifted his weight a fraction to the right, hoping to find a more comfortable position. He and Spencer were at the airport, sharing a space in the middle of a shipment of computer paper that was barely large enough for a midget. Uncomfortable though it was the position gave them a perfect view of the door through which Joey would enter. It also provided them with cover in the event bullets started flying.

McCai slipped his hand inside his jacket, then lightly palmed the butt of the pistol strapped beneath his left arm. He wore the gun only on special jobs these days. In the past it had been as much a part of his wardrobe as his shirt or shoes. He'd been fortunate, however, in that he'd never had to kill anyone. But on more than one occasion, his having a weapon in his hand, pointed toward the enemy, had saved his life.

The crackle of a two-way radio drew McCai's attention. He turned and waited while Spencer carried on a one-sided conversation with another officer.

"Don't let your guard down, Tony," Spencer was saying. "We don't know what the hell this is going to lead to. However, we have reason to believe that Tremont is involved, so that means trouble."

Another crackling response.

"Yeah, Mr. Squeaky-Clean himself. But maybe he won't be able to wiggle out of this one."

McCai's peripheral vision caught a movement to his right. He tapped Spencer on the shoulder, then nodded to where Joey Tate and an airport employee could be seen through the wide, glass doors, unloading three large airline animal crates from a van onto a wooden dolly.

Spencer ended the conversation, made a last-minute check of his men staked out over the area, then leaned back anxiously.

Joey entered the building behind the dolly, one hand in his jacket pocket, the other holding a manila folder. In the folder were the papers needed to ship the dogs to his contact in Mexico. His plans had been altered somewhat, but, Joey told himself, over the years he had learned to be flexible.

Back at his place his bags were already packed. His ticket to his sunny paradise was also there. At 9:45 in the morning he would be leaving his old life and beginning a new one.

A new life. A life with resp— He cried out as a ball of fire tore its way through his crippled leg. He bent and grabbed his calf with both hands, then turned and began hobbling toward the door he'd just entered.

André knew!

André knew, and he was trying to kill him, Joey thought. He was oblivious to the startled looks of bystanders or the shots being exchanged between the police and André Tremont's men, just as he was oblivious of his own whimpers—like those of a wounded, frightened animal.

André was going to kill him. He had to hide.

On the tail end of that thought another bullet found its way into Joey's thin, crippled body. It entered his upper back, the impact jerking him upright, then slowly he slipped to the cold, dusty floor.

McCai walked to the front door of the yellow bungalow. Since his hands were full, he pressed the doorbell with his elbow, then stepped back and waited.

When Phyllis Gliden opened the door a few minutes later, her eyes were swollen from crying. But when she saw the squirming bundle of fur in McCai's arms, she smiled.

"Ms Gliden," McCai said, nodding. "May Noah and I come in?"

"Certainly." She stepped back, waving them inside.

McCai walked over to the chintz-covered sofa and carefully placed the squirming, happy terrier on one of the cushions. He straightened, then turned and looked at Phyllis. "Noah's owner is very grateful to you for saving his life. As you know, his leg was very badly damaged. According to the vet, he'll always walk with a limp, which means he can no longer be a show dog. The owner would like you to have Noah. However, she reserves the right to use him at stud for one year. Are those terms agreeable to you?"

Phyllis couldn't trust herself to speak, so she nodded. She walked over to the sofa and went down on her knees in front of the dog. She gently drew him to her breast. Noah, delighted to see the pretty lady he'd grown very fond of, showered her face with doggy kisses, his stub of a tail waving back and forth like the frantic hands of a clock gone crazy.

McCai tapped Phyllis on the shoulder. She rose to her feet, so that she could watch him speak. "I'm sorry about Joey, Ms Gliden," he told her. "When I was hired to find the dogs, it was never my intention that anyone should die. Telling me about keeping the dogs for Joey was a courageous thing to do. Please don't feel guilty."

"Strangely enough, I don't. Joey decided his own fate, Mr. McCai," Phyllis said softly. "Knowing the facts as I do now, it's easy to see why he changed so drastically over the past few months. He once accused me of not accepting my deafness. I realize now that he was the one who was unable to cope. I was never aware of how badly he hated his disfigurement."

"Obviously no one knew."

"I'm glad he never learned that I was the one who ruined his chances for a new life. I . . . it would have been difficult facing him. Do you know I even tried to call him and tell him that you knew I was keeping his dogs?"

"No," McCai said, shaking his head. "I didn't know."

"He didn't answer the phone, and frankly, I was glad."

McCai, pleased to see that she really was all right, chatted a moment longer, then left. He'd already dropped in to see Richard LeJeune and settled Noah's bill. That left Tom Harper and one other person to see.

JENNY WAS STUDYING the sketch she'd made of the serving tables for the tea when she felt she was being watched. She raised her head.

McCai met her level gaze with his own.

They stared at each other for what seemed like aeons.

He took a couple of steps into the room.

Jenny moved from behind the mahogany desk.

They'd met in this room, she was thinking, so it seemed fitting that they should part in it as well.

"You've come to say goodbye."

"The case is settled," McCai said unnecessarily. There were so many things he wanted to tell her, but rigid training over the years held him as much a prisoner as Phyllis Gliden's deafness controlled her life.

Something snapped in Jenny. Something that made her want to push him, something that made her want to hurt him. She walked toward him then, slowly, her blue gaze never looking away from his green one. When she came to a halt, she was close—very close, but not touching him.

McCai stood motionless, his tall, solid body rigid. *What the hell?* he wondered.

Jenny slipped her hands behind his neck, her fingers interlocking. She went up on her tiptoes and kissed him hard.

"Now," she told him, stepping back, "you can go."

"Jenny, I—"

"Don't, McCai," she said. "What we shared was very special. Don't take away any of the magic with meaningless words." She turned and walked back behind the desk. "Goodbye, McCai." Without looking at him again, Jenny picked up her pencil and went back to studying the diagram.

CHAPTER SIXTEEN

JENNY SAT BACK in her chair, her gaze resting on Ed Bayliss's boyish features. His voice became a pleasant drone as her thoughts drifted back over the past few weeks.

Two of those weeks had been spent without McCai popping in and out of the Arbor. That was how long it had been since he wrapped up the case and returned to Dallas.

Two of the longest weeks of Jenny's life.

Not that there hadn't been hundreds of reminders of him, she thought. There had. The story of the dog-nappings and the misuse of the names of the nursing home residents had made the headlines in the Jefferson City and New Orleans papers as well on television.

Joey Tate had died shortly after reaching hospital, but not before naming his co-conspirators. Seeing his picture so often on TV and in the paper finally caused Jenny and a friend to remember that they had occasionally seen him at local dog shows. David Moreau lost his license to practice veterinary medicine and was prosecuted. André Tremont had fiercely denied any connection with Joey, and his lawyers were still hard at work to clear him of any charges. The show dogs, with the exception of the wire fox terrier given to Phyllis Gliden, had been returned to their owners.

The entire matter had been handled nicely and tidily, Jenny thought grimly as she reached for her wineglass and took a sip. She remembered Dolly's remark that the real problem—of dogs being stolen, then sold to research labs—would resurface after a while, and it would be business as usual.

Nicely and tidily—McCai's way. No strings attached. No loose ends.

Jenny chided herself for letting her thoughts dwell on him. But no amount of thinking or wondering or reasoning was going to alter the fact that Jonah McCai had been terrified of becoming more involved with her, and had run as soon as he possibly could.

At least she had the satisfaction of knowing she'd awakened something in his hard heart. She knew without a doubt that McCai cared for her. She'd seen it in his eyes, heard it in his voice and felt it in his touch. She'd seen it slowly unfolding before her very eyes from the first day he set foot in the front parlor of the Arbor till the last day he stood in that same room . . . almost in the same spot and told her goodbye. He'd gone from a hard, cynical individual to a caring human being. He'd shown that other side of him in so many ways . . . so many ways.

"Jenny!"

She blinked, looking at Ed in surprise. "Yes?"

"You haven't heard a word I've been saying," he said accusingly.

"Of course I have."

"Okay. What was I talking about?"

"The Army."

He was quiet for a moment, then frowned. "Well, you might have heard me, but your heart wasn't in it."

"For Pete's sake, Ed! What do you want from me? I've been listening to you play soldier in your mind since the first summer I spent with Aunt Kathleen when I was eight years old."

Ed grinned sheepishly, then ducked his head. "I've been at it that long, eh?"

"Yeah," Jenny remarked wryly. "The military should put you on their payroll as their best PR person. For the life of me, I can't figure out why you don't tell your mother that you're joining the Army, then do it. Why, in twenty years you could be retired and still be a young man."

"I'm afraid Mother doesn't see it that way," he said quietly. "And since she has no one else, I don't want to leave her. No matter that I'm grown and have my own company, I'm still her baby boy."

Jenny forced herself to listen. She'd been hearing the same story for years. In one sense it, along with Ed, was irritating, but it was as much a part of her life as breathing. Just as Matilda Atwood would approach her next year about using the Arbor during the Fall Fete and Jenny would say yes, and just as anyone or anything new in Jefferson City created a sensation.

She lived in a small town. It was progressive as far as industry was concerned, but on a more personal level, it still retained that small-town closeness, that almost closed mind to the outside world. In a way Jenny resented those things, but in another she'd come to love them. She only wished McCai could have been persuaded to accept such a life with her.

When Ed took her home that night, he was still talking. He'd spoken about the military, his mother and his plans for expanding his real estate business to New Orleans. By the time Jenny said good-night, she felt as if her ears were hanging from her head by mere threads.

The next morning when she double-checked the arrival time of a new guest, she was puzzled. Dolly had penciled in a name, but there was none of the usual additional information. Jenny wondered why.

At first Jenny had thought her Aunt Kathleen was silly for being so particular about whom she accepted as guests at the Arbor, but when Jenny took over the place, it struck her just how important it was for her to know a little about the people sleeping in her home and eating at her table. "Who is this Mr. Mitchell?" she asked Dolly a few minutes later as she entered the kitchen.

"Oh, just some man who called last night," the housekeeper said casually.

"A bachelor?"

"He didn't mention a Mrs. Mitchell."

"We usually don't get unmarried men."

"Is there some reason why we can't take them?"

"No," Jenny said rather shortly, "it's just that we usually don't. Did he say what line of work he's in?" Why was Dolly being so indifferent? Jenny wondered.

"I didn't ask. Should I have?"

"It's not written in stone that we have to, but we usually do. I thought he might have mentioned it."

"Well, he didn't."

"I wonder if we should say we're full when he arrives? Perhaps we could make reservations for him some other place."

"Nonsense. A paying guest is a paying guest," Dolly remarked.

"I suppose you're right," Jenny agreed, beginning to waver. "I see he's due day after tomorrow. That's the date of the ball. Did he say what time he'd be getting in?"

"Late. Said for us not to worry. If we weren't here, he'd find something to do till we returned."

"Hmm...seems to be a very accommodating person," Jenny murmured, still annoyed but unable to figure out why.

She put the matter out of her mind and went on with her tasks. After lunch she took the dogs to the nursing home. It was her second visit since Edna died, and even the news that her program had been funded for six months failed to erase the let-down feeling brought on by Edna's death.

"I'm glad to see you back, Jenny," Mrs. Dupree told her. "I know you miss Edna. We do, too. But we still need to see your pretty face as well."

Jenny bent down and hugged the woman. In dealing with her own unhappiness, she'd almost forgotten that there were innumerable Toms and Ednas, sitting in nursing homes, just waiting for a smile or a nod.

"You might be surprised to know this, Mrs. Dupree," Jenny said softly, "but I need all of you just as much." Somehow, those few words seemed to lift a burden that had been weighing heavily on Jenny's heart. Later, when she was helping Phil put the dogs back in the van, the sunshine seemed a little brighter than when she'd gone into the nursing home.

On the evening of the ball, moonlight showered the small town of Jefferson City. The temperature was in the thirties, and the steadily growing crowd at the Civic Center showed how the townspeople supported the efforts of the Sweethearts of the Nathan Bedford Forrest Society and the annual Fall Fete.

Costumes ranged from simple to outrageous. Except for one or two exceptions, everyone wore masks. Jenny's mask was a narrow black satin one that only covered her eyes. Her dress was made of crimson velvet, and had belonged to her Aunt Kathleen. It was simple in design, with puffed sleeves that reached to the elbows, a low square neckline, tight bodice and full skirt. In the back tiny covered buttons ran from the neckline to below the waist. She had on so many crinoline petticoats, she considered it a miracle she could even move. She was thankful she'd been spared having to wear a hoop.

"If that dress is any indication, your Aunt Kathleen must have cut quite a swath through the young men's hearts during her day," Ed Bayliss told Jenny while they were dancing. He was dressed as a pirate, and sported a comical patch over one eye.

"If that's the case, I wonder why she never found one she liked well enough to marry?"

Ed frowned, considered the question for a moment, then shrugged. "I don't think I ever heard Mother say."

Jenny couldn't help but laugh at his answer. On impulse, she cupped the back of his head with her hands, then let her forehead touch his. "You are a very special person to me, Ed Bayliss. Please don't ever change."

"Pardon me," said a stiff, cold voice, "but I believe Ms Castle promised me this dance."

Jenny's head jerked around, her gaze moving with hypnotic slowness upward past a black satin cummerbund, where it encountered the pleated front of a snow-white shirt with onyx studs, moved past rigid collar points and a black bow tie, to focus finally on a face wearing an expression as thunderous as a stormy night. Through the narrow slits of an abbreviated mask, hard green eyes were cutting Ed to ribbons.

"S-sure," Ed stammered. He stepped back, looked from Jenny to the tall angry man demanding her hand, then turned and headed for the bar.

"Did the old friend's daughter desert England and Scotland for a simpler life here in Jefferson City, McCai?" Jenny asked as she was drawn by two strong arms against a broad chest that was achingly familiar. For a brief moment she allowed her head to rest against that warm wall of human flesh. She followed his lead without effort. But then, hadn't it been that way with her from the beginning?"

McCai heard the question, but there was no way in hell, he thought, he could answer her. The warmth of her body in his arms was so satisfying, he wasn't willing to give up a single minute till the edge had been taken off the deep, aching hunger in him to see her, to hold her.

Jenny. Sweet, sweet Jenny.

He hadn't had a single moment's peace since he left New Orleans two weeks ago. He'd thought about her every minute during the day and dreamed about her every single night. In short, she totally dominated his mind.

After flying back to Dallas and meeting with Scanlon, then wrapping up all the loose ends of the case, McCai had planned to fly immediately to England and begin working on another case.

Plans. Plans that didn't materialize because he couldn't get Jenny out of his mind. In the end he'd sent someone else to England.

Because he'd done so, Jenny was terrified and delirious with happiness at the same time. Her heart was

beating wildly, and she was positive the couples closest to them could hear her knees knocking together.

Finally, when she thought she could speak again
without her voice trembling, she tilted her head to one
side and stared up at him. "Have you taken a vow of
silence, McCai?" she asked.

Slowly, tenderly, his features softened at the question. He looked deeply into her eyes and felt warmed
by the sunshine he saw there.

The sunshine of his life. Perhaps the figure of
speech was a bit sophomoric, he reasoned, but it was
an apt description of how he saw Jenny.

"McCai," Jenny said firmly, "I do not plan to
spend the rest of this evening engaging in a one-sided
conversation. Even Ed Bayliss and his never-ending
praise of the military is preferable to total silence."

McCai felt his lips relaxing into a lopsided grin. He
brought her hand he was holding to his mouth and
pressed his lips against it, then held it over his heart.
"I suppose I could say all sorts of things to you, Jenny
Castle," he began, "but I won't. As you well know,
I'm painfully blunt."

"Not to mention a lousy conversationalist," Jenny
added.

"Point taken, Ms Castle. As I was saying," McCai
went on solemnly, a very definite twinkle in his eyes,
"I can only tell you what's in my heart."

Jenny stopped dancing. Other couples had to hastily adjust their steps to keep from bumping into her
and McCai.

"What's wrong?" he asked. Was she in pain? Had he stepped on her foot?

"What kind of things?"

"Things like . . . I love you. Things like . . . I want to make lo—"

"McCai," Jenny interrupted him. "If you really are about to tell me what's in that black heart of yours, then it's darn sure not going to be on a public dance floor. I demand a moonlight setting with all the trimmings."

McCai hesitated only a fraction of a second. He cupped her elbow and escorted her to the edge of the dance floor. "As the lady wishes," he murmured smoothly, then stopped a passing waiter and held a brief, whispered conversation with the young man.

When he turned back to her, McCai grasped her elbow, then led her past small tables and laughing couples, through a pair of French doors onto a flagstone patio. He paused for a moment, his eyes searching the cool, brisk darkness. "This way, I think."

Jenny walked beside him, amused. When they reached a bench nestled in an alcove, McCai stopped, then motioned for Jenny to be seated.

He gestured toward the sky. "As you ordered, Ms Castle—moonlight, at its very best." To her utter surprise, he cast a rueful glance at the floor, then went down on one knee, his elbows resting on the thigh of his bent leg. "Your devoted swain at your feet. And," he said as the air was suddenly filled with the sound of a violin, "music."

"McCai..." Jenny began warningly, only to have him place a finger against her lips.

"Hush," he said softly. "Hush and listen." He took her hands in his then, his gaze holding hers. "I'm older than you are, Jenny Castle, probably too damned much so. I'm a hardened, cynical bastard, and those are probably some of my better points. I'm used to being alone, and I jealously guard what's mine. I—"

"McCai," Jenny broke in, "I know firsthand what a rat you are, but I love you anyway. And the answer is yes."

"The answer is yes?" he repeated with feigned innocence.

"Of course."

"But I didn't ask the question," he reminded her.

Jenny shook her head and smiled. "That's too bad, McCai." She glanced at the smiling violin player. He winked at her and grinned. Jenny turned her attention back to McCai. She really should let him get up, but she decided to wait. He was sadly lacking when it came to humility. "I think I'd like a June wedding," she said sweetly, then leaned back and waited.

McCai rose to his magnificent height, then reached down and hauled Jenny into his arms. "Now listen, honey. There'll be no June wedding. A week. That's how much time you've got."

"Mitchell Jonah McCai."

"In the flesh."

"No self-respecting female can get ready for a wedding in only a week," Jenny protested.

"Oh, you'll be ready, honey," McCai said gently. "Dolly and I have already discussed it."

"But a dress. I'll need—"

"We'll find the perfect dress," McCai assured her. "You may as well forget the excuses. I won't accept any of them."

"Overbearing as usual, huh?" Jenny smiled.

"Yes," McCai said, nodding. "But only to make you mine, Jenny. Afterward I'll let you lead me around by the ear."

Jenny's eyes became bright with tears as she stared into his face. For a moment she imagined him as a little boy, small and defiant, alone against the world. But the good Lord had let that little boy grow into a powerful man, able to fend off the cruelties of the world. Jonah had been given a mind that allowed him to succeed, and a wealth of love and feeling tucked away inside a warm and tender heart. She was going to love being his wife.

Jenny reached up and framed his face with her hands. "I love you, McCai. And I promise you, you'll never be alone again."

"I've never heard words as sweet, Jenny Castle. I worship you."

They sealed their vows of love with a kiss in the moonlight Jenny had ordered, and with the violin player weaving a magic spell with his music.

One week later—to the day—McCai and Jenny were married at the Arbor. Their honeymoon was spent at McCai's cabin in Colorado, high up in the snow-capped Rockies.

McCai's wedding gift to Jenny was diamond earrings and a necklace in an antique setting, the complete renovation of the Arbor and the one she favored most—his decision to settle in Jefferson City.

Harlequin Superromance

COMING NEXT MONTH

In April, Harlequin brings you the
world's most popular romance author

JANET DAILEY

No Quarter Asked

Out of print since 1974!

After the tragic death of her father, Stacy's world is shattered. She needs to get away by herself to sort things out. She leaves behind her boyfriend, Carter Price, who wants to marry her. However, as soon as she arrives at her rented cabin in Texas, Cord Harris, owner of a large ranch, seems determined to get her to leave. When Stacy has a fall and is injured, Cord reluctantly takes her to his own ranch. Unknown to Stacy, Carter's father has written to Cord and asked him to keep an eye on Stacy and try to convince her to return home. After a few weeks there, in spite of Cord's hateful treatment that involves her working as a ranch hand and the return of Lydia, his ex-fiancée, by the time Carter comes to escort her back, Stacy knows that she is in love with Cord and doesn't want to go.

**Watch for *Fiesta San Antonio* in July and
For Bitter or Worse in September.**

JDA-1

Harlequin
Superromance®

LET THE GOOD TIMES ROLL...

Add some Cajun spice to liven up your New Year's celebrations and join Superromance for a romantic tour of the rich Acadian marshlands and the legendary Louisiana bayous.

CAJUN MELODIES, starting in January 1990, is a three-book tribute to the fun-loving people who've enriched America by introducing us to crawfish étouffé and gumbo, zydeco music and the Saturday night party, the *fais-dodo*. And learn about loving, Cajun-style, as you meet the tall, dark, handsome men who win their ladies' hearts with a beautiful, haunting melody....

Book One: *Julianne's Song*, January 1990
Book Two: *Catherine's Song*, February 1990
Book Three: *Jessica's Song*, March 1990

Have You Ever Wondered If You Could Write A Harlequin Novel?

Here's great news—Harlequin is offering a series of cassette tapes to help you do just that. Written by Harlequin editors, these tapes give practical advice on how to make your characters—and your story—come alive. There's a tape for each contemporary romance series Harlequin publishes.

Mail order only

All sales final

TO: ***Harlequin Reader Service***
Audiocassette Tape Offer
P.O. Box 1396
Buffalo, NY 14269-1396

I enclose a check/money order payable to HARLEQUIN READER SERVICE® for $9.70 ($8.95 plus 75¢ postage and handling) for EACH tape ordered for the total sum of $_____.*
Please send:

☐ Romance and Presents   ☐ Intrigue
☐ American Romance   ☐ Temptation
☐ Superromance   ☐ All five tapes ($38.80 total)

Signature_____
Name:_____
                                           (please print clearly)
Address:_____
State:_____ Zip _____

* Iowa and New York residents add appropriate sales tax

AUDIO-H

The Adventurer

JAYNE ANN KRENTZ

Remember THE PIRATE (Temptation #287), the first book
Jayne Ann Krentz's exciting trilogy Ladies and Legends? Ne
month Jayne brings us another powerful romance, TH
ADVENTURER (Temptation #293), in which Kate, Sarah a
Margaret — three long-time friends featured in THE PIRAT
— meet again.

A contemporary version of a great romantic myth, TH
ADVENTURER tells of Sarah Fleetwood's search for lon
lost treasure and for love. Only when she meets her moder
day knight-errant Gideon Trace will Sarah know she's fou
the path to fortune and eternal bliss....

THE ADVENTURER — available in April 1990! And in Jun
look for THE COWBOY (Temptation #302), the third book
this enthralling trilogy.
